"What

"That I be ⋯⋯⋯⋯⋯⋯ before he kills me," she said.

Leaning forward and putting his head in his hands, Rick didn't respond to that. Maybe she was oversharing, but he was her only ally in this. He might not want to help her but she'd find someone else. She'd come too close tonight to give up and go home.

Rick lifted his head; his hair was rumpled and for the first time, she noticed him as a man. He stretched his arm along the back of the couch, her eyes were drawn to his biceps as he tipped his head back, staring at the ceiling.

"You don't have to help me," she said. "I can go back to my motel too."

Getting to her feet, she started for the kitchen counter where she'd left her bag.

"Stop. You're staying here and I'm going to be acting as your bodyguard until Vex is found—dead or alive."

Dear Reader,

I'm so excited to bring you Rick Stone's story. From the moment he rocked into the boardroom, drinking his Fanta and looking like he was about to fall asleep, I wanted to know more about him.

Jena is the perfect foil for Rick, who is so contained. She's a live wire who won't let him just be her bodyguard—she's determined to capture the man who murdered her best friend and let him know that it was a woman like Brianne who caught him.

One of the things I love about the Price Security team is how they all just are there for each other. Lee and Aaron are quickly brought into the investigation because it dovetails with Lee's work in the DEA.

I hope you enjoy this story!

Happy Reading,

Katherine

RELENTLESS PURSUIT

KATHERINE GARBERA

If you purchased this book without a cover you should be aware that this book is stolen property. It was reported as "unsold and destroyed" to the publisher, and neither the author nor the publisher has received any payment for this "stripped book."

MIX
Paper | Supporting responsible forestry
FSC® C021394

Recycling programs for this product may not exist in your area.

ISBN-13: 978-1-335-47172-7

Relentless Pursuit

Copyright © 2025 by Katherine Garbera

All rights reserved. No part of this book may be used or reproduced in any manner whatsoever without written permission.

Without limiting the exclusive rights of any author, contributor or the publisher of this publication, any unauthorized use of this publication to train generative artificial intelligence (AI) technologies is expressly prohibited. Harlequin also exercises their rights under Article 4(3) of the Digital Single Market Directive 2019/790 and expressly reserves this publication from the text and data mining exception.

This is a work of fiction. Names, characters, places and incidents are either the product of the author's imagination or are used fictitiously. Any resemblance to actual persons, living or dead, businesses, companies, events or locales is entirely coincidental.

For questions and comments about the quality of this book, please contact us at CustomerService@Harlequin.com.

TM and ® are trademarks of Harlequin Enterprises ULC.

 Harlequin Enterprises ULC
22 Adelaide St. West, 41st Floor
Toronto, Ontario M5H 4E3, Canada
www.Harlequin.com

HarperCollins Publishers
Macken House, 39/40 Mayor Street Upper,
Dublin 1, D01 C9W8, Ireland
www.HarperCollins.com

Printed in Lithuania

Katherine Garbera is a *USA TODAY* bestselling author of more than one hundred novels, which have been translated into over two dozen languages and sold millions of copies worldwide. She is the mother of two incredibly creative and snarky grown children. Katherine enjoys drinking champagne, reading, walking and traveling with her husband. She lives in Kent, UK, where she is working on her next novel. Visit her on the web at www.katherinegarbera.com.

Books by Katherine Garbera

Harlequin Romantic Suspense

Price Security

Bodyguard Most Wanted
Safe in Her Bodyguard's Arms
Christmas Bodyguard
Find Her
Relentless Pursuit

Visit the Author Profile page
at Harlequin.com for more titles.

This book is for anyone who felt less than and used
and had to grow into their own power.

Acknowledgments:

Special thanks to my editor, John Jacobson,
who gave me the freedom to write a story I wanted
and who was gentle with the limits they set for me.

Chapter 1

Jena Maxwell took a deep breath and forced herself out of her car. She didn't have any family—well, none that she counted on—but she had Brianne. Her best friend and partner in crime. They loved drinking margaritas on Friday night, binging the latest costume drama from the Regency period and dreaming that men in real life could be as handsome, loving and nice as the men on TV.

Reality was a bit different for the two women who'd met as runaways when they were sixteen. They'd both done things they wished they hadn't to make money, but at twenty-four it felt, at least to Jena, that she was finally figuring things out. When Brianne started dating a flashy player named Vex, Jena hadn't been thrilled. But he'd spoiled Brianne with clothes, jewels and trips to Los Angeles and New York City.

Jena knew it was too good to be true, and soon Brianne was at her door bruised and bloodied. She'd promised Jena she wasn't going to go back to Vex. The next time Jena saw her friend was in the morgue when she'd been called in to identify a woman found on the side of a road just outside Houston who listed her as next of kin.

The cops had found that the knife used to slit her throat had been tossed into a ditch with the body. There was no DNA on the knife or on Brianne's body. A dead end. But Jena knew who had killed her friend. She'd given the cops the name Vex, and they'd pretty much shut down.

Even if she could connect the nickname Vex to Tomas Vectra, the suspected leader of the Malus syndicate criminal gang, no one wanted to mess with the all-around bad dude.

They told her if she found hard evidence, and not just her hearsay information that her friend had been dating Vex, they'd investigate. But since Jena had never met Vex and had never actually seen Brianne with him, there was no physical evidence tying him to Brianne for now, and so they wouldn't be talking to him.

Frustrated, Jena had tried in vain to find something linking her friend with Vex, but he hadn't left any clues behind, and neither had Brianne. Even the jewelry and clothes that Brianne had said he'd given her appeared to have been purchased by herself. A few of the retailers seemed to remember a man with her, but other than tall, dark hair and tanned, they hadn't been able to give a description of Vex.

Left with no other options, Jena had resorted to desperate measures. The cops had said Vex was a drug kingpin, and from Brianne's trips (also all solo, according to the official paper trails) to Los Angeles and Manhattan, Jena suspected Texas wasn't his home base. She got in touch with her brother. They weren't close... Both had left their shitty-home sitch when they were teens, and other than getting in touch on Christmas—Joey loved the holiday—they never spoke. But he had connections in the drug world.

She'd asked for his help, and he flat-out warned her not to get involved, but it was too late to change her mind. No one cared about Brianne's death other than her. She'd overheard a deputy saying that Brianne had gotten what she deserved, which had pissed Jena off, and she'd confronted him.

What person deserves to be raped and murdered, with their body dumped on the side of the road?

No matter what she wore or how she acted, Brianne hadn't deserved that. Plus, the thought of Vex getting away with her murder...made Jena want to take matters into her own hands.

The deputy had walked away singed, but no more willing to do any real investigating than he had been before, and Jena knew that everything depended on her. Joey knew a guy on the West Coast who was a former DEA agent. He'd also used his contacts to tell her that Vex was in Los Angeles. There'd been some big arrests out there that had left a power vacuum. According to Joey, a bunch of mid-level crime bosses were out there trying to take it over.

She knew the odds were stacked against her, but she had a few cards up her sleeve. One was her brother's contact's name—Rick Stone. Another was the name of the club Vex was operating out of—Mistral's. She also had some over-the-counter recording equipment. Armed with all that, she'd taken her two weeks' vacation from the Green Valley Bank, bought the cheapest ticket she could find and headed to Los Angeles bent on getting the evidence she needed to bring Tomas Vectra to justice.

She had an idea of the type of woman Vex liked based

on the clothes she'd seen Brianne wearing, and Jena still had her best friend's ankle bracelet, which Vex had given her. She put that on with the shortest skirt she could find, a pair of lethal stilettos and a top that showed off her bosom.

She'd made it as far as the door of Mistral's when she got a good look at Tomas Vectra. He was bigger than she'd expected—at least six two and really muscly. He had a thin mustache and thick eyebrows over dark brown—almost black—eyes. His jaw was hard, and there was a scar on one cheek that made him look even more sinister.

But it was the bevy of women and large guards around him that made her take a step back. Approaching him would be harder than she'd thought. And even if she could get close, it definitely seemed unsafe to question someone that big and dangerous looking. She needed a better plan. She needed…maybe a date rape drug so she could get him a little drugged out before she tried to pump him for information. It might make him talk more freely—and if he did get upset or suspicious about her questions, she'd have an easier time getting away from him if he wasn't at his sharpest.

It took her a few days to find a seller—probably because she kept calling it "date rape drug," and most sellers thought she was a narc. But she'd done her research, realizing that the name of the drug was Rohypnol and that its "on brand" use was to aid those suffering with insomnia. She hit up a local college campus and was finally able to purchase Rohypnol after saying she had trouble sleeping and couldn't afford to go to a doctor.

So here she was again. Back at Mistral's, dressed this time in a sequin slip dress that ended at the tops of her thighs. In her purse, she had her phone turned on to record and the Rohypnol; between her boobs, she'd taped a wireless mic . She had a plan, she had a purpose and she wasn't leaving the club until she had his confession. No matter that her hands were shaking. Her heart beating so loudly like a drum tattoo following each step she took.

After taking a deep breath, she flirted her way into the club and past the VIP bouncers. Getting to Vex...that was the one thing she wasn't sure she knew how to do.

But then he noticed her. The long, black hair that hung almost to her ass. The short, tight dress that showed off all her assets. Apparently, he liked what he saw, because he invited her to his table.

Luck favors the brave, she told herself with more confidence than she truly had.

Even though he held the broken, dirty and somewhat ill-used cigarette loosely in his hand, Rick Stone knew he wasn't going to light it and take a drag. Or was he? It had been a long day, the longest in the last 863 since he'd stopped smoking. No one would know... There was no one around to see him at this hour, standing outside the building that housed the apartments of most of the Price Security team as well as their offices, an underground garage, a workout room and shooting range. But he'd know.

Somehow, despite a life spent working on the streets, or maybe because of it, he clung to his outdated sense of honor. When he made a promise to anyone, including himself, he kept it. He heard something behind him and turned, shoving the cigarette back into the pocket of the trench coat he habitually wore even though it was LA and didn't really rain that much. He liked the pockets.

He saw a woman lurch around the corner. She was wearing only one shoe, and the strap of her sequined dress was torn on one side and flopped down at the top of her left breast. Her mascara had run down her face; her hands shook when she noticed him and ran at him full tilt.

"Are you Rick Stone?"

"I am. Are you okay?" he asked her. She didn't look it. He kept glancing around to see if she'd been followed.

"No, I'm not. My brother gave me your name... I need help," she said.

She kept glancing furtively over her shoulder, and he sensed the urgency and fear in her. Unsure if he should touch her or not, he gestured to the secured and locked doors of the art deco–style building that housed Price Security.

"Come on, let's get you inside," he said, using his fob to gain entry. Once they were inside the bulletproof-glass doors, he moved her toward the elevator that led to the offices on the second floor.

She was still trembling, and when she got in the elevator, she hunched into herself. After shrugging out of his trench coat, he offered it to her, and she gratefully pulled it around her body.

"Where are you taking me?" she asked in a dazed voice.

"My office. I want to get a statement from you, and then we can call the cops—"

"No. I can't... Cops aren't going to believe anything I say. They never do," she said.

That was a lot to unpack and spoke volumes for her background. Having been in the DEA for a big chunk of his adult life and now working closely with law enforcement, he'd seen both sides of it. There were good cops and bad cops, just like people in general were good and bad. "Okay, no cops," he said to reassure her. Depending on what she told him, he might have to go to them eventually, but he'd hold off for now. "Why'd you come to me?"

"My brother, Joey, gave me your name and said you were solid. If I got into trouble...you'd help me."

Joey. Well, that wasn't much to go on. For now, he wanted to get her settled down and talking to him. But he'd need more later. "I have an apartment here if you'd rather go there than to my office."

She nodded, clutching his coat closer to her body. Her eyes were wide, hands trembling. Was she going into shock?

Hell.

He'd recently been on a case where teens had been trafficked, and some of them had had this look after the drugs wore off. Whatever had happened to her had clearly been rough, and now she was dealing with the aftereffects.

He escorted her into his apartment, making eye contact with the security camera, knowing that Lee and their boss, Van, would be watching. He needed time, which his look would tell them both.

Once inside, he escorted her to the couch, which was well-worn overstuffed leather. He loved that shabby couch, and more nights than not ended up crashed there instead of in the king-size bed in his room. He shoved a pile of comics to the side so she'd have space to sit.

"Want a drink?" he asked her while turning on the table lamps and heading toward the kitchen. His apartment was more of a warren of bookcases and comfy chairs. He knew that his coworkers' places were more luxurious, but despite making a very healthy salary, Rick was more comfortable with his secondhand furniture and cozy surroundings.

"Yes."

"What do you want?" he asked her. Her long, black hair was draped over her shoulder, reaching almost to her waist.

He started to take stock of the woman as if he were filling out a police report...the very thing she wanted to avoid.

But the cop in him was used to recording details. She knotted and unknotted her fingers before shoving one hand under her body between her thigh and his trench coat. She tugged the short skirt of the minidress lower, but it still only hit the top of her thigh.

She stared at him, lightly rocking back and forth. Damn. He had a feeling she wasn't going to like the idea of going to the emergency room any more than calling the cops. After opening cabinets until he found the bottle of Jack he kept for emergencies, he sloshed a good amount into a juice glass and walked back to her.

Without a word, he thrust it toward her. She grasped it with both hands, which he noticed were scraped and bleeding. Her eyes were huge as she took a big swallow of the whiskey and then gasped as it burned its way down her throat.

Perching on the coffee table close to her but giving her some space, he leaned in. "You're safe here. It's time to tell me what's going on."

She licked her lips, flinching when her tongue moved over the swollen abrasion in the corner. Tears burned her eyes, and her hands shook harder, until he took the glass from her, setting it aside and holding her hands securely in his.

"I'm here. You're safe," he repeated. Hoping that was what she needed to hear.

"I... I...don't think... I mean, I'm not sure... How can I be?"

"What happened?" he asked again, using a firm tone but keeping the level of his voice even.

"I...think I killed a man."

* * *

Rick Stone was hella good at masking his response. Nothing registered on the man's face. He simply nodded and then walked back to the kitchen to pour himself a glass of the same whiskey he'd given her.

Speaking of which… She picked the glass back up and took another swallow, as if booze could wipe away the images from the last forty minutes that were running through her head on a loop. Vex's people had noticed her hand over his his drink, and while he'd already taken a sip or two before they had, the drug hadn't been potent enough to have any effect on him that fast. She'd tried to flirt it out and make it seem like it was a party drug she'd given him so they could have some fun…but that had simply ratcheted the tension in the room up a notch. He'd dragged her toward the stairs that led to the second floor by her wrist. Telling his bodyguards he'd be okay with her.

Well, maybe not that lucky, since it still had hurt when she'd jerked her head back to keep him from pulling her up the stairs. She'd scrambled to her feet as he jerked her arm almost out of the socket. There had only been a few people left in the club. Most of them had looked the other way… Then it was a blur. Her running for the ladies bathroom. Him following, hitting her, her realizing there was a very strong chance she might die…determined if she did that at least she'd get his DNA on her body.

He'd held her up against the wall of the bathroom with his hand wrapped around her neck. Gasping for air, desperate, she'd tried kicking his nuts and scratching his hand. He'd pulled out the knife and asked if she liked things rough. Oh God.

She'd jerked herself off-balance and he staggered back, still holding her. She pushed the knife toward him as he lurched back to her and…the knife entered the side of his neck, blood spraying everywhere…

"So tell me what happened," Rick said when he came back.

The story spilled out of her—all of it except for Brianne, including the fact that she'd come from Texas. He didn't need to know about her friend. Right now it was enough for him to know just that she'd killed Vex.

"After I stabbed him, I turned and ran for the door. I didn't look back. But they were all frantic around him," she said. "I didn't want to go to the cops because I'm not sure they'd believe me that it was self-defense."

That was totally true. The cops seemed to never believe women when they came forward, especially dressed the way she was. "Were you raped?"

"No. It never got that far," she said.

"I'm glad to hear that. Now, we need to get you cleaned up and take your statement. I'm going to call in a coworker so you'll feel more comfortable," he said, taking out his phone. His fingers moved over the screen as he tapped out a message.

"I'm not sure we need anyone else," she said. The less people who saw her, the better. "I think I should disappear. You know, like move-to-another-country-kind of thing."

That had totally worked for Patrick Swayze in *Point Break*. Plus, she'd read an article about houses in Italy that could be purchased for one euro. Yeah, that's where she was heading.

Rick dropped his phone on the table next to where he sat, crossing his arms over his chest. The movement pulled the fabric of his button-down shirt taut across his arms, which surprisingly were muscly. He gave off a teddy bear sort of vibe, so seeing his biceps flex was a shock.

"Uh, what?"

"Well, I mean I killed him...and I don't want to go to jail," she said. Her mind was whirling. Ever since she'd heard the name Vex, things had been shitty. Brianne had been out of control and falling hard, then she was dead, and now... Jena was a killer. She'd been made into a murderer because of that man.

While she couldn't regret that he was dead and couldn't hurt another person, she hated that he'd forced her to take a life. Her hands started shaking again. Maybe she should stay here and go to jail. That was only fair. No one had the right to take another person's life.

Rick wiping her cheek with a tissue made her realize she was crying. "It's going to be okay. Let's take care of you. Lee will be here in a few minutes."

"Who's Lee?"

"My coworker. She's going to take your statement, and I'll make a few calls to verify that he's dead. Where did this happen?"

"A club in West Hollywood. Mistral's."

"Shit. Who did you kill?"

"Tomas Vectra, aka Vex. I think he's the head of the Malus syndicate."

"Hell. You sure he was dead?" Rick asked. "He's a big guy."

She gagged thinking about the body on the ground and all that blood around him. The smell had been strong. Her hands shook as she realized how close it had come to her body being the one on the floor.

"I think so. I mean, there was a lot of blood from his neck, and he hit the ground hard. His guards were all on him, and I ran. I didn't wait to verify it, but it looked to me like he was bleeding out."

"Have you ever seen a person bleed out?" he asked.

She shook her head. "Just on TV."

There was a knock on the door; he stood up to answer it. She took another sip of the whiskey since it calmed her nerves. Until Rick had asked, it hadn't occurred to her that Vex could still be alive. She needed to check the recording she'd made in the club, see what she'd captured.

Should she tell Rick about it?

There wasn't time to decide before a woman with dark hair in a ponytail, wearing jeans, a T-shirt and an easy smile, came over to her.

"Hi there. I'm Lee. I'm going to take your statement and get as many facts down as we can," she said.

"I won't talk to a cop."

"I'm not a cop. Neither is Rick. We're in private personal security. Now that you're here with us, you're our client."

Client.

"I don't have any money—"

"You don't need it," Rick said. "We're going to keep you safe."

Their eyes met. A feeling of warmth and safety seemed to wrap around her. This teddy bear of a man, with his soft eyes and muscled body, made her feel some security, and it had been a lifetime since she'd been able to say that.

There was a lot he didn't know. Things that might make him change his mind about whether she deserved his protection, but for this moment, while her body was aching as bruises formed on her arms and legs and blood dried on her arms and face, it was enough.

Chapter 2

Being unobtrusive was sort of his happy place. He thrived on blending into the background and observing—seeing everyone once their guard was down. It didn't take a genius to figure out that she was hiding something. Actually, she was hiding a lot of things. He didn't even know her name or the full name of the elusive Joey.

"What's your name?" he asked while Lee was setting up her laptop to start taking down the statement.

"Oh, it's Jena. Jena Maxwell," she said.

Which really didn't clear up this Joey she'd mentioned. "How do I know your brother?"

"He's a DEA informant in Brownsville, Texas," she said. "He said he worked with you about ten years ago."

At that time, Jena couldn't have been more than sixteen. She looked incredibly fragile and young sitting on the couch. He wanted to protect her. Not exactly a shock—everyone knew he had a white knight complex. Was that even a thing? It was what his sister had called it. Said he wanted to ride in on a charger and rescue everyone.

He'd failed a few times. In recent years, he'd tried to hide that knight away so he could function in the real world without losing his mind. It wasn't as easy as it should be at forty. He still wanted to help whenever he saw a damsel in distress—but he also had the insight to know when someone was trying to manipulate him. And right now, he was well aware that Jena was using her vulnerability to keep them from pressing her for more details.

He'd recently spent a lot of time in Mistral's helping to bring down the head of the La Fortunata crime syndicate. He easily pictured her cleaned up, making her way to the VIP section. The rest of her details were a little vague. In part because she was dazed. Fair enough. But he got the sense that there was more to it than that. There were things she was deliberately holding back. Missing pieces to this puzzle.

A date gone violently wrong didn't usually end the way she'd described. "Where's the knife you used on Vex?"

"Uh, I took it. It's in my bag," she said.

"We need an evidence bag," Lee said. "I'll be right back."

Lee left after giving him a glance that he pretended he couldn't read. She didn't like that Jena was here and not at a police station.

Jena fumbled for her cross-body bag, which he noticed now for the first time. The bag didn't go with the stripper heels and dress she wore. It was a large leather messenger-style bag.

Rick filed that away as well. Just another piece of the picture that didn't quite fit. He noticed strands of long, dark hair caught in the sequins on her dress.

"Wig?" he asked, not touching the strands since they'd probably have DNA on them too.

She nodded. "He likes women with long, dark hair."

Interesting. She'd known Vex's type before she'd gone to the club.

"We should be collecting all of this. I have a friend who's a detective on the force. I think we should call her."

Her hands shook again. "I... She'd have to arrest me. I killed a man."

"She will have to question you and collect evidence. Better to control the narrative of the case than to be called in after the fact. Were there any witnesses to your encounter in the club?"

"There weren't too many sober people left in the club. A couple of bouncers and the bartender," she said. "They aren't going to be helpful to me. They watched him drag me toward the stairs by my wrist and didn't lift a finger to help me."

A chill went down his back. How had she gotten away? There didn't seem to be enough strength in her to fight her way free.

Lee walked back in, followed by Rick's boss, Van. Jena shrank farther into his trench coat and back against the couch.

"Hello, there," Van said in that rumbly, reassuring voice of his. It was deep and could make a person feel like nothing could touch them. Van was of average height and muscled. He had a bald head and a tattoo of angel wings around his neck. He habitually wore dark suits and, even though it was the middle of the night, had one on now.

Jena nodded, but her eyes sought Rick's. He was her touchstone, not Van or Lee. He sat on the edge of the coffee table again, awkwardly patting her arm in a way he hoped reassured her.

"Jena, this is my boss, Giovanni Price," he said.

Van smiled easily and reassuringly at them, but there were questions in his eyes.

"Call me Van. Everyone does," he said. "Rick?"

"I mentioned Detective Miller," he informed Van. "Are we good to call her?" he asked Jena. "We'll all be here with you."

"What if she has to arrest me?"

"We have a very good lawyer on retainer that will keep you out of jail for now," Van said.

Rick appreciated that it might be a hard decision for Jena to make, but the fact that Van was in the room already told Rick that his boss had made the call. He didn't disagree. There was a lot about Jena that had to be preserved. Her appearance spoke volumes as to what had happened. It was all evidence that would be crucial in proving she'd acted in self-defense.

"Okay," she said. "Please know I never meant to kill anyone."

"Of course, sweetheart," Van said. "You don't have that vibe."

"You do."

He thought she was talking to Van, but her eyes were on Rick. And if that was what she thought of him, then she wasn't wrong. It wasn't a stretch to say he'd killed in the line of duty, but had she picked up on the other deaths... the ones that had nothing to do with work and everything to do with vengeance? Those people lived in his memory, sometimes haunting him, but they weren't his only ghosts. He'd also held victims as they died of overdoses, self-harm and gunshot wounds. Death had been dancing around him since he was a teen.

"Only when I'm pressed." Hopefully, that reassured her that she was still safe.

"I'm glad."

There was a knock on his door. Van opened it to let in Detective Miller, who looked as exhausted as she always did. Cops were always stretched thin, and he knew that Detective Miller picked up more cases than most. That woman was determined to mete out justice for as many as she could.

"Good thing I said yes," Jena said dryly, and for the first time, Rick saw the woman she must be when she wasn't the victim of violence. No matter the outcome, she had been beaten and threatened. But there was a strength and resilience to her all the same. It told him that she'd get through this.

"Good thing."

She gave him a slight smile, even as she winced a little from the wound on the side of her mouth. It was still one hell of a smile. The kind that made it all the harder for him to see her as a client rather than a woman. At the same time, though, the wound just emphasized her vulnerability, her need for help. *His* help.

If he had a type, it would definitely be a woman in need of his protection. It wasn't just burnout that had led him to leave the DEA and come work as a bodyguard for Price Security. It was also that damn white knight complex that was going into full-on overload as he tried not to look at Jena.

Detective Miller took photos of Jena's every scrape, cut and bruise. She also talked to her privately to verify that she didn't need to use the rape kit. Jena was grateful she could honestly say no. The panic was still in the pit of her stomach from Vex's gravelly voice asking if she liked it rough.

The other woman was shorter than Jena's own five foot, seven inches. She had brown hair that hung to the top of her shoulders and wore a pair of black pants with a matching blazer. Her white shirt had an open collar, and she wore sensible shoes. She looked a bit like some of the social workers who'd used to come and check on her and Joey when they were children.

"Can you use a rape kit posthumously?" she asked.

"Usually the autopsy includes that. Why?"

"My friend was raped, beaten and murdered. The cops told me they didn't find any trace of the man who did it," Jena half whispered. There was still a white-hot pain deep in her gut whenever she thought about how Brianne had looked when Jena identified her body.

Detective Miller squeezed her hand carefully. "I'm sorry for your loss. If the assailant wore a condom, it can be hard to find any DNA unless the detectives found the condom too," she said.

Of course Vex would have. He left no trace. That was why Jena was pretty sure she'd have ended up dead, her body dumped in the trash somewhere, if she hadn't managed to get away. None of those people at Mistral's would have done sweet fuck-all to help her.

"Thanks for trusting me to take these photos. We will try to get DNA from your clothes. I'll take them when you get changed."

Like she'd had a choice about the photos. Jena had never been big on letting anyone help her and wasn't sure how she felt about it now. What she did know was that changing into fresh clothes sounded fantastic. But what was she supposed to change in to? Should she return to her motel room? "Okay."

Detective Miller glanced over at Rick where he was talking with his boss and Lee. They'd all been really nice to her, but the panic was still there. Was she about to get booked and charged with murder? Or would the police believe she'd acted in self-defense? Right now Detective Miller had sent a unit to Mistral's to retrieve the body and mark off the crime scene.

Rick came over as Detective Miller moved away to process everything she'd taken from Jena, the photos and statement. It was hard to be believe it was almost seven in the morning when she glanced at the clock.

"You doing okay?" he asked, his voice low and husky, soothing the panic that still kept trying to consume her.

"Yeah." She shrugged back into his trench coat. Now that she wasn't intent on seducing the truth from Vex, the dress felt too short and exposing. She pushed her hand into the pocket, felt a cigarette and pulled it out.

Rick's eyes went to the cigarette, then back to hers. She tried to hand it to him, but he shook his head. "That stays in the pocket."

"Why?" she asked. The cigarette was the distraction she needed. It wasn't any big deal that he smoked, but the way his entire body had changed when he saw her holding the cigarette told her there was more to it than just a smoke in his pocket.

"Uh…" He shoved his hand through his hair and gave her a rueful grin. "It's there just in case."

That made her smile even though the side of her mouth hurt. "Just in case of what?"

"I quit a while back, but the craving is still there. So I

keep that in my pocket to assuage that need. I pretend that if things got really bad, then I'd use it. So far they haven't gotten that bad. So yeah."

Rick Stone. This man wasn't what she'd expected at all. After days of watching Vex and his gang enter and leave Mistal's, she could see that there was the same tension in Rick when he'd first brought her up to his apartment. He'd been on guard. Tense as if expecting someone to attack. But since that moment, he'd settled down. A calmness exuded from him, helping her to battle her nerves as she came down from her adrenaline rush.

"I like that. Habits are really hard to break," she said, more to herself than to him.

"What habit are you trying to break?" he asked.

She didn't know him well enough to share it. But in her heart, she knew it was trying to fix people. That was how she and Brianne had become friends. That was why she'd walked away from Joey—to save herself from her impulses. If there was a way she could wrap everyone she knew in something protective like Bubble Wrap and ensure they only trusted people who had their best interests at heart, then she'd do it. But that wasn't possible, even with the people she loved most.

"Just the usual stuff. Binge-watching too much TV. Screen time."

His eyes narrowed, but he only nodded. "So why are you in LA?"

"Uh." God, she'd hoped he wouldn't ask. She had no good reason. Her mind whirled with things she could say, and none of them made any sense. "Vacation."

"On your own?" he asked.

Just me and the ghost of Brianne. Which she totally didn't say. "Yup."

"Why did your brother give you my name? Did you anticipate getting into drug-related trouble?" At the moment, Rick didn't look like the cuddly teddy bear he had earlier. Steely determination was in every tensed, rigid part of his body. He wanted answers, and he didn't seem to buy her half-baked story.

"I... I just mentioned I was going to be here and he..."

"Said there's a former DEA agent I used to know who lives there now?" Rick suggested.

Yeah, when he said it out loud, it sounded even dumber than it had in her head. "Okay, there's a little more to the story than that, but I can't get into it with all these people around. Joey mentioned you in case I got into trouble."

"Which you did. So what were you really doing at Mistral's?" he asked.

She took a deep breath, realizing that the room had gone quiet. Rick wasn't the only one interested in her answer. God, she wasn't ready to tell him or a cop why she had come to LA.

Detective Miller's phone pinged, and she read the message before turning to Jena. "There's no body at Mistral's. Right now, there's no proof that you killed anyone."

Detective Miller, Van and Lee all cleared out of his apartment while Jena went to grab a shower, and get some sleep. Detective Miller took her clothes in an evidence bag with her. She was going to talk with witnesses at the club who had come forward to mention concern for a young lady who matched Jena's description. Detective Miller had Rick's contact information, and Jena had lost her phone in the escape, so she gave that number to Detective Miller as well.

Lee was tracking down the phone based on pings from

the cell phone towers nearby, and Van was using his contacts to find out where Vex's hang was.

Rick, who didn't have any task to take care of, was restless and edgy. Perfectly understandable, given the night he'd had that had bled into morning. Not that he was at all ready to deal with it being morning after a night of no sleep. Fortunately, his apartment had blackout shades because he preferred it cool and dark, which meant that he could block out the morning sun.

Jena had handed him back the trench coat before going through his bedroom to get to the bathroom to shower. He put the coat on a hook on the wall, reaching in to check on his cigarette before turning away.

A smoke wasn't going to take the edge off. Nothing would until he got the truth out of Jena. He was sure she'd been attacked, and believed she killed Vex. But he was equally certain that she wasn't in LA on vacation and that her brother hadn't just given up his name.

She'd been on the verge of telling him something. He would bet that cigarette in his pocket it wouldn't have been the truth. There was no way she was coming clean with a man she'd just met or the cop who had been called in despite her wishes.

This mess she was in shouldn't be his concern, except the minute she'd walked up to him asking if he was Rick Stone, her problem had become his. Protecting her was one thing. He could keep her safe here at Price Tower. But the truth was, he wanted more. He wanted those secrets he saw lurking in the back of her eyes.

Wanted to understand that nervous way she fiddled with her hair when she thought no one was looking at her. Wanted to hear the out-there story he had no doubt she was cooking up in the shower to tell him. Wanted to uncover the truth.

There was something innocent behind the bruised body. He couldn't put his finger on what it was, except to say that she wasn't the kind of woman he'd expected to see in this situation. The dress clearly made her uncomfortable; he'd noticed the way she kept trying to pull the hem lower.

So why had Jena put on that dress, gone to Mistral's and ended up at Vex's table? One explanation could be she was drawn to dangerous men. That was completely buyable. He didn't think she was the type, but he'd been wrong before, so he definitely wasn't ruling that out.

He did wonder about the knife. It had gone into an evidence bag, but Detective Miller had left it, along with Jena's torn dress, here at the Tower for now. Locked in a vault that no one could get into without a security code.

But the knife didn't fit the LA gang profile either. It was one of those hunting knives that was used when they were torturing informants to get information. That was it. He suddenly realized why he was uncomfortable with her story.

He'd seen a knife like that used on two women during a case he'd worked when he'd been in Brownsville. One of them had been seeing a gang leader for the Malus syndicate and had agreed to be an informant for Rick. She'd been beaten and tortured to death before her body was dumped outside of town. And the murder weapon had been a knife very similar to the one Jena had brought into his home.

It was a leap, he told himself.

But she was from Texas...maybe Brownsville. And she'd shown up at club that was still a gang hangout despite the arrests that had been made six months ago. He still couldn't figure out how all the pieces of the puzzle came together though. Everything he was coming up with wasn't making sense.

The door to his room opened, and she stood in the doorway, in his sweats. They were too big for her, but she'd rolled the waist at the top to make them shorter. He could see the bunched-up waistband under one of his T-shirts, which she'd also borrowed. Her hair was dark blond from the water and only about shoulder length. She looked younger without the makeup on.

Innocence radiated around her as he glanced at her body, which was so much more appealing draped in his big clothes. "Thank you."

He nodded. "I think we need to talk."

"I guess it's too much to hope that you'd be happy with the explanation of 'wrong place, wrong time'?" she asked as she came into the living room and sat on the opposite end of the couch from him. She curled her legs underneath her and leaned her head against the back of the couch.

"Definitely."

She chewed her lower lip and then shook her head. "What do you want to know?"

She was clever, not revealing anything until he showed his cards first. But then, that didn't surprise him. His gut was saying this was a woman looking for answers and maybe justice or revenge. Asking him a question when he asked her one was a tidy way to ensure she didn't expose more than she had to.

"What do you do when you're not on vacation?" he asked.

He noticed he'd surprised her, which had been his goal. He didn't want to hear her rehearsed story; he wanted her relaxed and talking so that the truth might slip out.

"I'm a loan officer at Green Valley Bank on the outskirts of Houston," she said.

"So, not Brownsville where your brother is?"

"No. We grew up there though," she said. "That's how I know about you. Joey told me about when you asked him to help you. He said you were a decent guy. A trustworthy man."

"I am," he told her. Once someone earned his loyalty, they had it for life. And Joey Maxwell had done that when Rick's case in Brownsville went south. That kid had been solid. He wanted to believe his sister was too, but he'd have to get to the truth first.

Chapter 3

The plan she'd come up with in the shower was to ask him to help her find a new identity. Then she'd take her meager savings and move to Europe and try to buy one of those one dollar houses that were always being advertised on travel shows.

But she couldn't ask him for anything yet. Not when it was clear he still didn't trust her. He was watching her with a level gaze that made her feel like he could see straight through any lie she might be tempted to tell him. It was enough to keep her silent.

At the same time though, she found herself wanting to confide in him. Her brother trusted Rick. That was the only thing that had made her run to him. That, and she'd had nowhere else to go and very clearly needed all the help she could get.

It was scarier than she'd thought it would be to be trapped in that club with a killer. A part of her wasn't sure what "no body" meant. Had she killed Vex and his men took the body someplace? The true crime podcasts she listened to were usually full of bodies found in out-of-the-way locations—usually hidden by the killers to keep their crimes under wraps. But she certainly hadn't hidden Vex's body. So who had? And why?

And were those same people going to come after her?

"Jena?" he asked.

"Yes?" she responded.

"Why were you at Mistral's?"

She took a long breath. The truth…well, she wasn't ready to reveal her hand to Rick Stone. No matter how trustworthy he might be. His boss had still called the cops when she asked him not to.

Even though Detective Miller had been very helpful in taking a statement from her and collecting evidence from her attack, Jena wondered if that would have helped Brianne. The first time she'd seen her friend bruised after a night with Vex, should Jena have taken photos as proof?

"I told you—just wanted to get out of my hotel room," she said.

He stood up and walked away from her toward the windows with blackout shades that lined the far wall of the living area. They were tinted and bulletproof, something Van had mentioned earlier. Supposedly that made it safer for her here.

But the truth was, she didn't feel safe. She felt scared and angry and unsure. There hadn't been time to listen to the recording she'd made on her phone. She'd lied about losing it to the detective because she thought the woman might want to take it into evidence as well.

Plus, the voice recording, if it had been clean, would

definitely reveal that she'd been coming on to Vex. It also would have caught his accusation that she'd drugged him.

It was a lot more than she wanted to get into. In fact, she really just wanted to sleep, but Rick clearly wanted answers. She got it. She'd shown up on his doorstep, bringing a mess and possibly murder with her.

"How about I make some guesses and you tell me if I'm right?"

His suggestion was welcome. She didn't want to lie to this man any more than she already had. He gave her a smile that was gentle but determined.

"Okay."

"A chance meeting with Vex brought you to his attention. He liked you, gave you gifts and then invited you to join him for drinks tonight. You showed up ready for a fun night with the handsome—"

"He's not handsome," Jena interrupted. There was a cruelty to Vex that couldn't be masked with Hugo Boss.

"He's not? Then why did you go?"

Yeah, Jena, why? She could only fall back on what Brianne used to say. "He's surprisingly charming and splashes money around."

All true. There had been a few moments tonight before things turned violent when Jena had a glimpse at the man that Brianne must have fallen for. The man who was attentive and sensual.

"Ah, so you're at the club, things get heated between you and then you realize—what? What is it that makes you stop? Does he get violent?"

Uh, no, he caught me putting the Rohypnol into his drink. But she wasn't about to admit to that.

"It was... I'm not into hooking up in bathrooms at clubs," she admitted.

Though she had planned to entice Vex into the VIP bathroom with just that promise, if only so she could get him alone and ask questions about Brianne. He had seemed dazed at first but then snapped out of it. That was when Jena had realized her plan was going to backfire and there was a very real possibility that she might die too.

Rick didn't say anything. He just watched her. "He put his hand around my throat and was strangling me. I tried kicking and punching him, and he pulled a knife from his pocket...asked me if I liked it rough and..."

The rest was a nightmare blur. She'd managed to claw at his face with her long nails, and he'd loosened his grip on her throat to pin her against the wall. As soon as she'd seen the knife, her gut had screamed that it must be the same one he'd used on Brianne. A sort of red mist had come over Jena. She had to get the weapon from him.

She'd fought him for it, and maybe the Rohypnol had kicked in enough to help her, but she'd been able to get it from his hands.

"But you don't, and that's when the fight started?" he asked.

She nodded. Well, really, it had escalated when she'd accused him of killing Brianne and told him that she had evidence it was him. He had told her that she was a crazy bitch and come at her.

That moment when she'd stabbed him...her heart had been beating so fast she thought she was going to have a heart attack. She'd thrown up as he'd crumpled to the floor of the bathroom, his blood all over the place.

He was gurgling something as she shoved the knife in her bag and walked out of the bathroom and then out of the club.

"Yeah... I'm not even sure how I was able to get the knife from him. But if I hadn't, I'm pretty sure I'd be dead," she said.

He felt like he had a rough idea of what had happened. Her hands had stopped shaking, and she looked small sitting on the edge of that couch. There was something in her eyes though that was more than fear. It looked closer to anger—which he got, but made him feel like he hadn't gotten the entire story.

"You're lucky you aren't," he said at last.

Her ragged exhalation drew him back to the couch. "Not every woman who crossed Vex's path was so lucky."

Maybe this was the piece of the puzzle he'd been missing. "Ah, who was she?" he asked.

"My best friend. A sweet girl, really. It was like you said. He saw her in Houston and showered her with gifts, swept her off her feet. Then slowly things started to get rough between them. Like not on her first few dates. He sent her money to fly to New York for a weekend... When she came home she had bruises. She was scared."

"I bet she was. What did you do?"

"There was nothing I *could* do. I tried talking her out of seeing him again when he came back to town a few months later. Told Brianne she deserved better. But...he gave her a Cartier watch and money to get a nice apartment...and it just kept escalating until I got a call to identify her body. She had been found on the side of the road. I tried to tell the police it was Vex."

"They didn't believe you?" Rick asked.

Jena shook her head. "I didn't have any proof. I had never met him. All the gifts he'd given Brianne had been purchased with cash, and even the plane ticket she'd paid for and he reimbursed her. There was no paper trail linking the two of them. Just my word. And that isn't enough."

"Which led you here?"

"Joey was really helpful. He told me everything he knew about Vex. He still works with the DEA. He tried to talk me out of coming, said that Vex was a big-time player known for being sadistic and dangerous. Two things that I already knew."

Rick sat down on the couch. His own sister had fallen for a midlevel drug dealer. Rick had a pretty good idea of how Brianne's relationships with Vex had played out. The gifts, cars and money that started the relationship, and then the slow escalation of violence. "What did you hope to accomplish?"

"I wanted to get him to confess," she said.

A confession. That was tricky. Rules of evidence meant that a confession couldn't be used in court if it had been coerced, something he was pretty sure that Jena, with her need for vengeance for her friend, hadn't been thinking of. That was why this sort of thing was better left to law enforcement. But given what she'd said about the cops not believing her about Vex, he could see why she'd felt she had to take action herself. No doubt she'd been trapped between wanting someone to pay for her friend's life and the reality that there wasn't much she could do.

He was starting to figure out what had caused the confrontation between her and Vex at Mistral's. That solved one question he had…which was how things had gotten so out of hand in the first place. Men like Vex usually didn't indulge in their hobby of hurting women in public. Too many witnesses.

"So you confronted him?"

"I did. Well, first I tried to drug him to sort of loosen his inhibitions."

"Good God."

"Yeah, it was tricky, and he's bigger than I expected. Maybe I should have used more."

His mind was spinning. The fact that she'd made it out of Mistral's alive was something of a miracle. Ownership had changed since Lee and her DEA undercover-agent boyfriend, Aaron, had taken down the La Fortunata crime syndicate that had operated from there. But once a hot spot for drugs, always a hot spot for drugs. He doubted they'd even bothered boarding up the old secret entrance.

Drugging Vex wasn't smart. If the man had noticed her doing that… Honestly he was still processing the fact that she'd made it out of there alive. "That plan—"

"Would have worked if I'd had more drugs, right? I just needed him to confess. I really hate the idea of him out here living like nothing happened, with Brianne as just another murdered girl who doesn't get any justice. It's not right."

Rick couldn't agree more. He had his own demons when it came to the unsolved murders of women. He'd never been able to run far enough or fast enough to escape them.

"So what was the goal here?" he asked, still not sure why she'd come out here to Los Angeles and done something so foolish. He could tell she wasn't reckless by nature. Something had pushed her to this.

"Get evidence and then turn it over to the cops so they arrest him."

That wasn't easy to do. "Do you really work for a bank?"

"Yes."

His incredulity must have shown on his face, because he put her hand up toward him.

"I listen to a lot of true crime podcasts, watch a lot of TV and movies, and read a lot of thrillers. I know that one woman can get justice," she said. "I just didn't realize how scary it would be. Also, when I thought I'd killed Vex... I mean, I still might have, right?"

"Yeah, you might have. Detective Miller will have people out searching for a body. We can watch the club. Lee was undercover there not that long ago as a bartender. She can't go back, but she put in some passive surveillance equipment. I'll see what she can find out."

"Thanks, I really appreciate that. You've been great tonight," she said with a small smile.

"Yeah? It's the least I could do."

"What happens if they don't find Vex's body?" she asked.

"What happens to you, you mean?"

She nodded.

"I'm just guessing, but Detective Miller will probably file an assault report on your behalf, putting on the record that he got violent first. So if the body shows up, that will already be recorded. If he's not dead...what will you do? Are you going back to Houston?"

"Do you think he might not be dead?"

"Until we see a body, everything is possible."

"I'm not leaving until I know he's dead or arrested for Brianne's murder."

There was no use pretending she was going anywhere. Not until she'd done what she came here to do. Maybe if she was a different person, she could have gotten justice in some other way, without getting her hands dirty. If she had better computer skills or understood how to hack, then she could have looked into his financial transactions. Maybe caught him that way.

But that wasn't an option for her, so instead she was stuck doing it the risky way. "Could you teach me how to use a gun? And is California an open-carry state?"

"No, and what?"

"If he's not dead, he's probably going to come after me," she pointed out. "I straight up told him I know he killed Brianne."

"Of course you did. What were you thinking?"

"That I better get him to confess before he kills me," she said. "Just so you know, he never even tried to deny it. Instead, he tried to strangle me, so yeah, I'm sure he did it."

Leaning forward and putting his head in his hands, Rick didn't respond to that. Maybe she was oversharing, but he was her only ally in this—for now, at least. If he didn't want to help her, she'd find someone else. She'd come too close tonight to give up and go home.

Also, the more time she was away from Vex, the less scared she felt. She'd come damn close to getting the information she needed to go to the police. Next time she'd succeed. She was sure of it.

Rick lifted his head; his hair was rumpled. For the first time, she noticed him as a man. He stretched his arm along the back of the couch, and her eyes were drawn to his biceps as he tipped his head back, staring at the ceiling.

"You don't have to help me," she said. "I can go back to my motel."

Getting to her feet, she started for the kitchen counter, where she'd left her bag.

"Stop. You're staying here, and I'm going to be acting as your bodyguard until Vex is found, dead or alive."

"Uh, that's not necessary." How was she going to find

Vex and force him to confess if Rick was with her all the time?

"It is. So let's start at the beginning. Did you follow Vex to figure out where he was?"

"Yeah. Joey knew he was in LA and said that Mistral's would be a good place to start. So I went in looking like regular me and no one noticed. I followed Vex to a house in Beverly Hills with a high gate. I've driven by it a few times, but despite what I've seen in the movies, I'm not sure I can get over the fence and into the house without being spotted."

"What kind of movies are you watching?"

"*Lethal Weapon*…the entire series, and *Beverly Hills Cop*. Again, all four movies," she pointed out. She'd gotten a few ideas from watching them. They'd been available through her library and had been the first hits when she googled cop movies set in Los Angeles.

"So you prepped by watching cop movies. Anything else?"

"I bought Rohypnol near the college campus."

"Great. So have you talked to anyone about Vex?" he asked.

"Not really. Just followed him around while I got my hands on the drug. Then I waited until I had enough courage to go and confront him."

He gave her a sympathetic smile. "It's not easy."

"How would you know?"

"I was an undercover DEA agent, remember? Every time I would start a new assignment, my nerves were shot waiting to see if they'd buy my cover," he told her.

"That's how I was. But also, I had to build my cover all by myself. I just knew I had to try to be the kind of woman Vex would go for... It took me three tries before I got into the VIP area."

Rick shifted around so he faced her and put his hand on her knee. The heat of his touch was warm and comforting, but also stirred more awareness of him as a man. "I promise you that I will see that Vex is brought to justice. Even if he's dead, I will investigate and find the evidence to prove he killed your friend."

Distracted for a moment by his green eyes, which were so pretty this close up, she didn't respond. Then his words sank in. "Great. I'll help you. I have to see this through. I have tons of information on him. Together we can catch him. I need to do this for Brianne."

There was a few tense moments, and then he sighed. "I get that. Okay. Well, if we find your phone, that might lead us to him. They'd want to remove anything you dropped or left behind tonight."

Oh f— Her phone. Which was currently in her bag on the counter. What was Lee going to tell him when she traced the signal and found it here?

But Rick was still talking, so she didn't have a chance to tell him the truth.

"First thing tomorrow morning, we can head over to Mistral's and stake it out."

"I get to go too, right?"

"Yes. There's a old movie called *Stakeout* if you want to do some more research," he said with a grin.

"Smart-ass." But she liked that he teased her. It made her feel a little more normal, like she might be able to sleep tonight without nightmares keeping her awake. But no, the nightmares were probably inevitable. Never in her life had she been so scared or so unsure of making it out alive.

Brianne had no doubt felt that and so much worse because her friend had thought she loved Vex. That Vex loved her too. How wrong Brianne had been.

"You're probably ready for some sleep. You can take my room—"

"I'm not sure I can sleep. You can keep your room. If it's okay, I'll just sit here and watch videos," she said.

"Or I can keep you company and we can watch *Stakeout*," he said.

"I'd like that." She guessed he'd figured out she didn't want to be alone. Maybe if she was lucky, the movie would lull her to sleep with no nightmares. But the truth was, she wasn't counting on that. Nothing had gone her way since the moment she'd set foot in LA. except meeting Rick Stone.

Chapter 4

He knew the exact moment she drifted off to sleep. Immediately he lowered the volume on the comedy he'd put on to distract her. On paper, the cast of Emilio Estevez and Richard Dreyfuss shouldn't work they were both so opposite, but it did its job as far as he was concerned.

He'd been on enough stakeouts to know they were long and boring most of the time. His phone vibrated in his pocket. Careful not to disturb Jena, he got up, made sure she was covered with the blanket and went into the kitchen for a Fanta. He'd given up so many vices but had never been able to quit the sugary orange soda.

Lee: So...her phone is in your apartment.

Fuck. Just fuck. Trust was hard to build, so he shouldn't be surprised that she'd lied to him, but he was. Because he'd been starting to see her as a woman he wanted to trust.

He had been halfway there even though his gut told him she was hiding stuff.

Turns out he was hella right on that one.

Rick: Thnx.

He shoved his phone back in his pocket. Out of the corner of his eye, he saw his trench coat on the back of the chair where she'd left it, and almost went for his crutch: that damn dirty old cigarette he'd been toting around for too long.

On his way to the chair, he noticed her bag on his kitchen counter. Given that she'd changed out of that skimpy dress and into his sweats, he didn't have to put that much effort into deducing her phone must be in the bag. He didn't feel the slightest tinge of guilt as he opened it.

But guilt surged a moment later when a photo of two women fell out. In it, Jena looked much the same as she did now, but with light makeup, and the woman with her… she looked so much like Andi. That had to be her friend who had been murdered by Vex.

He hated to say it, but there was that blend of vulnerability and bravado in her eyes. This was a woman who'd been hurt badly by life but was still trying to find someone to protect her. A man with the money to keep her safe. Too bad she'd found Vex instead.

His heart ached for both of these women. He set the photo carefully on the counter so it wouldn't get damaged and then reached into her purse, pulling out the other items. He set aside her wallet to go through later. Next, he found a small bag that housed an e-reader and Chapstick, as well as sunscreen and some random receipts, her keys and finally her cell phone.

The screen was cracked and smudged, and he wasn't a safecracker, so he didn't even try guessing her passcode. He was tempted to use facial recognition and hold the phone over her face...

Texting Lee, he let her know he'd found the phone.

Lee didn't message back, just thumbs-upped his message.

He wanted to know why she'd lied about the phone. There had to be something on there, and he deserved to know what it was. She was in his home and in the tower where his family lived. No, they weren't blood relatives, but they were closer than any family he could trace through his DNA. The women and men of Price Security meant more to him than anyone else. He'd always protect them.

Had he brought trouble to them by letting her in?

Jena didn't look like trouble...as if trouble had a look, right? She'd been bleeding and thought she killed a man when she arrived. Sure, she'd tried to explain it, and that picture he'd found had him believing that that part of her story was the truth, but there were so many other half-truths between them. So many other things he wasn't sure he could believe about her. At the same time, he was struggling with so many...regrets. Part of him needed her story to be honest so maybe he'd be able to fix some of the bad karma left over after Andi had died.

But karma didn't work that way. Lord knew, Rick had spent all his late teens and most of his adult life trying to prevent another woman from following Andi's path.

This phone...

Fuck it.

He walked over to the couch and squatted down behind where she slept. He had no clue if this would work. Lee would be laughing her ass off if she saw him attempt to use facial recognition by holding the phone over Jena's sleeping face.

It didn't work the first time. He was about to try again when her eyes popped open. She screamed, and he shot to his feet, putting his hands up by his shoulders.

"I wasn't doing anything creepy," he said, trying to sound reassuring.

"Except going through my bag... That's my phone."

"The one you said you lost. How do you know I didn't find it downstairs?" he asked. "Why did you jump to me going through your bag?"

She wasn't wrong, but he wanted to hear her lie to him again.

"We both know that's where it was. I was going to tell you...just things were starting to feel almost normal and I wanted that for another minute, you know?"

Yeah, he got it. Her arms wrapped around her middle, and she watched him with wide eyes that beseeched him to understand.

"So what's on here?" he asked. He wasn't going to allow himself to get thrown offtrack by her big brown eyes or her rumpled hair, which had dried and curled around her face and shoulders.

She licked her lips, and he noticed the mark near her mouth was starting to get even darker. "Want some ice for that?"

"Yeah, thanks."

"Sit at the breakfast bar and tell me what you're hiding—and don't pretend you aren't hiding anything," he warned her.

"I wouldn't," she said.

Again, he wanted to trust her, but he wasn't that gullible. Jena Maxwell, whatever else she might be, was on a mission. Nothing and no one was going to keep her from getting what she wanted from Vex, and he knew she wouldn't hesitate to lie to get her way. So he'd take everything she said with a grain of salt and pretend he still didn't want to protect her...even from herself.

The catnap she'd taken on the sofa hadn't been enough sleep to make her feel rested. Her body still ached though the ice pack he'd made for her and handed her to put on her mouth helped. For a split second when their hands touched, she felt a small shiver go up her arm. He had such nice eyes, she thought, then shook her head.

Vex hadn't had bad eyes. What an expression. She looked down at the counter, trying to figure out what to say. That photo of her Brianne caught her eye, and she knew that whatever else she did, she needed to see this through for her friend.

"Did you go through my wallet too?"

"Not yet."

"Don't you have any embarrassment?"

He shrugged. "Not when it comes to keeping those I care about safe."

Did he care about her?

"Me?"

As soon as the word left her mouth, she mentally kicked herself. "Don't answer that. We're strangers."

"We are. That's why it's disturbing to learn that you weren't honest."

Honesty. God, if only life really worked out when you told the truth. But it didn't. She'd been brutally truthful with the cops in Houston, and they'd said it was just her word against someone else's. That was what everything came down to.

"I was trying to get proof that Vex killed Brianne. I needed to capture his confession."

"What?"

"Yeah. I know. So I got one of those wireless mics and taped it between my books, then I started a voice note and had my phone in this little bag so it would pick up on anything he said. I wore it the entire night, until I got away from Mistral's and put it into my purse as I ran. I haven't had a chance to listen to whatever was recorded," she said, pulling her phone toward her. She unlocked her phone with her code since her bruised face wasn't recognizable.

"What were you doing crouched over me? That was unnerving."

"Your scream was a good indication of that. I was trying to use facial recognition to unlock it," he said.

"Can't your IT woman break into my phone?" she asked. Lee had the look of a woman who could find her way around any tech barriers.

"Probably, but I didn't want to bring her back down here. I'm not sure what I'm dealing with."

"Me?" she asked again.

"Yeah, you. You've given me enough information to know you're in trouble, but not enough to figure out if it's all of your own making."

"Hey, I told you all about Brianne."

"Also that the cops weren't sure she dated Vex."

"Yeah, well, she did."

"You mentioned you'd never seen her with him. Did she have any photos on her phone of him?"

"Actually…she did. But when I looked at her phone, they were gone. Do you think he deleted them?"

Rick shrugged again.

"What kind of answer is a shrug?" she demanded, getting worked up because she was frustrated. All this time, and even after tonight there still might not be anything to link Vex to Brianne's murder.

"It's an 'I'm not sure' answer. Lee can look into your friend's phone and cloud files. It's hard to completely erase every trace."

Finally. "That would be great. The guy I talked to at Best Buy mentioned that but said I had to install software on her phone to access it. And the cops had it, so that was out of the question."

"Guess breaking into evidence lockup wasn't covered in your movies?"

She gave him the finger. He was so annoying. Not everyone had a background in law enforcement. "I worked with what I had."

"Did you really think he'd confess to killing your friend?" he asked.

She rolled her eyes and shook her head.

"What kind of answer is that?"

"Your question was too stupid to answer," she said before hitting play on the voice note.

Her own voice stating the date and time and her location came on first. When she'd gotten to the club, she had to wait in line, and she heard all the conversations around her, pulling her back to when she'd been waiting to go inside.

She wasn't sure she could listen to this. Her heart was racing the same as it had been when she'd been anxiously trying to get past the VIP bouncer. Back then, in the club, she hadn't had time to focus on her nerves—she'd been too intent on becoming, through sheer force of will, the woman she'd needed to be. One who would do anything to get answers.

"You sound…different."

"Yeah, I knew I had to be if they were going to let me in," she said.

"Good job. That's the first rule of going undercover. Be the person you need to be, not yourself."

"How many rules are there?" she asked, even though she was pretty sure he was just trying to put her at ease. He was fun to spar with, and her heart, body and soul were so broken and bruised and sad that she needed this.

"Lots. More than you can learn in one movie."

She smiled to herself, but it faded away as she heard Vex's voice. It was a low, deep rumble of a voice with a slight accent to it. He spoke such good English that she thought maybe he kept the accent on purpose just because he knew that women liked it. And they definitely did.

She hadn't been the only one trying to get close to him.

Rick leaned closer to the phone as he heard Vex's voice. "That him?"

"Yeah."

"Can you turn it up a little? It's hard to hear over the music."

"It gets slightly quieter once we go to his private banquette toward the back," she said.

"What's your name, baby?" Vex asked on the tape.

"Gia," Jena answered in a huskier version of own voice.

Rick paused the recording. "Why did you give him a false name?

"In case Brianna had mentioned me. Also it's close to Jena so maybe if she had, he'd draw a link," she said.

"Nice thought."

"Yeah. It didn't work. He called me Jay for the rest of the night."

"Doesn't matter. Did you get him talking about Texas?"

"I did and it was... Well here, you listen to it."

***

She'd done a pretty good job of flirting and leading the conversation where she wanted it to go at first, but Rick could tell the moment she got frustrated that Vex wasn't answering her questions the way she wanted him to.

"You are being too..."

"Obvious. Yeah, I hear it. But at the time I realized it was getting late, and he has a roving eye. I wasn't sure how long I would be able to keep his attention," she said as she hit pause.

"You did good. It was your first time, right?" he asked her, still amazed at how much work she'd done to try to get close to a man she believed had killed her best friend. That took real guts. He admired her.

Okay, so there was more than admiration going on over here. But flirting with her and bantering with her was all he'd allow. For one, she was too young for him. Second, she didn't belong in his life. There was no place for personal relationships. He had work and Price Security, and that was enough for him.

So, yeah.

"Rick?"

"Huh?"

"Bored already?"

Her sassiness wasn't what he'd expected. "Not bored. What'd you ask?"

"I asked if you're ready to listen to more. I think this is when I spill my drink to distract him while I put the Rohypnol in his glass."

"That you weren't caught right away is amazing," he said.

"I spent a few days practicing at the hotel before I went to the club," she said.

"Did you drug other people's drinks?"

"No. I'm not a monster. I just practiced putting my hand over my own drink a bunch of times. I saw this show on how sleight of hand is done. You have to really practice it so it becomes almost second nature."

TV and movies were clearly a big thing for her. He wanted to know more, but listening to the recording had to take priority. At the same time though, there were telltale signs that listening to the recording was getting to her. Probably forcing her to relive the entire experience. She shouldn't have to do that.

"Why don't I listen to the rest on my own? I can tell you if there's anything we can use on there," he said.

She put the ice pack on the counter and shook her head. "I have to do this."

"Why? You already did the hard work for your friend," he reminded her.

Her face got really tight, as if she wanted to keep arguing...but then her shoulders slumped a little and he saw her give in. "Okay. I don't want to hear him when he started to attack me."

"You don't have to. Go finish watching *Stakeout*. I've got some headphones," he said.

"I'll try to stay awake this time," she said, attempting a smile and failing.

Whether she'd been fully honest with him or not, he knew that she had good motives for what she was doing. She was a decent woman; it shone through in the way she acted toward him and even toward the people at the table with Vex on the recording. Her anger was all directed at the one man. That was it.

She settled onto the couch, and he paired his headphones to her phone and then leaned against the counter to continue listening.

It was disturbing, listening. Especially once Vex realized she'd been trying to drug him. He barked to his men not to follow.

"Did you kiss Brianne like this?" Jena asked. Her voice wasn't as husky as it had been earlier. This time it was closer to her own voice.

"Brianne?"

"Brianne Jones. The woman you were dating in Houston."

"What are you talking about?" he asked.

"You know what I'm asking," she said, then the rest of her words were cut off. Rick assumed he grabbed her wrist then and drug her from the table.

There was a bunch of grunts. Vex was strangling her until he heard the man grunt and cry out.

"Bitch!"

"*I'm* a bitch? You were just strangling me," Jena said, her voice a sort of croak. "Is that what you did to Brianne?"

"That bitch liked it rough. I'm guessing you do too. That's why you're here, right?" he asked.

"I'm here to get you to confess to killing her," Jena said.

"Ah, baby, that's not happening," Vex said.

Then there was the sound of flesh being hit and Jena's cries of pain until she must have gotten the knife from Vex and stabbed him. There was a thud as he fell to the floor. He could hear Vex's gasping breath as Jena leaned over him.

"It's too late. You're going to die. Tell me…you killed her, didn't you?"

"Fuck you."

Then the door to the bathroom exploded in; he heard the

door hit the wall and then Jena crying and pretending to be worried about Vex. She somehow escaped the bathroom.

He heard her ragged breaths and tears as she ran from the club. A few concerned patrons asked if she was okay, and then the recording ended.

He took off his headphones and looked over at the couch. He wasn't surprised to find she was watching him and not the TV.

"Anything?"

"No. He never admits to killing her. He doesn't deny it…but he doesn't actually say anything that could be used against him."

"I hoped I was wrong. I guess that was all for nothing…but at least he might be dead. I know that makes me sound mean."

"That guy strangled, beat and cut you, not to mention what he did to your friend. I think it's okay to be glad he's not alive to do that to anyone else."

"Yeah? Yeah, you're right. I just… I wanted him to admit he knew Brianne."

"He does. He says she liked it rough," Rick pointed out.

"Oh, that's right. I forgot about that," she said. "So if your friend can find photos on Brianne's phone…maybe the cops will look into him as a suspect for her murder?"

"Does it still matter now that he's dead?"

"Yes. Justice always matters. I want the man who killed Brianne to be in jail."

Chapter 5

She'd managed a few hours of sleep. With that rest, and the coffee Rick had gotten for her at the drive-through, she was feeling mostly alert and clear-headed. But that didn't stop her mind from constantly replaying the moment she'd stabbed Vex with the knife. She wondered how long it would take for the sharp edges of the memory to fade. Would she carry it with her back to Texas? Into next year? For the rest of her life?

It pissed her off that she was upset she'd killed a man like him. But she was. Her hands shook if she wasn't careful with them, and her already-broken heart felt even more bruised and shattered. This wasn't at all the life she'd envisioned for herself or fought so hard to avoid. She could have stayed in Brownsville if she wanted to end up embroiled in the world of criminal gangs.

But instead, she was here, with Rick—ready to dive into a new day while they worked on their investigation.

At least she was in her own clothes now. Rick had driven her to her hotel to collect her bags, and she'd taken the opportunity to change into a pair of shorts and a blouse made of a light, flowy material to suit the hazy LA heat.

The car Rick had them in wasn't much to look at on the outside, but inside it was clear it had all the bells and whistles. There was an in-dash screen with a map, messages and some other tracker. He'd told her the car was bulletproof and had power under the hood. Whatever that meant. She shrank back farther into the thick bucket seat. Trying to disappear into it.

"You okay over there?"

"Yeah."

"Lee's working on trying to access your friend's cloud storage. I also have a friend from my DEA days who still works in Texas. I've asked him to look into Vex's connections in the area. The homicide cops might not know of him, but the vice ones might," Rick said.

That was good news. "When did you have time to do that?"

Sure, it was 10:00 a.m., but he hadn't gone to bed until almost 4:00 a.m.

"I don't need much sleep," he said.

"Why not?"

He shrugged, his lips quirked and he shook his head. "Not an answer, right? I just never have. My sister used to say I was wired. I guess I still am."

She couldn't help smiling back at him. Her mouth didn't hurt as much this morning. "Your vibe is totally not wired."

"I know I give off a chilled-out image, but it's not real. It's just the result of a lifetime of working with people who are on edge and trying not to get busted. I learned how to project calm to keep situations from spiraling out of control."

She tipped her head to study him as they sat in the back of the parking lot across from Mistral's. If they'd met under different circumstances, she'd be totally into him. Not that she wasn't now, but given the situation, she wasn't sure he would welcome any flirting from her. After all, he knew what had happened to the last guy she'd flirted with.

"What?"

"What *what*?" she responded.

"You're watching me with a look...what do you want to know?" he asked.

How he kissed. But no way in hell was she uttering those words. "Just curious about you."

That was a safe answer.

"I'm pretty much what you've seen so far. I work, I chill and repeat."

That wasn't entirely true. "What about the people you care about? Who are they?"

"You've met two of them. Lee and Van."

"Come on, you saw the same movie I did—you should know that now that we're on an investigation together, we're meant to talk in the car and tell each other our backstories," she said.

"You want a list or something?" he asked her. "Who do you care about?"

"Brianne and my elderly neighbor, Rina, who has mobility problems," Jena said. She had coworkers who were okay, but she wasn't close with any of them. She'd never really learned how to make connections with people.

"That's it?"

"Yeah. I grew up...rough, I guess. I wasn't encouraged to bring friends home, and most people didn't want to see me," she said. That way of living had made it so easy for her to be invisible. Invisible had equaled safe for a long time. But ever since she'd come to LA, she had made bold moves that brought plenty of attention.

Killing a man.

Not getting the justice she wanted for Brianne.

She'd give anything to be invisible again.

"That's... I'm sorry," he said at last.

"Not your fault. Some people weren't meant to have kids."

Jena was pretty sure she was one as well, so she wasn't going to take any chances. The doctor wouldn't give her a hysterectomy until she was thirty, but as soon as she could, she was getting one. The line of addiction and abuse she'd inherited from her folks ended with her.

"True. What about Joey?"

"Joey definitely shouldn't have kids. He's still working with the DEA," she said. "Not sure if you knew that."

"Yeah. He's an agent now," Rick pointed out.

"Uh, I didn't realize," she said, more to herself than to him. They weren't close. Seeing him reminded her of a past she'd worked damn hard to forget.

"I can see why getting Vex's confession is so important to you," he said.

He'd understood before, she suspected. He owed her nothing; she'd shown up on his doorstep and brought this to him. Instead of backing away and sending her home with Detective Miller, he'd invited her to stay at his place and had offered to help.

God, it was hard not to let that matter. But it was so new to have someone she felt she could count on. She'd been on her own basically all her life. Having someone here with her was a lot to process.

Emotions were choking her. She was struggling to process a mix of like and gratitude all directed at one man... and that was weird. Very unlike her. And so uncomfortable too.

But there was also that warmth that promised she'd was safe with him. Her instincts told her that was a false security and that she shouldn't trust him.

It was too late, she thought as her eyes got heavy. It was quiet in the car, the air warm because they only had the windows cracked. The panic that had gnawed at her the closer they got to Mistral's ebbed. With Rick by her side, she knew she was safe.

That was her last thought as she drifted off to sleep.

It was safer for him to glance over at her when she was sleeping. That vulnerable look was back on her face. The bruises on her body were still fresh, but the cuts on her face were healing. Soon...this would all be behind her—at least, if he had his way.

He got that she wanted to follow this through for her friend, but the truth was, the only way she'd be able to move on was to return to her life. To remember there were good things in the world. Though there were times when he still struggled with doing exactly that. That was where his family came in.

He'd call Luna and go hang with her. She got that he just needed someone to be with at those times. They didn't really talk, usually just went for walks around Echo Lake Park or even drove out to the beach. Trouble was, he'd lived here his entire life, worked the streets as a young DEA agent and been undercover so many times. He'd thought going to Texas would show him a different world, but while the landscape was different, the people and life were the same.

So maybe Jena had the right idea, staying here to figure out what happened to her friend and the man she'd killed.

Lee had pulled photos of Tomas Vectra, aka Vex, sending them to Rick's phone so he could ID him. Detective Miller was going to do a courtesy call on his home later today to see if he was there.

The cameras that Aaron and Lee had installed at Mistral's must have all been taken down, because Lee couldn't find a trace of them anymore, so if they wanted to know who was going in and out of the place, a physical stakeout was their only option.

This parking lot made the back of his neck itch. He'd been in a shoot-out in the coffee shop at the end of the strip of stores the Christmas before. Then earlier this year, he'd helped take down a smuggling ring that had been running out of Mistral's.

It wasn't like law enforcement agencies weren't aware that criminal activity had picked right back up again after the dust of the raid had settled. But they were overworked, and as long as there wasn't a major crime, they were content to watch and wait. There was always a bigger fish. Vex wasn't a big fish though he had been on his way to becoming one. He was a player with interests on both coasts and Texas.

Texas, Arizona, California—those were the places the DEA usually focused, wanting to stop the flow of drugs over the border. But there were other ways for illegal drugs to enter the United States. Other places that served as transport hubs. He'd been toying with returning to the DEA and had taken a few shifts when his old boss needed someone to help out.

Seeing Jena and hearing about Brianne was enough to remind him that there was still work to be done. Still lives that needed saving.

A dark-windowed, souped-up sedan pulled up in front of Mistral's. Four people got out of the car. One of them was big and bald. Even from this distance looked like he would be tough to take. One of the other men had a bandage around his neck. He was wearing dark glasses and moved as if he'd had too much to drink the night before.

Was that Vex?

He nudged Jena awake, even as he double-checked to make sure he was recording with the built-in cameras that Xander had set up in this car. Lee would be able to zoom in and verify if what he suspected was true.

"You recognize him?" he asked Jena, handing her his binoculars.

She put them up to her face, then dropped them. "It's him."

Her hands were shaking, and she laced her fingers together as she continued watching until all four men entered the building. He tapped out a message on the screen to Lee letting her know they'd positively ID'd Tomas Vectra. He also asked her to sharpen the image.

He didn't know what to say to Jena. Her skin was washed out to the point where even her lips were gray. There was anger and fear in her eyes. It was probably good that she was scared. Because a man like Vex was going to come for her. She'd overplayed her hand by mentioning Brianne. Oh, yeah and tried to kill him.

Rick wanted to do something to bring back her spark. It took him a minute to think of something, then he pushed his sunglasses up on his head and turned to face her.

"Good news—you aren't a murderer."

Letting out a ragged breath, she shook her head. "I guess so. I think I would have rather he was dead."

"Now we have a chance to get him and put him behind bars."

"Yeah," she said. "But first, I'm going to need a different wig, and maybe you can teach me some self-defense moves. I'm pretty sure he's going to recognize me when I get close."

"You're not getting close to him again," he stated. Over his dead body was she going anywhere near Vex again. Having had a good look at the man, he could now say it was miracle that she'd gotten away from him the first time. Maybe it was the drug she'd used or just the element of surprise, but Jena had been very lucky.

Rick knew you didn't get lucky twice.

"Then it's a good thing I don't listen to you. I'd like your help, Rick, but if you don't want to help me, that changes nothing. Vex is going to pay for what he did to Brianne—"

"And to you. Remember, he attacked you. That gives Detective Miller grounds to arrest him. But you'd have to press charges."

Her face went tight, but she didn't say a word. He guessed she was weighing her options, which was fine. Whatever decision she made, Rick knew that until Vex was behind bars, he'd be her shadow. He wasn't losing another woman he cared about.

And he did care about her—whether she was being fully honest with him or not.

What was she going to do now? Vex was still alive, and she knew he wasn't going to admit to killing Brianne. She got that. The man wasn't going to spill anything—unless she gave him no choice.

Rick thinking he had any say in what she did wasn't something she'd entertain right now. It had been nice to toy with the idea that she wasn't alone, but that had never been her. And it wasn't now.

Her mind was caught in a cycle of thoughts that wasn't really helping anything. "What did you mean about pressing charges?"

"Detective Miller got evidence and photos of you last night. We can have Vex charged with assault for what he did to you. I'd like to talk to Van. He's better at strategy than I am. There's nothing else to see here for now, so are you okay with heading back to Price Tower?"

She nodded. Already she was going over the patterns she'd found for Vex's movements. It was Sunday, so he shouldn't be at the club at all today. "Do you think they have cameras your friend can't access?"

"Why?"

"He doesn't normally come here on Sunday. There has to be a reason for him to show up today." Jena asked.

She took out her phone and opened the note she had on Vex. She skimmed down to Sunday. Normally it was some kind of meal at a home in East LA that she couldn't get close to—or at least, that was her best guess at what he was up to the two times she'd driven by the house. She'd been following him for two weeks.

Her boss at the bank had extended her unpaid leave for an additional week, but Jena knew she was probably not going to have a job when she called him tomorrow to ask for more time off. Now that she'd confirmed Vex was alive, she wasn't leaving LA until he was behind bars.

"Good point. What are your thoughts?" he asked as he put the car in gear.

"Wait, shouldn't we follow him?"

He put the car back in park and turned to face her. "Are you ruling out going to Detective Miller?"

"I'm not sure yet. I think we'd do better to see where he goes. Normally he spends Sunday afternoons at a house on Euclid," she said. "I want to know what else has changed."

"How long have you been following him?"

"Awhile. I couldn't just walk in blind. I needed to know more about him and the best place to try to pick him up. I tried at a coffee shop on Rodeo Drive but couldn't get close to him. Plus, I just blended into the background there."

Rick put his arm on the back of her seat, leaning in. "What else?"

"What do you mean?"

"What else does he do on Sundays?"

"He spends four hours at the house on Euclid, and then he goes to some clubs that I couldn't get into. I mean, if I was dressed like last night I probably could, but I only had that one dress..."

Rick watched her like she'd grown a second head. "That's good detective work."

"You think so?"

"To be honest, I wasn't sure what you'd done, so this is impressive. I really think we need to strategize and figure out next moves. If it's okay with you, I'll get someone from Price to watch the parking lot while we go back and come up with our next steps."

"Who?"

"Probably Luna or Xander. I'll reach out to my DEA contacts and Aaron and find out who owns Mistral's now. Then see if we can get some leads on what Vex is doing out here."

Yes. This was the kind of information she hadn't been able to get on her own. She could tail him—she'd taken an online class on following someone without being spotted—but knowing where he was didn't give her any insight into what he was actually doing.

"Okay. But you have to teach me self-defense," she said.

"I'm more of a street fighter."

"Even better. I scratched his face last time, but my nails are shot. Kicking him in the nuts was impossible from where he held me up. I need to know how to break away next time."

"Sure, but you're not going to be that close to him again," Rick said. "I'm your bodyguard now."

"I didn't hire you, remember?"

He shook his head but didn't respond as he tapped out a message. Xander quickly answered he would be there in five to take over the stakeout.

"Stop ignoring me. I'm going to be the one to get Vex's confession. I want to see his eyes when he admits to killing her."

"What will that get you?"

"Satisfaction in that moment when he's caught and knows that a woman like me got him."

Rick shook his head sounding frustrated with her. "No."

Which she hurt her feelings, but hey, she could do this on her own. "Then I guess we're done here. I'll get an Uber back to my hotel. Thanks for helping me out last night," she said opening the Uber app on her phone.

"Like hell."

She ignored Rick as she tapped in her current location, but then he took her phone from her hand, tossing it on the dashboard where she couldn't reach it.

"Stop being a dick."

"I'm trying to protect you."

"I don't need protecting."

Their eyes met and something electric passed between them. She felt fear and the anger, but also a new emotion. Lust mixed with need and…and pleasure at the idea that he wanted to protect her. But she knew that no man could. She had her own back and life was much safer that way.

He leaned forward his mouth opened to say something, but all she saw were those full lips and the compassion in his eyes as she leaned forward and brushed her mouth over his.

Chapter 6

Kissing her wasn't smart, he knew that, but the moment her mouth brushed his, he was all in. His hands were gentle when he put them on her shoulder, leaning closer. She smelled of his soap and the strawberry body lotion she'd used. She tasted... Oh man...she tasted so good.

Given the turmoil she'd experienced in the last twenty-four hours of her life, he didn't want to pressure her, so he only let his tongue touch hers when she deepened the kiss. She'd distracted him from what he'd been saying, but he had no regrets about that. He wanted her. He had from the moment she'd looked up at him with those wide, wounded eyes and asked him for help.

Being her savior was something he needed. Protecting her was a done deal as of that moment. She might believe she was in charge, but that wasn't the case. He'd keep her safe, whether she wanted him to or not.

And he knew damn well she didn't want him to.

So kissing her was damn stupid. It was also addictive. He shoved his hands into her hair and took the kiss he wanted. Sucking her tongue deep into her mouth and taking everything she offered him before he pulled back. His body was on fire, and stopping now the last thing he wanted.

But he needed to.

She was a client.

She had lost her best friend and been attacked.

That had to matter more than his desire for her. He suspected she needed some kind of release, a nice touch after Vex.

He lifted his head. She watched him, her eyes wide and questioning.

"That was…"

"Good. Actually better than I was expecting. Not that I was expecting anything. It's just…you get to me, Stone," she said, shifting to lean against the door and watch him.

I get to her?

"Same," he said. He was trying to process how off-balance she kept him. All his life he'd been a loss cannon and had fought hard to become logical and methodical. Probably two things that had kept him safe and off drugs and out of gangs. He'd seen a way out and taken it.

Right now he saw a path to keeping Jena safe, but she wasn't letting him take it. Maybe it was unfair of him to be upset with her for that. She couldn't know that her words and actions were so intriguing it was all he could do to keep his hands on the steering wheel where he'd placed them to keep from reaching for her and pulling her back into his arms.

"'Same'… Wow, your chatting game is on point."

"Stop. You know we can't do anything—"

"Why not?"

"You're out here trying to get vengeance for Brianne. You had the scare of your life last night and came closer to dying than you're willing to admit."

"Yeah. I know all of that," she said, swallowing hard. "I was there, so I effing know how close I came to not making it out alive. Yeah, my life is one big scary 'what the fuck' right now. But why does any of that mean I can't be with you? You feel solid when everything else is up in the air," she said.

Her words had come out fast and rough. That just made him want to pull her into his arms even more than earlier. But that last part…she relied on him and the only way he could make sure he was 100 percent focused on protecting her, not allowing any distractions to get in the way, was for that kiss to be the only one they shared.

"I've got you," he said.

"Sure. As long as I do exactly what you want me to," she retorted. "Don't bother denying it."

"I wasn't going to," he said, shoving his hand through his hair before canting his head to the side to get a better look at her.

"Vex is the first gang member you've tried to take down. I've been doing this for twenty years," he reminded her. "I know my stuff. Trust me to help you and get justice for Brianne. I'm a man of my word."

She touched his hand where it rested on the steering wheel. A tingle went up his arm and straight to his groin. It was too soon to touch after that kiss, which had awakened everything masculine inside him.

"Rick…"

Just the sound of her saying his name that way turned him on. He cursed and pulled his hand out from under hers.

"My entire life," she said, "it's just been me. Then I had Brianne for a short while and I couldn't keep her safe. I let her down."

He got that all the way to his soul. There were no words he could offer that would make this better for her. She had to find her own way to peace. Rick realized he was trying to keep her safe from a world she'd already been exposed to. Him thinking she'd be better off back in her old life wasn't a reality. She had no old life to go back to.

Vex had wrecked it to hell when he'd killed Brianne.

"Okay."

"Huh?"

"You can stay and try to get justice for your friend," he said.

"Jeez, thanks for your permission. I mean, it's not like I hadn't already decided that for myself."

He gave her a hard look. "I'll help you. With your knowledge of Vex's movements and my undercover experience, we will take him down. We'll get your confession. I promise."

She smiled then and nodded at him. Xander pulled into the parking lot in a pickup truck, drove past them and took a spot on the other side of the mall. "That's Xander. We good to head back to Price Tower?"

"Yeah," she said.

As they drove back, she was quietly working on her phone. Fingers tapping something, but he had no idea what. He should be paying attention to the traffic, and he was—but on a low level, he was also very aware of every move that Jena made. The way she cracked the window open to let the hot breeze blow on her face and wash away her tears.

Grief. He got it. It took eons to get over losing someone close. There were times when he still cried about his sister. Little moments when he saw the sun set the way it had on that last night they'd been together. Stuff that no one else would understand.

But he totally got where Jena was. He reached over absently to squeeze her shoulder, and she put her hand on his, holding it there. He wanted to keep his distance but knew he wouldn't. She needed something only he could give her.

That feeling of not being alone anymore.

"So is Price Tower like Titan Tower?" she asked as he pulled into the underground garage. She had to admit she didn't know of any place like it. Rick lived and worked out of the same building. From what he'd told her, the rest of the team did as well. He'd tried to make it sound normal since bodyguard work took them on the road and it made more sense to have all their accommodations in one location.

But he'd gotten serious again, and the longer they were in the car driving, the more her fears started to materialize. Despite what her current actions might suggest, she was normally a very shy and quiet person. But murder changed a girl.

"What are you actually talking about?"

"You know, like on *Teen Titans*. The Titans all live in the tower, and then when evil is in the world they go and fight it," she said.

He flushed. "I guess. Who are these Titans? Are they, like, strong warriors?"

"Yeah, sort of. They all have some kind of ability. Beast Boy can turn into animals, Raven can manipulate emotions... She's the daughter of an evil being from—"

"I'm going to stop you there. No, we're nothing like them. We are just all trained bodyguards and investigators. Some of us, like me, are former law enforcement or government agents. Others are good fighters. Van has a feel for what makes a good bodyguard."

"He's your leader," she said just to needle him since it was clear that Rick didn't want to be compared to a team of superheroes.

"He's the boss."

Rick got out of the car, and Jena followed him to the elevator, unable to keep her eyes off the way he moved. That kiss had cleared away the image of him as a teddy bear. Now all she could see was his strength and that innate sexiness that he kept on the down low. But it was there. He watched her with hungry eyes when he thought she wouldn't notice.

But she had.

Vex had left her feel icky. There was no other way to put it. Listening to the recording of it last night had made her want to shower again. She needed a palate cleanser, and Rick Stone would fill the bill nicely.

Except it didn't take a genius to realize that he'd decided that one kiss would be it between them. She didn't blame him. She was the hottest mess she'd ever been. Today was slightly better than all the days she'd had since Brianne died, but she was consumed with making Vex pay. No man with any sense would want to get tangled up with a woman like her, hell-bent on a vengeance quest.

There had to be some way to make herself feel clean again without compromising what she needed from Rick. His knowledge of drug gangs and law enforcement connections were too important for Jena to mess it up.

He was quiet on the ride up in the elevator. She noticed the smell of his soap and aftershave, and the way he made sure to keep his body slightly in front of hers. He'd done it every time they'd been together.

"Are you trying to protect me?" she asked.

"Duh. I'm your bodyguard."

"Do you think there is a threat here?" It hadn't occurred to her that Vex might be able to get into Price Tower. The place felt like an impenetrable fortress.

"No. Just habit," he said with a shrug of his big shoulders, which drew the fabric of his shirt tight against them.

"It's cool. You don't have to take a bullet for me or anything. Just show me how to defend myself—"

"Why do you need that?"

Because she was going to get close to Vex again. Now that she knew he was alive, there was no way she wasn't going back and getting the confession she didn't get last night. Next time she wasn't failing.

"I just do. I mean if Brianne had known some basic self-defense...maybe she'd be alive."

"Fair point. You just have a wild look in your eyes... You're not planning something wild are you?"

"Define wild."

"Jena."

"Rick. I'm serious. Everyone has a different definition for that word. It's subjective. By my standards, no I'm not."

The elevator doors opened before he could respond, and she pushed past him as she exited. They weren't on the floor where his apartment was. Instead he led the way down to a large conference room. When they walked in, Lee and Van were already there, along with a tall, muscly guy she hadn't met and a woman with a slicked-back brown ponytail who seemed very quiet.

Van smiled at them as they walked in. "Xander's tail-ing Vex. We'll see if he hits that house on Euclid. Kenji's out today, so we can get started."

"Who's Kenji?"

"Another team member," Rick said, holding out a chair for her.

She took the seat feeling very out of place in this room. These people were all...seriously intense and clearly shared a deep bond and connection, she realized. Van went around the table and made the introductions. The woman was Luna Urban DeVere, married to the millionaire Nicholas DeVere. The guy was Lee's boyfriend and DEA agent Aaron Quentin.

Some of the intimidation she felt melted when Van told the team all the recon she'd done and they all nodded at her with approval. "Good job."

"Thanks. I just tried to be logical about things when I got out here. My brother gave me some locations where Vex might be, but he couldn't tell me who Vex works for."

"He's independent, from what my street contacts say. He's got a large network across the country. So far no one has been able to get close to him."

"Jena did."

Rick knew how rare Jena was. She'd managed to do what even the DEA hadn't been able to accomplish by getting that close to Vex. It was something she should be proud of, especially since she had no training. But the rest of them did have training—and that meant it was up to them to strategize the next steps.

She was quiet as Van, Aaron and himself discussed what to tell Aaron's boss at the DEA and what to keep at Price. He wasn't sure if she was overwhelmed or just trying to figure out how to use them for her objective.

He knew she wanted justice...but justice was another word that meant something different to everyone. For him, that meant getting the bad guy arrested, putting him on trial and seeing him convicted and incarcerated. But there was a look about Jena that suggested for her it might have a different conclusion.

"His crew is tight. From what I hear he keeps the same four people around him wherever he goes. He has no play on the West Coast," Aaron was saying. "But he wants to pick up where the cachorros and the chacals left off. I can't get close to them anymore. I could take a stab at talking to Jako in jail or maybe Ramos. But they're still pissed because I betrayed them."

"Yeah, not the best idea for you to talk to them. Jena, could you describe anyone that Vex talked to while you were following him?" Lee asked. "I can run them through the database and see if we get any hits."

She fumbled for her phone. "I took pictures everywhere I followed him. Some of them aren't very good. The camera on my phone is old."

"That's great. Your photos are a huge asset," Rick reassured her.

Lee had Jena connect her phone to the Bluetooth-enabled screen at the end of the room. The shades went down as Jena's photos flashed up on the screen. The first one was of her car at the rental agency.

Rick couldn't help but smile at those. She was a conscientious person. Safety was her first instinct. How had she ever made herself confront Vex so directly?

"My brother gave me the name of three places, and I drove by all of them the first day. Mistral's was my last stop, and I saw several men... I didn't know what he looked like. So I wasted two days following the wrong person."

"Why didn't you know what he looked like?" Luna asked.

"I never met him while Brianne was dating him. Which told me that he was careful about who he lets see him. And he beat her up and I didn't like him so she never shared any more photos with me. So all I had was one photo of his hand and some cocktails. He has a tattoo around his wrist of barbed wire and something in Latin," she said. She scrolled through her photos, past one of her and Brianne, until she found the one she was looking for. She zoomed in on the tanned hand and the tattoo.

"That's it. When I got close to the first guy, I realized he didn't have that tattoo," she said. "I went back to Mistral's and spotted Vex. I started following him, and then later that day, I accidentally took his coffee at the place he goes to on Rodeo Drive. I saw his hand and the tattoo. This is the photo of it."

She switched to the photo that definitely matched the picture her friend had sent to Jena.

"Nice. Would you mind giving Lee a copy of all of these photos?" Van asked.

"Not at all. Rick mentioned we needed a strategy. I mean I think I should use makeup and a different colored wig once I'm healed up and go back in."

"That's not going to work again," Rick said. "Plus, that's not happening."

Jena started to argue, but Van put his hand up. "He's right. After last night, Vex isn't going to let any woman past his VIP bouncers that hasn't been vetted. And if those bouncers recognize you, it'll be all over before you get anywhere near him. Luna or Lee might be able to get close to him if it comes to that."

Jena didn't look happy about that.

"What about Jena pressing assault charges against Vex? It's bold and would let him know that she's not going quietly," Rick said.

Jena went stiff next to him. Her distrust of cops was still strong. She had already let him know that she didn't like the idea.

"I like it. Would definitely give Detective Miller a reason to bring him in and question him. But that puts a big target on Jena," Van said.

"She's under my protection," Rick said. "I'm her bodyguard now."

Van nodded. "I think that idea has merit. Do you, Jena?"

Rolling her phone between her hands, she took her time answering Van. "I'm not sure. I don't trust cops. They aren't big in believing women can be victims when they look like I did last night. There's a sure bet he's going to tell them that I hit on him."

"Hitting on a man isn't an invitation for him to beat on you," Rick reminded her.

"Not everyone sees it that way," she said.

"Detective Miller isn't like those cops you talked to in Houston. She wants to see men like Vex behind bars for good. She works hard to keep the streets safe for everyone." Rick tried to reassure Jena, but he understood that she'd have to get there on her own.

"Is there anything else we could do?"

"Lee is already looking into photos from Brianne's phone, and we have the ones from yours now. We can watch him until we find a point to try to infiltrate his close circle. But that's a long game. How much time do you have?"

"I'm supposed to go home tomorrow," she said. "Will it speed things up if we go to the cops?"

"Yes. He'll know where you are, it might make him do something reckless," Rick said.

Chapter 7

Calling her boss netted the result Jena expected. If she wasn't back on Monday, her job wouldn't be waiting for her. A quick check of her bank confirmed that she had enough for rent for the next three months before she'd absolutely need to line up a new job. And Lord knew she could live cheap.

Rick was talking to his boss but left when she pocketed her phone.

"Got it sorted?"

"Yeah. Um…would you take me to return my rental car? Also, is it okay if I stay with you until Vex is arrested?" she asked. That would save her a lot of money. She could eat cheap. She'd pick up ramen and a bunch of bananas and be okay for a week.

"Sure, though I'm not sure how long it will take for Vex to be arrested," Rick started.

"I can stay somewhere else, if that's better."

"Not what I was saying, lady. Your boss okay with you on indefinite leave?" he asked.

She heard the other people in the room talking, but her focus was solely on Rick as he moved so that he blocked her from everyone else. "Yup."

Jimmy had definitely agreed she'd be on indefinite leave unless she was at her desk tomorrow at eight, which wasn't happening. So yeah, she was here for the long haul. Maybe she'd try to get a job out here. But for right now she was good, if she could stay here and return the car. She'd already checked out of the hotel at Rick's urging in case Vex tracked her there.

"Then you're good to stay here. Makes it easier to keep you safe," he said. "Van suggested he come with us to the station when we go meet Detective Miller."

"Why?"

"I think he's taking it personally that you were treated poorly by the cops and wants to make sure it doesn't happen again," Rick said.

"That was Houston. Was he a cop?"

"His dad was and two of his brothers still are. Not here. Up in Northern California," Rick mentioned.

"I don't mind if he comes with us. Do you think if I press charges, Vex will mention I drugged him?"

"Does he know you did?"

"Yes. I was hoping he'd know he felt a little out of it," she said. "Or maybe he'll just think it was all the effect drinking."

"I just don't want to get arrested for drugging him."

"I thought you said you'd practiced."

"I'm not a pro. His bodyguards definitely saw my hand over his drink... I really don't want to be arrested," she said. She wouldn't be able to get closer to Vex again that way. Also, being arrested scared her. A lot.

"I think we can keep you out of jail," he said.

Lee overheard that bit as she came over to them.

"Actually, you two both being in rough shape, the police might dismiss it as a drunken dispute. You both sort of roughed each other up."

"Yeah," she said. The way Lee painted it made sense. In an odd sort of way, justice had been served. They'd both been wronged by each other, and each of them had made the other pay.

"Okay, so when do we go?"

"Van is wrapping up a call. Would you object to me adding a tracking app to your phone? That way I can keep tabs on you… I get how that sounds."

It sounded a little like Big Brother, and she wasn't sure why Lee needed to keep track of her.

"Why?"

"Just in case you and Rick get separated. It's something we do for all clients. It's part of how we can guarantee your safety."

Put that way, it seemed less creepy. She handed her phone to Lee. "Did you get anywhere with Brianne's cloud account?"

"Actually, since you knew her password, I was able to get right in. Someone deleted a shit ton of photos, messages and notes the night she died. I'm going through old saves to retrieve the data. It's slow going, but I'm making progress. I think I'll find something."

"Great. I'm not sure that the cops are going to investigate a man who I attacked based on his tattoo."

"Yeah. I'm going to run that tat to see if it is a known gang one. Aaron's going to be asking around. He's working in the office now, but he's still got some good people out there."

Jena didn't know how to respond to that, so she just nodded. Rick squeezed her hand as Lee walked away. His presence throughout this entire morning was keeping her from really wigging out.

Balancing her fatigue, fear, desire for vengeance and this burgeoning awareness of Rick was taking a toll. She wanted to curl up in a ball and stay there until time reversed and Brianne was still alive.

Too bad that wasn't ever happening.

Detective Miller had been considerate the night before, so Jena wasn't afraid to talk to the woman again. But she hated police stations. Not just because of the visit to to confront officers and try to get them investigate Brianne's death. It was all those trips as a kid to see if her dad was in lockup.

He'd had so many drunk and disorderly arrests back then, the sheriff had just kept him in a cell knowing that her and Joey wouldn't be able to make bail. How were two under-tens going to manage that on their own? Or maybe he didn't know. Dad had always made it sound like their mom was still around.

Maybe that was part of why she didn't trust the cops to deliver justice for anyone. They'd always believed everything her father had told them. Never actually looked for the truth. And that was all she was after.

Detective Miller talked to Jena over the phone rather than making them go into the station, which he thought made Jena happy. Miller already had all the photos and evidence and statements so once Jena said she wanted to press charges Detective Miller filed the paperwork. She told them she'd keep them posted once she talked to Tomas Vectra.

"What will we do now?" Jena asked. "I think it might be good to talk to his mom. I'm pretty sure that's the woman he visits on Euclid. She didn't look like his usual type of chick."

"We'll wait on that for now. How about some self-defense lessons?" he suggested. Rick needed to do something physical to get his body focused on something other than Jena.

"Really? Yes! I really need to know how to use a knife and maybe a gun. Martial arts would be cool, but it seems like it would take a long time to learn," she said.

"Slow down. We're going to start with basics. You're not learning to use a gun," he said.

"Why not?"

"Do you know how many people get shot with their own weapons?"

"No. A lot?"

"Yes. Chances are that would happen to you. You don't need a gun."

They got off the elevator in front of his apartment. He'd brought her bag up earlier and stowed it in the bedroom. As they entered his place, he remembered she wanted to return her rental car.

"When do you want to take your car back?"

"The sooner, the better. I don't want to have to pay for another day," she said.

He glanced at his watch. "Let's go now. I'm assuming you got it at the airport?"

"Yeah."

"Where is it parked?"

"I left it a few blocks away from Mistral's in a Jack in

the Box parking lot," she said. "Figured it would be better kept out of sight in case he'd noticed me following him during the week."

It amazed him, all the things she'd thought of. Jena had a natural instinct for investigation. "Another thing from a movie?"

"Nah." She grinned at him. "*Law & Order.*"

It was cute the way she'd consumed media in order to avenge her friend. But while they could laugh about movies and TV shows, he knew that this self-appointed mission was one she took very seriously. He sensed she wasn't going to be happy with Vex just going to trial. She wanted him behind bars or dead.

"Well, it worked."

She fiddled with the radio on the ride to get her car before finally giving up and listening to KISS FM. Rick typically listened to blues. He was a sucker for Stevie Ray Vaughn. Based on his dating past, he knew it wasn't to everyone's taste.

They got to the Jack in the Box parking lot. Her car was where she'd said it was. He pulled up next to it and got out when she did.

"What are you doing?"

"Just checking to make sure it's safe."

Dropping to the ground, he looked under the car to ensure there were no fresh leaks underneath it and checked the tires before he got back to his feet. Standing a few feet from the back of the car, she had her arms crossed over her chest.

"No one knows this car is mine," she said as a black Audi with dark windows and a rear spoiler pulled up behind them. The window started to lower, and Rick moved with lightning speed as a semiautomatic handgun came of the window and two shots were fired.

He felt one graze his shoulder as he tackled Jena and rolled with her to the ground, keeping his body between hers and the gun.

"Crawl to the front of the car. Don't stand up."

She hesitated, but when he shoved her butt to get her moving, she did it.

The person in the Audi fired again as Rick reached for his weapon and rolled to his back, firing at the assailant's hand and hitting it hard enough to make him drop the weapon. As soon as it clattered to the ground, the Audi took off.

Rick tried to memorize the plate. People rushed out of the restaurant. He got to his feet and walked over to where the gun was, kicking it out of the way of traffic because he didn't want to spoil any DNA on it.

Jena rushed to his side.

"Oh my God. What the hell was that? You're bleeding," she half screamed at him.

He glanced down at his shoulder. It was burning, but he could tell that it was just a graze. "I'm fine. Call Van. Tell him what happened. I'll call the cops."

Before he could, a police car pulled into the parking lot. One of the officers coming over to them while the other started talking to witnesses.

"I'm Officer Larkin. Do you need an ambulance?"

"Nah, I'm good."

"What happened?"

"We came to pick up her rental car... She was attacked at a club last night and was scared to come back by herself," Rick said. "Before she could get in, an Audi 3000 pulled up behind us. I saw the window lowered and then a weapon. I knocked her to the ground—"

Realizing he hadn't checked on her, he turned to Jena. "You okay?"

"Scraped knees, but yeah, I'm good."

"The bullet nicked me, and I shoved her toward the front of the car. I got off one shot—I'm licensed to carry concealed—and hit the shooter's wrist. He dropped the weapon, and they sped away.

"I got a partial plate."

"I got a photo of the car," Jena said.

Of course she had. He'd been worried she'd be overwhelmed with everything that happened, but she had more guts than most.

Inside, she was freaking out. She'd never been shot at before, and it was scary and Rick was bleeding and oh God it was a good thing she hadn't eaten because she was going to throw up. She gave the cop her phone and turned to try to find a place to barf that wasn't on the concrete parking lot, but there was no green anywhere, so she hurried to the front of her rental car.

It was mostly dry-retching. Her stomach hurt, and tears were burning in her eyes. She felt a gentle hand on the back of her neck. Rick. He gathered her hair and held it back as she kept gagging until her stomach had had enough. She stood up. He handed her a tissue to wipe her mouth, then pulled a bottle of water from his pocket.

She took a swallow, rinsed and spit it out. Then took another sip to soothe her throat. He watched her quietly.

"Getting shot at is a lot."

Understatement of the year, although last night was way worse. She wasn't even hurt right now. But the fear that had flooded her when she'd noticed the gun was unlike anything she'd ever felt before. If Rick hadn't jumped and knocked her down…she'd be dead.

"They were going to kill me."

"Definitely. But you've got a bodyguard now."

"Yeah. I don't want them to kill you either," she said.

"They won't," he said. "Officer Larkin wants to take your statement when you feel able."

"I'll do it. Do you think he knew I was following him?"

"We'll figure that out later. Just focus on what happened here. We don't know who shot at us," he said firmly.

She understood that Rick wanted to keep everything with Vex between them. Well, her investigation, at least.

The officer was really nice to her and took her into the Jack in the Box to take her statement. Rick followed and stood close to her. She understood he was protecting her—as was Van, who arrived about ten minutes after the cops.

It was hard not to notice the big bald man when he arrived. He stopped to talk to the officer who was still outside, which distracted Jena. "Is that all?" she asked Officer Larkin.

"Yes. Here's my card. If either of you remember any further details, call us. Good thinking to get a photo of the car. With the plate that Rick got, we should find the vehicle quickly. What's the best number to reach you?"

Rick rattled off his number while Jena just sat there in a daze. She didn't feel safe anymore. It was funny, because for the last two weeks, while she was trailing a man she knew had murdered her friend and trying to buy drugs, nothing had fazed her. But last night had changed everything. And now, she'd been shot at.

In movies, she'd always sort of thought "suck it up" when someone was screaming or freaking out, but now she got it. She'd always just taken being safe for granted. But she wouldn't be able to anymore. They'd shot at her in the freaking Jack in the Box parking lot.

A fast-food restaurant... That wasn't what she'd expected.

"You okay?" Rick asked, sitting next to her on the bench as the officer left.

She scooted over but not too far, taking comfort from being close to him. Her emotions were boiling over; she was about to break down. Like, really break down—which wasn't what she wanted to do. Not in public. Not in front of Rick or his super-scary boss.

With a small sound, she turned toward Rick. He pulled her into his arms and let her bury her face against his chest, his hand moving down her back. He was saying something. The words didn't register, but the tone did. It made her feel safe and okay. Told her that it was fine if she cried. He wasn't going to let anyone hurt her.

She was vaguely aware when Van came into the restaurant and sat down across from them.

Pulling away from Rick, she wiped her eyes.

"You okay, sweetheart?"

It was almost a dichotomy for such a stern-looking man to speak so gently. "Yeah. Rick's hurt."

"What?"

"Graze. It's fine. I put a Band-Aid on it."

Van nodded. "Good. We need to get you back to Price Tower."

"My car."

"I'll take care of it," Van said. "You two go back to the Tower."

"Sure thing, boss," Rick said.

"The rental car needs to be filled up," she said, panicked. Her credit card was close to the limit so if they didn't fill the car up where it was cheaper it would max the card out completely.

"I'll take care of it," Van said.

There was something reassuring about him. Not the same way Rick was. She preferred Rick. Though she'd seen evidence that he could be scary and lethal when she was threatened, there was something unnerving about Van.

Van left a few minutes later, and they were back in Rick's car, but this time she wasn't feeling quite as confident that she'd get Vex's confession and walk away from this whole thing unscathed.

"He's going to keep trying to kill me until he does," she said at last.

Rick didn't answer. But really, what was he going to say? Some platitude? Tell her that she was imagining things?

They both knew that wasn't true.

"Do you think he knew I was following him before the club?"

"Maybe. He definitely knows who you are now," Rick said.

"How? I used a fake name last night," she pointed out.

"Bringing up Brianne narrowed it down," he said.

Brianne. Of course. It had always been the two of them. Everyone she worked with knew Brianne. They'd been close and texted and talked a million times a day. Sent each other endless Reels and DMs.

Vex didn't strike her as someone who left loose ends, and now that she had played her hand and lost…well, she was glad Rick had taken on the role of her bodyguard, because she had a feeling she was going to need one.

That scared her. She was still angry and wanted justice, but for the first time, she was afraid she might not live to get it.

Chapter 8

Self-defense training wasn't something Rick was particularly great at. Most of his training had come from growing up on the streets, then basic weapon and hand-to-hand combat training when he'd been studying criminology in college before joining the DEA. He'd been so focused back then on being the best, but his inherent nature wasn't as intense as someone like Kenji.

There was a gym and a shooting range in the building. He wasn't sure that giving Jena a gun was a good idea. She had gone quiet on the ride back from Jack in the Box. The way she held herself told him that the impact of her actions was just now sinking in. It was odd for her to be so quiet, so he knew something was up.

"Want to talk about it?" he asked as they entered the gym. There were changing rooms with some basic black workout gear in all sizes, and they'd both changed and met back on the mats.

It didn't take clairvoyance to guess she was reliving the shooting. Some clients in the past liked to dissect every moment and try to figure out what they could do better the next time.

"What? How you almost got shot instead of me?" she asked.

"That's my job, Jena."

"How is it a job? I'm not paying you. I'm the sister of a guy you knew years ago. Let's face it, you shouldn't have been shot for me," she said at last.

"I made it my job. Money doesn't make me your bodyguard."

"What does?" she asked, moving closer to him.

"My desire to keep you safe," he said. "I gave you my word."

"Your word is your bond?"

"You know it."

"Well... I don't want you shot at because of me again. I'm the one who started this," she reminded him.

As if that was going to make any difference to him. She'd pulled her hair up into a ponytail, and he saw a long scrape on her shoulder and collarbone. The signs of the previous night were all over her body.

The rage he worked hard to keep under control flared for a second. Tomas Vectra was going to pay for what he'd done to Jena. It was personal. He didn't ruminate on the fact that a woman he hadn't known twenty-four hours ago was now so important to him.

She was.

That was all he needed to know.

There were faint shadows under her eyes. She needed sleep more than him training her, but she was too wired to rest. Shifting from foot to foot as she watched him and waited.

"So what do you want to know first?"

"I have no idea. Vex is big…not bigger than you though. Also, he attacked me and Brianne with a knife. I was lucky I got it from him. Maybe show me how to disarm someone?" she suggested.

"Do you have any defensive skills?" he asked.

"I signed up for kickboxing and did two lessons. So I know how to do a side kick and a roundhouse kick."

Rick went to get some training pads for kicks and put them on his hands. "Show me."

It was clear almost immediately that she hadn't done the kicks since the classes. Her form was loose and sloppy.

Moving next to her, he positioned himself at her side. "Your stance is off. You need to find your balance on both legs."

"Like in warrior one or warrior two pose for yoga?"

"Show me." Yoga, he had no clue about.

She did.

"Yes. Ground through your feet, but bring your legs closer together. When you start your kick…this is a front kick. Put your hands here in front of your chest and neck. He's probably going to be targeting them. Then thigh up, weight on your back leg and kick with a snap. Push your power down your leg through your foot."

She was flexible and a quick learner. He had her dog reps of the front-snap kick for a few minutes, trying to get her to kick higher.

"Try to kick here," he said, holding the pad up near his head.

"What if I hit you?"

"I'll be fine. I'm told I have a hard head."

"I can believe that."

The first few times, she was unsteady but then she got into a rhythm and hit the pad with enough strength to knock it back into his face.

"Good. So first of all, try kicking your assailant in the head. Snapping their head back will give you time to run away, which should always be your goal. Get as far away as you can. Got it?"

"Okay, so I kick him in the head. What if nothing happens and he gets his knife and tries to stab me?"

"You're going to disarm him. We can work through this a few times, and then I'll get a training blade for us."

"Work through what?"

"Everything is a series of moves. You're going to have to memorize and practice them, so if you are ever in that situation again you know what to do."

Her face got tight, and she gave a small nod. "I'm ready."

"Defensive stance," he said, showing her the foot placement they'd just worked on with her arms in front of her chest.

She mimicked his moves.

"This is my knife hand, coming down to strike you. You move inside the path of the knife," he told her.

She stepped closer, his arm brushing her arm. "Bring your far hand over and aim to hit my neck just above the clavicle. Make a fist and I'll show you."

She made a fist, and he showed her where to hit him.

"Use all of your strength for this. Either use the flat side of your fist where your hand and wrist meet, or let this knuckle stick out and hit me."

"Why are there two methods?"

"Depends on what feels more comfortable for you," he said.

Their eyes met; he felt the warmth of her breath against his neck. Her eyes widened as his gaze dropped to her mouth. He'd promised himself he wouldn't kiss her again, but she was so close…so tempting. He shook his head and stepped away from her.

Focus.

Except all he could focus on was how she looked in her workout gear. He struggled to keep his mind on the lesson and off how much he wanted her. But the bruise on her shoulder reminded him of the real reason why they were here.

"Next, use the hand you punched me with on the back of my neck. Draw my head down as you grab the wrist of my knife hand."

He showed her, moving closer again and trying to ignore the tingle that went down his back from her hand on his neck. "Push me toward the floor, move around behind me as you force me down. Then climb on my back, use your knees to pin me to the floor and remove the knife from my hand."

She tipped her head back, and her forehead bumped his chin. "I'm not sure I can do that."

"You can. We'll try it a few times and you'll see."

"Okay," she said, not sounding particularly confident.

"Just remember that this is your chance to get the upper hand. Basically if you can't kick or hit him and get away, this is your chance to save yourself."

"Right. Brianne didn't have a chance, but I will," she said.

"Exactly," he said, even though there was no way he was letting her go anywhere alone until Vex was behind bars or dead. That much he'd already decided.

This was still good for her to know and would make both of them feel better.

They moved through the steps a few times, and she grew in confidence until she finally got him to the ground and pinned his arms with her knees.

"Your back is so broad," she said.

"Is it?" His face was on the mat as she sat on his back. Her weight wasn't much at all. He liked the feel of their bodies moving together and watching her get more confident with each time they practiced things.

"Yup, but I still pinned you. I'm like Nala in *The Lion King*."

Another movie he hadn't seen. He just wasn't a movie or TV watcher. He preferred books.

"Sure. But don't let your guard down."

"I'm on top of you," she said.

Putting his hands next to his shoulders, he did a push-up, lifting them both off the mat. Then he carefully bucked her off, rolling until she was under him. "I guess I'm Nala now."

Emotions moved over her face as he held her hands lightly next to her head. "You're definitely not Nala... She's a girl."

"I figured. But I pinned you," he pointed out.

She twisted, but he held her wrists in an unbreakable grip. "Want to learn how to get out of this?"

Rick on top of her was sending messages all through her. It took all of her control to keep from arching her back and rubbing her breasts into that hard muscled chest of his. But no, she needed to stay focused on what they were doing. His lessons were key to her being able to disarm Vex the next time she was close to him.

It was slightly reassuring. Maybe she wouldn't die getting him to confess to killing Brianne.

Maybe.

But right now, with Rick over her, that big firm mouth of his so close, it was all she could do not to kiss him again. Or nip at his lip to try to get him to let her go. His hands on her wrists didn't hurt her, but she felt very pinned by him. His legs were on either side of her thighs, his core pressed her into the floor.

"I might know how to do this," she said, squirming underneath him until she felt his erection against the top of her thigh.

He pushed himself up to his feet, offering her his hand. She took it.

"Why'd you stop?"

"I was…distracted," he said.

"Is that what you call it?"

He groaned and turned away from her.

"Jena. Don't."

"What?"

"Don't flirt with me. Keeping you alive—"

"You've already demonstrated you can do that even when you're not really paying attention," she said, going up behind him and touching his back. He had a small birthmark on the back of his neck. She'd seen it repeatedly as they'd worked through disarming him. She'd wanted to lean up and kiss it, but she'd resisted.

It wasn't fair to him for her to keep pushing this way. But she couldn't help herself. Some basic instinct drove her. This need she had for Rick wasn't going away. The more time they spent together, the more she found to like about him.

"I wasn't distracted. I saw the car when it pulled into

the parking lot. Kept an eye on it. But I still should have moved closer to you before they had a chance to get a shot off," he said. "That was sloppy. It won't happen again."

She turned him to face her. "You were great. I didn't even clock what was going on before you had me on the ground. There is nothing sloppy about you, Rick."

She put her hand on his arm just above the bandage she felt under the fabric of his T-shirt. "You saved me. That's all that matters, right? Not the how of it, the result."

"The *how* of it matters to me," he said dryly.

"Why?"

"Ego, I guess. I would rather have had you back in the Dodge. I should have made you stay in the car."

"Made me?" she asked. They needed to set that straight right now. She wouldn't do anything to put herself or him in jeopardy, but she was the only boss of herself.

"Yeah," he said, cocking his head to the side. "What are you going to do about it?"

There was a challenge in his eyes. God, this attraction between the two of them was taking over the room. She guessed he wanted her to show him her disarming moves, but the only move she wanted to make was putting her arms around him and kissing him.

Not like the one they'd had earlier. But one that was hot and sweaty and didn't end until they were both breathing heavy and satisfied.

She made a fist with her hand and brought it toward his neck but opened her hand to touch him, let her fingers skim over his skin until she was rubbing her finger over that birthmark at the back of his neck. Going up on tiptoe, she tipped his head down toward hers.

Their lips met, triggering a warm sensation that spread down her neck through her breasts and straight to her center. His hand was on her waist, but he didn't draw her closer. That was fine; he didn't push her away either.

His mouth opened when she pushed her tongue against his lips. He tasted so good as she sucked his tongue into her mouth. His fingers on her waist caressed her in a slow languid movement that made waves of pleasure spread down her body until she was wet and hungry.

She felt so empty, needing something that only he could give her. She shifted, trying to get closer to him, but he used his strength to keep space between the two of them. His other hand was on the back of her neck as he tipped her head back and deepened the kiss.

She had the sensation of falling and found herself on her back on the mat with him over her. He held his weight off her, but she felt the brush of his chest against her breasts as he slowly lowered himself over her.

She tore her mouth from his, and their eyes met as she pushed her hand up under his T-shirt. Stroking her hand over his chest, she noticed it was furry. She hadn't expected that. The hair on his chest made the tips of her fingers tingle.

He shifted back to his knees, which were braced on either side of her, whipping his T-shirt off and tossing it aside. Her breath caught in her throat. His chest was tanned and muscled—not a surprise—but she was taken aback when she saw it was covered in puckered, healed wounds and scars. She ran her finger over the one closest to her, on the left side just above his belly button.

"What's this from?"

"Gunshot. Got that in Texas, actually," he said. "Occasionally my cover got blown. Stuff happens."

Stuff happens. This man's body told her that he'd lived his life on the edge. Her teddy bear was really a grizzly.

A big warrior who had the scars to show from the battles he'd fought. "Guess today's graze isn't big like these."

He leaned down so quickly she was shocked. He kissed her hard and fast. "That one matters more because if I'd been a split second slower, you'd have been hit."

"You would never let that happen." Everything she'd learned about Rick told her he would have to be dead himself than let someone harm her.

That was a bigger turn-on than his rocking, hot body. She'd spent a lifetime relying only on herself, and now there was Rick.

The kiss deepened, and she stopped thinking about anything but the feelings that were moving through her. The heat that made her reach between them to caress his erection as his hands caressed her body, touching her so softly.

He lifted his head, kissing the long scratch on her shoulder with a feather-soft touch. "I—"

The door to the gym opened, and Rick rolled off her, getting to his feet and holding out his hand as he turned to face the visitor.

It was Lee.

"Sorry to interrupt. Thought you might want to know that Detective Miller called. Jena, you need to go down to the station. Vectra has witnesses who saw you put something in his drink. He's saying he's normally not violent and that the drug you used made him behave that way."

A shiver went through her, and Rick stepped in front of her. "How long do we have?"

"If she doesn't show up today, they'll come tomorrow to arrest her and bring her in for questioning."

"Let Detective Miller know we'll be there first thing tomorrow."

"I will," Lee said and then left the training room.

Rick turned back to face her. "What drug did you use?"

"The date rape one."

"Where did you get it?"

"Why?"

"We need to know everything about the drug you put in his drink. Normally Rohypnol doesn't make anyone violent."

"Do you know someone who can test it?"

"Yeah, at the DEA. We're going to have to work fast. I need a shower. I'll take one here if you want to go back to my apartment. Lee added the key to your phone when she put the tracker on there."

"She did? What else did she put on there?"

"The ability to unlock the outer doors to the Tower so you can get in when you want."

Her body was still pulsing from making out with Rick. Her mind was sort of mush. She needed to think and make a plan. This wasn't what she'd expected. Putting all her faith in Rick and his DEA friends being able to prove that the drug she'd given Vex hadn't made him violent took a lot of trust.

She'd already acknowledged she trusted him with her safety, which was disarming. The attraction she felt for him was all mixed up in him saving her. She'd never been that girl before.

Was she now? Was this just her trying to keep this scarred warrior by her side, or was the attraction real? And did it matter?

Rick nodded to her as he walked to the shower rooms, and she left the gym no closer to figuring anything out than she had been when he'd been lying on top of her.

Chapter 9

Jena showered and dressed in a pair of jeans and a nice blouse. She wasn't sure if her hair would dry, so she slicked it back into a ponytail. But since her hair was only shoulder length, she then decided to twist it into a bun. Groaning, she put her hands on the bathroom counter, letting her head drop down.

All this focus on what she looked like wasn't going to change anything. Detective Miller wasn't going to be pleased that Jena hadn't mentioned she'd drugged Vex. She wished she could say that she hadn't or that the witnesses were mistaken but it wouldn't take too many questions to find out the truth.

The first question would probably be "why did you drug him?"

Which, honestly, what was she going to say? He was a big guy? She wanted him to know what it felt like because Brianne had mentioned when she'd been in New York that

Vex had given her a drink that had made her feel woozy and the rest of the night was a blur?

It had seemed like the perfect way to get him pliant so she could get his confession?

Rick's idea of getting the drug she'd purchased tested... she liked it, but this was getting out of her control. What had started out as a straightforward mission to get a confession and then turn it into the cops was turning out to be more complicated than she'd ever imagined. Maybe it had been out of her reach to begin with.

Teasing aside, Rick had been right when he'd said that watching movies and TV shows wasn't the background she needed to learn how to get Vex to talk. Even drugged up and beating her he hadn't lost his composure. He definitely knew Brianne, but getting him to admit to anything more than that wouldn't be easy. No wonder Rick wanted her to leave the investigation to the experts.

That was the smart option. Her intelligence was one of things Jena prided herself on. At the same time though, her mind didn't hold sway on this. Her need to avenge Brianne's murder was emotional and came from the heart. That bastard had to pay, and she wanted to see justice done personally.

There was a rap on the bedroom door while she was still in the bathroom. She'd been in here longer than she needed to be. Debating how she should look to get Detective Miller to understand why she'd done what she'd done.

"I'm coming."

She turned off the bathroom light, picking up her bag and putting it across her body before she exited his bedroom.

Her heart beat harder as she saw him standing there. He wore a pair of slim-fitting jeans that hugged his legs and a button-down shirt left hanging loose. His blond hair was darker, as it hadn't fully dried, and he'd shaved. Her fingers tingled with the need to touch his face and see if it was as smooth as it looked.

"Sorry to rush you, but if we're going to get to the station by five, we need to go. Where did you make your buy?" he asked.

Detective Miller had time to see them this afternoon and everyone thought it best to get down there and press charges against Vex before there was another incident.

There was a guarded wariness to him as he asked the question. "Did you say it was near the UCLA campus?"

"Yeah, at some apartments. I saved the location on my phone," she said.

"So you could go back for more?" he asked as she Air-Dropped the location to him.

"No. I figured it was one and done." Honestly it had never occurred to her that she'd fail. Her plan had seemed practical in every sense.

"Are you a user?" he asked.

"What? No. Why would you think that?"

"Just had to ask. You knew what drug to get and where to go."

"For Christ's sake. I spent three days asking people if they knew where I could buy the date rape drug before a bartender took pity on me and told me the street name. He said I sounded like an idiot."

Rick stared at her incredulously.

"I started to ask for the actual drug name and someone pointed me to a dealer. I got a number to text and then met them near campus." She sort of got why he needed to know if she was a drug user, but she hoped that he got now that that wasn't her at all. She'd seen her father so stoned out of his mind too many times to do it herself. She'd seen the way a life could totally fall apart.

"I hope you believe me when I say that I'm not using drugs," she said after a moment.

"Jesus. How the f— did you not get hurt? That was stupid and dangerous," he said.

"Yeah, I know. That's why I saved the details on my phone in case something happened to me. Joey knew I was in LA, so maybe he could have found me." Talking about it made her ears ring and her palms sweat. There were so many times that things could have ended badly. "The fact that everything worked out made me believe I could get Vex to confess."

He shoved his hand through his hair and shook his head. "Let's go."

He looked so frustrated with her that she started feeling defensive. Yeah, she'd had to take some chances, but it wasn't like she'd done any of this just for the thrill of it. She'd done what she needed to do to get justice for her friend—because no one else had been willing to even try.

"No one cares about dead women unless they have rich parents or husbands or look like they should be modeling," she said. "You're a dude and a cop, and you believe that they help everyone…but they don't. If you're poor and white trash, they don't give two shits about. So I had to take chances."

Rick stalked back toward her. "I care about you. If you'd come to me when you landed in LA and told me all of this, I would have helped you." There was nothing but honesty in his eyes.

"Men usually don't," she pointed out.

"I'm not most men."

"I'm beginning to see that," she said.

For a moment his eyes dropped to her mouth; her lips tingled as she remembered how good his had felt against hers. He cursed under his breath and turned, walking out of his apartment.

In the car with her again, he was at least more prepared for the scent of her body spray and the way she fiddled with her purse strap. Or maybe the reason he wasn't distracted by her at the moment was because her words were playing over and over in his head.

He got what she was saying. His sister hadn't been rich or pretty and had fallen into that same space where cops hadn't really wanted to put in the effort to find her. They'd been poor and he'd been a troublemaker, so it was almost as if the authorities thought they'd gotten what was coming to them.

Truth was, that kind of thinking pissed him off. Especially if Jena's case could have led to another death. It didn't make communities safer. It made them more dangerous because when you felt you had nothing left to lose... you usually lost.

He knew that better than most.

"Text your guy and set up another buy," he said to her when they were out of the parking garage.

He listened, still processing everything she'd said and his own PTSD, while she talked about "her guy." It stirred memories he'd thought he'd dealt with. Hell, he'd even told the therapist that the DEA had sent him to that he was cool now. Totally past it.

But he wasn't.

Just thinking of Jena using had made his skin tight. Of course it had only taken him spitting the words out for him to realize she wasn't anything like his sister.

"You okay?" she asked, making him jump a little in his seat.

"Yeah, why?"

"You keep squeezing the steering wheel," she said.

He shrugged. "Sorry. Yeah. I'm solid."

"You don't have to be. You're human, you know. Stuff is allowed to bother you," she said as he turned onto the 5.

"Thanks," he said wryly. "I thought I had you convinced I was a robot."

"Ha, that session on the gym mat proved you're not."

He looked over at her, then concentrated on the road. "Should I apologize?"

"Not to me," she said. "Are you beating yourself up about it?"

"Not really. I'm your bodyguard, and you've had a tough time lately. The last guy who kissed you wasn't great."

"Ya think? Nah, I'm cool with that. I wasn't into him at all."

He wasn't sure what that meant. "And?"

"I like you, Rick. You're funny."

"Geez, really?"

"What's wrong with that?"

"I can't think of one time I was trying to make you laugh," he said.

But the truth was, he had a few times. He liked seeing her smile instead of the fear-anger-grief thing she had going on.

"That's a straight-up lie. So what are you touchy about if it's not kissing me and rolling around on the mats?" she said.

His body reacted to her words, and he realized that this was her way of distracting him. Funny that she had figured out he was in his head. Most of his clients never noticed it. Probably because they were too worried about their own shit.

Jena should have her mind on hers. But instead she was probing and trying to make him feel okay.

"My sister. She was a user. Got in way over head," he said. Because that was the story of Andi, as far as every living person was concerned. He didn't get deeper into that. He wasn't going to unload on Jena.

"Ah...so you thought I might be too. I'm not. My dad was a hardcore user. My earliest memories are empty syringes and him in a daze in the corner."

She was so blasé about it, which was a dead giveaway that those memories were traumatic. Traffic slowed to a stop, and he looked at her again. Was this her PG version she shared with people? He suspected it was. Not exactly a pretty picture, but he could easily guess how much worse the reality was.

"People don't know how to react, right? That's how it is when I bring up my sister. Everyone is like 'you couldn't save her, she made her own choices'...but I was her kid brother, and we were in it together."

"Yeah, like me and Joey. He got out his way and didn't want me to follow him. He's the reason I live in Houston and work at a bank. One of us had to be normal, have a chance at a real life," she said, blinking and wiping away a tear that escaped.

He reached over and squeezed her thigh to comfort her as traffic started moving again.

"Yeah. Andi...that's my sister. She didn't have a chance to tell me to do something else."

"She died young?"

"Yeah. Not unlike Brianne. Just another young user in a short dress whose body was found on the side of the road," he said, hearing the bitterness in his voice. Usually, he worked to hide it, but with Jena he didn't have to pretend.

She got it, unfortunately.

She put her hand under his and laced their fingers together. They didn't say anything else as he continued to drive. She just held his hand, her thumb rubbing over his knuckles. He didn't want it to be as soothing as it was, but that wild part of him that was always called to the surface when he talked about Andi felt a little less savage.

When they got close to their destination, she got stiffer and he knew she was remembering coming here. He parked the car a few blocks from where they were going to meet the dealer in a nearby park.

"I'll go with you," he said. "I want to talk to the dealer."

"Yeah, but you look like a cop," she said.

"I can be chill," he said. "I'm actually good at making buys without tipping anyone off."

"Yeah?"

"True. I've had a lot of experience. I found the guy who killed Andi that way. Worked my way up the gangs until I got to him."

"Like me," she said.

Exactly like Jena, except he'd been tougher than she was. Joey had done a good job of keeping his sister protected in a way that Andi hadn't been able to do for Rick.

The drug dealer, Kyle, was just a normal-looking dude with a skateboard and that chill California vibe. His hair was longish but nice looking, blond—obvs. He was friendly, which had surprised Jena. All her drug dealer images were from TV, and she expected him to look strung out or like Al Capone in *Scarface*. Which she was pretty sure would make Rick smile if she mentioned it.

This guy. It was like everything he did and said just made her like him that little bit more. Right now that wasn't part of her plan. She was dedicated to getting Tomas Vectra in jail. Only then could she move on with her life.

So her body was just going to have to stop reacting every time their hands brushed or he did something sweet like open up about his past. Just no.

"Hey," Kyle said when they were close to the bench where he'd been sitting. Maybe this was his version of an office. It actually unnerved her how nice and easygoing he seemed, given that he was selling a date rape drug. Last time there hadn't been a chance to be judgy, but this time... she was having all the feels, and most of them were violent.

Like, "don't be a dickhead and sell drugs that end up with women being violated."

But she needed the product to prove he wasn't selling something to her that was laced with another drug that might have made Vex more violent.

"Hey. I need another dose."

Rick's eyes rolled so hard in his head as he stepped around her. "Babe, I'll handle this."

"Will you? I thought it was odd that she was buying. Who are you?" he demanded of Rick, not as chill as he was before.

"Her boyfriend. It's just a little kink she wanted to try," Rick said, slinging his arm around her waist and squeezing her ass. "We had some side effects though. Made her a bit violent."

Kyle put his hands up at his shoulders. "Whatever set her off can't have been what she got from me. This is straight from the pharmacy. She told me she couldn't get a script for her insomnia... I don't know what your kink is, but that's not what I deal in."

Covering his ass, no doubt. Last time he'd been all like "chicks dig this and don't notice a thing."

"Sure. Can we get some more?" Rick asked.

"You a cop?"

"Do I look like a cop?"

"Yeah, and you're both freaking me out," Kyle said, getting up, putting his skateboard down.

Jena couldn't believe how quick Rick moved, but Kyle was off his board and sitting back on the bench in a clinch hold seconds later. Rick had him so tight around the neck, she wasn't sure Kyle could breathe. "I used to be a cop, but I'm not anymore... You know what that means?"

Kyle shook his head as he tried to pry Rick's arm from around his neck.

"Rules don't apply to me. Are you going to sell to us or not?"

Kyle reached into his pocket and pulled out a tiny baggie, then tossed it to her. Jena was shit at catching and fumbled it but got it before it hit the ground. She almost smiled at Rick, but she knew better. He got up. Tossed some bills to Kyle.

Rick took her hand as they walked away.

It wasn't hard to guess that he was mad, but for the life of her she couldn't figure out why. She waited until they were in the car. He took photos of the location and of Kyle, along with screenshots of her texts messages. "Detective Miller will want all of this."

He put the car in gear, and she realized he was going to keep driving angry and not talk to her.

"What's up?"

"*I need another dose?* Really. What the hell were you thinking?"

It was sort of ridiculous, considering he must have guessed she wasn't really part of the drug world. "That we need to buy some more."

"Did you ask for it that way last time?"

"Yes."

"Goddamn."

He was truly pissed, but she wasn't catching why. "Sorry I'm not a pro at buying drugs."

"Not a pro? That doesn't even begin to cover it. You could have been hurt, really hurt. You know that, right?"

She crossed her arms over her chest, looking out at the scenery passing them as they got back on the 5. "It worked out."

"Yeah, you live under a lucky star."

"Fuck that. I make my own luck," she said.

He shook his head, then threw it back and let out a laugh. "God knows you do. I thought you were going to drop the bag when he tossed it."

A smile teased her own lips. "Me too. You were awesome. How did you move that fast?"

"I'm nimble. Plus, I give off such a chill vibe most of the time, people aren't expecting it from me," he said.

"Yeah, that's me. I give off such a sweet, girl-next-door vibe, so most of the dealers I approached were sort of protective of me. I told them a dude used it on my friend and hurt her and I wanted to get him back…they were all sympathetic, but still said no."

"I can see that. I hate that you put yourself at risk," he said.

She didn't regret it. It was the only way she had gotten close enough to Brianne's killer. All that stuff she'd done that scared her had gotten her here—in the car with Rick and on her way to a police station.

So yeah, not exactly going to plan, but after Rick's outburst, she realized things did seem to always work out for her.

Chapter 10

Jena was tense when they entered the station. Detective Miller had an interrogation room booked for them.

Detective Ramona Miller was about five seven and habitually tired. She worked hard for the city of Los Angeles to try to keep the streets safe, but it was an uphill battle that shone on the lines around her eyes and mouth. She was probably close to forty like Rick was. Most days, it wasn't easy to guess today wasn't one of those days.

"Do you want to have an attorney present?" Detective Miller asked as they both entered the interrogation room. She'd already ascertained that it was all right with Jena if he accompanied her.

"Do I need one?"

"Right now I've got a *he said, she said* situation. I saw you and I've seen him. You clawed the hell out of his face, by the way, and he has a thick compression bandage on his neck," Detective Miller said, gesturing for them to sit down.

"Can I talk to Rick alone for a minute?" she asked Detective Miller.

"Sure. I need more coffee. Want me to grab you a Fanta?" she asked him.

He nodded.

Detective Miller glanced at Jena. "Water, coffee or sugary soda?"

"Uh, diet anything," she said absently. Her hands were knotted together in her lap.

The detective left and Rick turned to her. "They have recording equipment set up so they can document your statement. I trust Detective Miller, so I think it's off but I can't guarantee it."

"Great. This is why I didn't want to call the cops," she muttered. "Do I need a lawyer? I don't even have one."

"We do. Let me text her," he said.

Taking out his phone, he sent a quick text to Kenji's wife, Daphne Amana. She was an international rights lawyer by trade, but she was the only attorney he knew that he could hit up last minute.

She called back instead of texting.

"What's up?"

"My client has been brought in for questioning, and they asked if she wanted an attorney present. Her name is Jena. I'll let you talk to her," Rick said, then passed his phone to Jena.

Jena caught Daphne up on everything that had gone down. Most of the details matched what she'd initially told him, but he noticed she added in a few extra truths that it had taken Rick a while to get out of her. Daphne must have started talking, because Jena went quiet and then nodded a few times.

"I don't know. I mean, all I have to say is what I've told you. Okay. Thanks."

Jena handed the phone back to Rick. "She wants to talk to you."

"Hey."

"Hi. We're about two hours out of the city, so I can't get down to the station, but I can ask Cass from my office to come down there. I know it's Detective Miller and you can count on her to be fair, but if the questions get into an area where Jena doesn't feel comfortable, then stop the interview and wait for her to arrive, okay?"

"Yes. We got the drug that Jena used and want to have it tested to make sure it wasn't laced with something else," Rick said.

"Van is on his way there. Kenji texted him. I think having a private firm test it will be better. Jena mentioned it's her word against Vex. I think Detective Miller will want to see what shakes out when she questions Jena. I wouldn't mention the drugs you purchased today She shouldn't volunteer anything."

"Okay."

"She wants to defend herself, which I totally get, but this is the time to be cautious. I mentioned that Detective Miller is simply gathering information, she's not going to make any judgments. Try to keep her from defending herself. Listen to the accusations Vectra made and then simply restate her story. Don't go for a point-by-point defense."

"I'll try to keep that from happening."

"I gave her the same advice. Wish I was closer. Kenji's going as fast as he can to get us back. It's okay to stop the questioning at any time and tell her you want to come back with me," Daphne said.

"If it gets dicey, we will," Rick said. Then hung up.

"What are you going to do?" he asked Jena.

"I don't know. I mean, I want to defend myself, but it sounds like that's the worst thing for me to do," she said. "Should I just not say anything?"

"I think stick to what you've said so far. Let's hear what he said about you."

She rubbed her hands together. "I can't believe he's still alive. He was bleeding so much I thought for sure I'd killed him."

"Yeah, neck wounds bleed like a mother."

Detective Miller knocked on the door before opening it. She took a can of Fanta from one pocket and then a can of Diet Coke from the other before handing them disposable cups she'd carried in her other hand.

"What's the verdict?"

"I'm being represented by Daphne Amana. She can't be here today, but I'd like to hear the charges that are being leveled against me," Jena spoke, but Rick heard Daphne all over that statement.

Detective Miller did too, sighing as she sat down across from them. "I have your original statement when you thought you'd killed him."

Jena didn't add anything to it.

"Okay. You're being accused of drugging a guy you picked up at the club and then leading him to the bathroom when the drug kicked in and telling him you liked rough sex. Then he hit you at your request—"

"I never—" Jena interrupted, then stopped herself. Her face was tight and angry. "Sorry for that."

"It's okay. He said he got out a knife because it excited

you, and then things got rougher, ending with you stabbing him. Then he says you leaned over his body, took a key from his pants pocket before running from the bathroom. His guards saw you leaving with the blood on your hands and went to check on Vectra before you disappeared."

The story Jena told and the recording he'd listened to painted a very different version of events. Except for one thing. Jena had never mentioned she'd pickpocketed Vex while he was on the ground. He glanced over at her and her face was stone. She gave nothing away.

Stole a key from him? Where had he gotten that idea? She certainly hadn't had her wits about her enough to pat him down. She just lit out of there before his men could finish the job that Vex had started.

Glancing at Rick, she noticed his face was tight and he wouldn't look at her. Did he believe Vex? Of course he did. Bastard. He should trust her. Except she'd lied to him about a few things before this, so she guessed maybe that was where his head was.

Still.

"Uh, I didn't take anything from him," Jena said. "I was scared and just got out of the bathroom. I thought his men would kill me if they found me with him."

Detective Miller jotted that down. Daphne had been clear that she shouldn't defend herself. Daphne mentioned that was where suspects ended up incriminating themselves.

"He says you took a key."

"A key or his keys?" Rick asked, sounding less stiff. She couldn't wait until they were alone so they could have this out.

"A key," Detective Miller repeated.

"What kind of key?" Jena asked.

"He didn't add anything to that. Do you have a key?" Detective Miller asked her.

"No. I have bruises and nightmares, but that's it," she said.

"Got it. Did you drug him?"

"I think I should wait for my attorney to answer that," she said.

Detective Miller proceeded with her questions, and Jena stuck to what she'd either told Detective Miller the other night or said that she wanted to wait for an attorney. It felt like they were in the interrogation room for hours, but in reality it was only forty minutes later when she and Rick were back in the parking lot. He texted Daphne's attorney friend and told her she wasn't needed. Van was waiting for them in the busy parking lot. The downtown police department was only a few blocks from Price Tower.

"That was quick."

"Jena wasn't answering anything outside of what was in her statement earlier."

"Good play. Let's get back to the Tower and talk. Daphne will meet you there," Van said to her.

All she could muster was a weak nod of agreement. She still felt sort of sick at the way that Vex had described the night—mostly because she couldn't really refute much of it. She *had* picked him up, she had drugged him but the rest of it was pure fiction.

She'd gone from potentially being an avenger to a murderer to a possible date rapist. Her head hurt, and she really wanted to curl into a ball somewhere and pretend that the real world didn't exist.

Except that had never worked. Not back when she was thirteen and not now that she was twenty-four. So she had to get her ass in gear. Now that she knew his version of events…of course he knew hers as well. And what key was he talking about?

"You okay?" Rick asked when they were in his car.

"No."

"What's wrong?"

"You think I stole from him."

He didn't bother to deny it. "You wanted proof that he killed Brianne. Did you think he had it on him?"

"What kind of proof would I look for in his pockets? And what would I do with a key? I doubt he kept anything of hers. He certainly didn't leave anything behind in her apartment—I was the one who packed it up and cleared it out after she died, and I would have noticed."

Rick tipped his head back against the seat and closed his eyes. Was he seriously taking a rest right now?

He didn't do anything but sit there for like three minutes and then his eyes popped open. "Did you bring her purse to LA with you?"

"Yes. It's in my suitcase," she said.

"What if… I'm reaching here…would Brianne have a key that was Vex's? Something that would link him to her murder?" Rick suggested.

"Oh, shit. I didn't even look. I mean, I got her key chain out to go through her apartment, but I didn't look to see if there were any extra keys. Also, he kept referring to it as one key. No one keeps one key by itself except for the self-start for the car," she said.

Was that the link she needed? She hadn't even thought to sort through her friend's bag. She'd been too busy making her avenger plot. Plus, it made her sad to look at Brianne's stuff.

Their favorite Fenty lippie would be in there, her wallet with the pictures of the two of them from that trip to Six Flags they'd taken the weekend before Brianne had been killed. Stuff that made Jena's heart ache so painfully.

"Let's go take a look," Rick said.

"Not until you apologize."

"For what?"

"Thinking I'm a liar. I came clean with you," she said. "You want me to trust you with everything, right?"

His only response was a grunt as he put the car in gear and drove out of the parking lot.

"Well," she continued, "it's a two-way street. I need to know you have my back."

"I'm just supposed to take everything on blindly?"

"No. If there's something you want to know, ask me about it," she said. "But don't just assume I'm lying."

He gave a heavy sigh as they turned into the underground parking for the Tower, hitting the button to open the heavy garage doors. "You're right. I should have heard your side."

"I know I'm right," she shot back, crossing her arms over her chest as he backed into his spot and turned the car off. He reached for the door, but she stayed there. One of the hardest lessons she'd learned and was still learning was to ask for respect for herself. He owed her an apology. She wasn't leaving here with him if he couldn't give her one.

It was dark in the garage and cool. But she was hot and tense, waiting to see if Rick was the man she thought he was or if she'd read him wrong.

He shoved his hands into his hair. "I'm sorry. I have issues with women."

"Duh."

She opened her door and got out of the car, hearing him do the same. They both had more baggage than any two people should be lugging around, but that didn't mean that they had to unpack it all right now.

Rick watched her walking away from him. Respect was all he felt for her right now. She'd been right to call him on being an ass. He could come up with as many excuses as he wanted but trust worked both ways.

Maybe that was the problem, he thought as he followed her out of the elevator and down the hall to the big conference room. He wasn't being 100 percent honest with her. There were parts of himself that he'd never willingly share.

Too many broken pieces, too much rage-filled behavior. One of the many therapists he'd seen over the years said that he had to forgive himself. But there were some actions that just couldn't be forgiven.

No one knew that better than he did.

He kept things solid by being chill. He'd used cigarettes for a long time, but a spot on his lung had stopped that. He didn't have cancer. He couldn't have handled it if he had. People—the Price team would have felt sympathy toward him. No way was cancer easy; he knew that, but for him it would've have been a relief. He'd been so low when that scare had hit. He'd gotten lost in the job and his own karmic balancing act. So he'd quit smoking and started to get himself clean and in a better head space.

He'd never been addicted to drugs or drink; those two things never tempted him. But putting his life in danger, taking risks that brought with them the adrenaline rush of life or death... Hell yeah, that was home to him.

"You okay?" she asked as they entered the conference room. "It's not like you to just follow me."

"I like the view," he said slowly. Because he needed to get out of his head, and it was the truth. She had a fine ass, and the outfit she'd put on to go to the police station flattered her.

Tossing her head, she smiled at him. "I'm glad."

That feisty woman was going to be the death of him. Because every time she sassed him, it made him hard. Made him want to say the hell with everything else and take her to his apartment and then just take her. Up against the wall, on the couch. Then, after the edge was off, he'd pull her into his bed for a long leisurely "learn all her secrets" kind of session.

But she was his freaking client.

Something that mattered way more to him than his own lust.

He had nothing in this life but his honor. It had been the thing that kept him from going too far when he was on the street. After he'd avenged Andi, he kept that monster locked away.

But he knew that it was still there deep inside him. These feelings that Jena stirred were awakening emotions and desires he'd done a damn good job of hiding from until now.

They were alone in the conference room. Jena stood by the window. He had a flash, remembering a similar window when they'd started protecting Nick DeVere and someone had shot at it.

"Get away from the window."

"I thought I was safe here," she said, moving back and leaning one hip on the table.

"You are, to an extent," Rick said. "Or at least as safe as you can be."

"Do you think Vex will try to kill me?"

"Not until he gets that key he's looking for," Rick said.

"Should I go and grab Brianne's bag?" she asked, moving toward the door.

"We'll do it together after the meeting," he said as the door opened. Van, Lee and Aaron were back.

"Detective Miller's not happy you lawyered up. I just got off the phone with her. Vectra's lawyer wants blood," Van said as he walked in and took a seat.

Rick dropped into a chair next to Jena, and Aaron and Lee sat across from them.

"I guess I stirred up something."

"You sure as hell did. Word on the street is that Vex wants you. He's put a nice-size bounty on you too," Aaron said. "My guy said no one seems to know why you're worth that much."

"Once they get a look at him, they'll know," Rick said, remembering the description that Detective Miller had given them of Vex's condition after tangling with Jena.

"What does that mean for me?"

"I'm your shadow until he's in jail," Rick said.

The soft smile she gave him didn't help him maintain the tight control he needed over his dick and his emotions. He wanted those sweet smiles, but he wanted them when they were alone and he could do something about it.

"What have you two got for us? Did you get the pill?"

"We did," Rick said, passing it down the table to Van. "How did you get that in his drink?"

"I ordered blue velvet martinis for both of us."

"Risky," he said.

"Yeah, we were doing shots of tequila in between. I waited until the third martini to drop it in," she said.

He was impressed by how much work she'd put into getting that confession from Vex. The fact that the drug turned liquid blue and she'd ordered something with blue curaçao in it was genius.

"I'll wait for Daphne. I want to make sure we use a lab that is court approved. Also, we'll need to be able to give a portion of the same pill to his team to test," Van said.

"Am I going to be arrested?" Jena asked.

Rick heard the fear in her voice. "Not if I can help it. Aaron, can your guys get us close to Vex?"

"What are you thinking?" Aaron asked.

"Make a deal with him. He accused her of stealing a key. So he's looking for something," Rick said.

"Do you have it?"

Rick looked at Jena she shrugged. "It might be in Brianne's personal effects."

"It might save your life."

Chapter 11

Back in Rick's apartment, she hesitated to open Brianne's bag. She knew there were a ton of memories that would wash over her when she opened it up. Rick sat next to her at the table, giving her as much time as she needed.

Finally she drew the knock-off Gucci bag toward herself. "Brianne got this in Chinatown on that trip she took to New York to meet Vex. I asked her why she didn't ask him to buy her a real one, since he was always splashing cash."

"What'd she say?" Rick asked as he waited with that patience he often demonstrated just at the right moment.

"That she wasn't with him anymore... That's the thing that really bothers me. Like, why did she go out with him again? She knew he was bad news," Jena said, remembering the bruises on Brianne's neck and wrists.

"We'll never know. Want me to open the bag for you?" he asked. "You don't have to put yourself through it."

"I can't let you do that. This is her private stuff. A woman's purse is sacred," she told him.

"Believe me, I'm not at all tempted to look in anyone's handbag," he said dryly.

"Except mine," she said.

"Touche."

She took a deep breath, hesitating for another minute, and then undid the clasp on the bucket bag. The scent of Brianne's perfume wafted out, and tears stung Jena's eyes. She swallowed hard, reaching inside and pulling out her wallet, which was a Hobonichi weekly planner.

Opening the cover, she saw her friend's credit and loyalty cards, a picture of the two of them tucked into the front pocket and a sticker that she knew Brianne had made that read *2024 is your year. Shine, girl!!!*

She traced her finger over the raised letters of the vinyl sticker. Hating every minute of this. How was she supposed to deal with this?

Rick put his hand on top of hers and squeezed. "Want to just dump it all out? If there's a key, it should spill out."

Blinking and swallowing to keep her emotions under control, she turned it upside down. More things spilled out. Their matching engraved Yeti tumblers that Jena had gotten them for Christmas. Fenty lipstick, a few receipts that Rick reached for, putting them aside. There was a stress ball, Brianne's keys, and a pouch she assumed had makeup or medicine, a tampon, a pad.

"No key," Rick said.

Yeah. But she was looking at this stuff. This was her friend's life summed up in a bunch of random things that were with her at all times. She saw the effect that her friendship had on Brianne, and in her heart she knew that Brianne knew how much Jena had loved her. But this hurt.

She took the bag from him and pushed her hand down into it. Feeling in the small pocket that wasn't in a real Gucci bag but was in this one. There it was. She pulled out a key and set it on the table.

They both looked at it. Was this the key that Vex wanted bad enough to kill Brianne and come after her?

She turned it over in her hand and realized that it was a safe deposit box key. Which she recognized because her bank branch had them. "Safety deposit box... But which bank?"

"You sure that's what it is?" Rick asked.

"I do work at a bank."

"That's right. I really can't picture you as a bank teller."

"I'm not. I'm a loan officer," she said. Or at least, she had been a loan officer before she'd decided to stay in LA instead of showing up for her shift. That was it. "I'm not sure which bank this is for."

"I bet that Lee can find out. She can usually get any intel we need."

"She does seem pretty efficient," she said.

"Yeah, she is. Do you need a few minutes? I want to take this to Lee and the team. Maybe someone else will recognize it," he said.

"Give me a second to put this all back," she said.

But as she touched it, she knew she didn't want to just shove it all back in the knock-off Gucci. She wanted to linger over it and remember her friend. But not yet. Not until Vex paid for what he'd done to her. So for now, she started to put her things back into the bag. But then a photo fell out of the back of her planner wallet. One of those Instax ones. She picked it up, her hand trembling when she realized it was a photo of Brianne with Vex. He had his arms around her.

He looked straight at the camera, but Brianne's head was tipped back, looking up at Vex with so much love on her face. Jena's heart broke seeing that photo.

Rick glanced down. "Proof he was with her. Nice job."

That's right. The cops couldn't deny she'd been known to him anymore. "I wish I hadn't been so afraid to look in here."

"No use beating yourself up over it. Grief takes time to process," he said, one arm hugging her. "She was really into him."

"Yeah. Looks like he was into himself," Jena said.

Rick made a grunt of agreement.

She put the photo on top of the receipts that Rick had set aside. Her hands trembled. She hated that.

"You okay?"

"Just so damn angry. Not like that's new. I've felt that way since the moment I got the call that she was dead. The moment they asked me to come down and identify her body. Vex is going to pay. If I have to go to jail to make that happen, so be it."

"I think we can come up with another solution. You've got more evidence against him than he knows. The key... that's crucial."

"It is. I don't want to give it to Detective Miller," she said.

"We're not going to. We need to find out where the safety deposit box is. The contents are crucial to bringing him down—and the fact that she had it might even prove to be his motive for killing your friend."

Jena was more subdued than he expected. He'd seen her scared, angry, sassy and determined, but not subdued. It didn't take a genius to realize that she was too in her head.

He wanted to distract her—and he could think of plenty of fun ways to pull that off—but there wasn't time.

He couldn't help noticing the way she worried her lip when she thought no one was looking. This was taking a huge toll on her, and he wished there was some way he could convince her to...what, to go back to Texas?

He definitely didn't way that to happen. He wanted her here, next to him, where he knew she was safe.

There was this feeling in his gut that a clock was ticking. Probably because they'd only be able to keep Detective Miller at bay for so long. But that wasn't where his head needed to be right now. Daphne wouldn't be over to talk to Jena until later and Van had gone with Aaron to the DEA offices to find out more about the threat to Jena. At the moment, his only task was to keep her safe and to find out where that safety box was.

They took the key to Lee, who immediately started running a search on her computer. She had four monitors on her desk. Rick was lucky to get by with his phone and would go nuts if he had to sit in front of the computer like Lee did most days.

"How do you do it?" he asked her.

"Smarts," she said with a wink.

"Smart ass, more like. I meant sitting here all day," he said, pulling a chair over for Jena and then grabbing one for himself.

"My time undercover with Aaron was enough excitement for me. My love language is protecting the people I care about. You know that. I have to be here watching and monitoring keeping you guys up to date...and safe."

"It's kind of scary how easily you are pulling this information," Jena said.

"Not really. I just know where to look. Speaking of

which I finally got into your friend's cloud account. I have WhatsApp messages and photos of her and Vex. Also, it seems like she was on to him."

"She was?"

"Yeah. She left you a note. I can put it up on the screen or Air Drop it to you," Lee said.

Jena tightened her mouth, her jaw hard as she nodded. "The screen."

Lee hit a few keys and the note popped up.

Jena—
You were totally right about Vex. He's not Prince Charming. In fact he's probably the opposite. Sorry I got so mad when you asked about the bruises. It's embarrassing to admit I was so wrong about him. In fact I can't even say this to your face.

In New York I saw a totally different side to him. He's not a nice man. I think he killed someone. I mean I was in the car and drunk...don't judge! I was on vacay. I heard a gunshot. Hard to miss those having grown up like we did.

When he got back in the car he had this...well, big smile on his face. He pocketed his Glock and then took my hand and told his driver to take us to his place. You're going to be pissed but I asked him what was going on. You know I have no filter when I'm drinking.

He told me to mind my own business. Which I totally didn't. I'm tired of men treating me that way. He got a little rough...you saw the bruises. But then he calmed down and we had sex before he left to go to a meeting. He told me to stay put.

I was freaking. I thought about calling you but

*he's dangerous. I can't do that to you. I found some
stuff in his desk and tried to take a picture of it but
my hands were shaking and I heard him come back. I
grabbed a key that was hidden under his mousepad.
I don't think he knows.*

Two weeks later

*Okay, that key...he wants it bad. I've put it in my new
Gucci. I know you hate when I do this, but I left it at
your apartment. I didn't want it on me when I go to
meet him. His bank is a big one in Manhattan, but I
don't know which one. I got my own safety deposit
box at one of your branch offices and am going to
give him that key. They look very similar.*

"Oh my God. What was she thinking? She took too many chances," Jena said. "I didn't even question it when she started using her small phone bag instead of this one."

"Probably the same thing you were when she died and no one would listen to you," he said. "She was trying to sort her life out through whatever means she could find."

"And it ended up killing her," Jena said. "I wish she'd told me."

"She clearly believed if she did, you'd end up dead," Lee said quietly. "At least we know the bank is in New York. I'll start digging there. Almost all of them are flat keys with a small *f*."

"I wonder if he thought the key she gave him was the real one?" Rick asked.

He wanted to distract Jena before she had time to realize what he had noticed as he'd skimmed the note from Brianne. The fact that Vex knew her name—well, first name—and that the key that Brianne had given him was a fake. It wouldn't take him long to work out which bank Jena worked at.

"Why didn't he come after me?" she asked in a low tone.

"I'm guess you making a fuss with the cops in Houston made him retreat and regroup," Rick said. It was the only logical conclusion he could reach.

"Yeah, and then I showed up out here and let him know exactly who I was."

"At least you had the upper hand," Rick said as Lee worked on her keyboard. "If you hadn't, he would have probably come back to Houston and killed you. You wouldn't have had a chance."

"Yeah. He knows where the key is if he read that note."

"I'm pretty sure he did. He deleted it."

Chaos. That's what her head was filled with. Rick and Lee were talking, but she couldn't hear them at all—the only thing she was thinking about was Brianne's note. Her friend should have just told her that Vex was a dick. Not that it would have been a shock.

Which was probably why Brianne had kept silent. Jena herself hadn't shared the details of her most shitty relationships. Like it was somehow either of their faults that they'd gotten involved with shitty men.

It seemed to her that it all came back to honesty. Probably why she had a hard time trusting anyone. People lied. Not always because they were cruel or inherently dishonest but just to protect themselves. She got that. She did it herself when coworkers asked about her family. She had her go-to *Boy Meets World* fake family she used.

When she'd been a kid that show had been her escape. She'd gotten so caught up in the idea of parents that cared deeply for their kids and taught them life lessons. Even the teachers at Cory's school liked him. Her reality had been different...except for Ms. Kieffer. She was the only teacher who'd really seemed to see Jena, and who'd believed in her potential. She'd helped her get a Pell Grant to go to community college, where her grades had gotten her a scholarship to finish out her degree.

It made her feel better to remember how far she'd come. The obstacles she'd overcome. This was just another stumbling block. She was going to avenge Brianne. Her friend had left her some good evidence and clues. Now it was up to Jena to finish the job.

She promised herself and Brianne she would. Tomas Vectra was going to end up behind bars.

"I'm going to go for a walk," she said to Rick. "I need to get out of here."

She felt like she'd been cooped up all day—especially in the police interrogation room. And after reading that letter from Brianne...she needed some solitude, needed fresh air and a chance to clear her head.

"I'll come with you."

"No. I need to be alone."

"Vex put a hit out on you. So going out on your own is a no go," he said. "You can chill in my apartment or the gym."

She wanted to kick something or punch Rick for making her stay here. She got it. He wasn't wrong. If she was dead, then she couldn't avenge Brianne. But she needed to be outside. To walk around, see people living a nice normal life to remind herself that there was some good in the world.

Rick picked up on her vibe.

"I'd have to go with you to keep an eye on you, but

you could walk on your own. Let me figure out where it would safe," he said.

He pulled out his phone, those long fingers of his moving over the screen, tapping out a message or searching something. She remembered his hands on her—even though they hadn't been on her nearly enough. She wanted him.

Also dangerous thinking.

Weird to think she had only met him thirty-six or forty-eight hours ago. It felt much longer. Like a lifetime had passed since Brianne had been murdered. She almost couldn't remember her life before that.

Her focus had been on finding Vex. She'd pushed herself outside of her comfort zone and was paying for it now. She needed to move and get rid of some the energy that was building up inside her. She needed some place to ugly-cry and maybe kick something. The gym was probably a good place to start, but she felt like she couldn't breathe in this building. Maybe it was because it was so enclosed, so secure. All her life, Jena had been one to leave a window open basically year round.

And there were none in this building.

No place to get fresh air.

Ah…she was spiraling.

"I'm going to the gym."

She left Lee's office without waiting for Rick's reply, taking the fire stairs instead of the elevator. Running up them as fast as she could. Her work pants weren't really made for exercise and pulled tight on her thighs with each step she took, but she didn't care. When she got to the top, she opened the door and went to the gym, grabbing a pair of exercise shorts and sports bra from the lockers and going to get changed. As soon as she was in the changing room, her composure finished shattering.

She screamed—one long guttural sound she couldn't control. Tears streamed down her face as that violence that she'd been trying to contain spilled over; lashing out, she hit the wall as hard as she could. Pain shot up her arm to her elbow, and she hit it again.

This kind of pain was what she needed. Anything to distract her from her heart, which was breaking again. How could it keep hurting more? It wasn't like Brianne could be any more dead than she already was.

The pain was so sharp in her chest, burning in her stomach, that her knees gave way. She crumpled to the ground, dropping her head to her hands as she just let go. She heard herself making sounds like an animal that was trapped and couldn't figure a way out.

She *had* a way out; she had a plan, but her mind couldn't focus on it. Not right now. Not with Brianne's voice fresh in her head from reading that note.

Someone came in. She had the thought that she should get up and pretend things were cool. But before she could, Rick was next to her on the floor, pulling her into his arms. She hesitated for a second before she burrowed closer to him, put her face in the crook of his neck, letting the storm within her rage until it was done. He kept running his hands up and down her back.

He let her have her time. Then, as she calmed down, their touches changed. His mouth found hers, the kisses reminded her of something other than pain.

Chapter 12

She wanted space, and he'd struggled to actually give it to her. Protecting her didn't just mean from bullets to his mind. This emotional crap could cut way deeper, and he didn't want her to have to face it alone.

To see her on the floor sobbing, her knuckles bruised, nearly broke his heart. He'd held her while she cried out her rage, and he'd felt filled with a new purpose. To fix this, to fix her. But when had he ever been able to do that?

He kissed her as she calmed down, which was a world-class mistake. God, the way she tasted should be illegal. He was addicted to her and didn't want to stop. Her arms snaked around his middle, pulling her breasts flush against him.

He was hard. Had been since she'd stopped crying and their lips met. There was no walking away this time. He had to square that with himself. Because this was happening...unless she changed her mind. Then fuck it, he'd walk away.

Jena had endured enough. A man pushing himself on her was the last thing she needed. But her hands on his back, nails digging into them as she shifted around until she straddled him on the floor, was a huge affirmation.

"You sure about this?" he asked, checking in just to be sure. "There are other ways to process emotion," he said.

"Shut up, Rick. Kiss me like you mean it. I want you and I need to forget all the bad stuff," she said, peppering his face with kisses as she spoke. "Will you help me do that?"

"Hell yes."

He undid the buttons of his shirt, shrugging out of it. Her hands were immediately on him, caressing all of the scars she'd already seen. She touched them like they were badges of honor...even the dumb ones he'd got from going off half-cocked into dangerous situations.

The heat from her fingers was making him harder, and he realized he had a lap full of willing woman and hadn't touched her. He pulled her shirt off and tossed it on top of his. Then unhooked her bra, catching her breasts in both of his hands.

She moaned, pressing her chest into his palms. The tight buds of her nipples poked him. Leaning down, he took the tip of one into his mouth while he undid the fastening of her pants, pushing his hand in deep until he cupped her ass, bringing her on top of the ridge of his erection.

God, yeah. That felt so good. That was what he needed as she rocked back and forth, rubbing her center up and down his length. He reached between her legs, cupping her pussy. Her hands moved beneath his, directing him to her clit.

He stroked it as she fumbled with the opening of his

pants. He shifted back, taking his mouth from her breast. They were both frantically trying to get each other's clothing off. He stood up, shucking his pants and underwear. They got caught on his feet, but that didn't matter.

She was bare-ass naked the next time he looked at her. He lifted her up on the counter with the sinks and stepped between her legs. Her hands were in his hair, her eyes wide. The first brush of the tip of his cock against her center was warm. He couldn't wait to get inside her, but she stopped him.

"Condom."

That one word, bit out, froze him in his tracks.

"Fuck."

"Do you have one?"

"In my apartment," he said. Though from now on, he was carrying one with him at all times.

"Uh..." she said.

"Later," he said, dropping to his knees. He needed to taste her, to give her the release she'd been asking for.

It took her a second to realize what he was about to do, then her hands were on his shoulders, pulling him in. He parted her, flicking his tongue over that sensitive bud. Her thighs rubbed along the sides of his face as she arched her back.

God...this taste. All of Jena had intrigued him from the moment they met but now, she was a craving in his soul, and he couldn't stop himself. His mouth still on her as he pushed his fingers into her.

Her pussy clenched in response. She was so tight. He reached down to stroke his dick with his other hand as he pushed deeper into her. Her back arching, her cries echoed in the bathroom as he drove her higher and higher.

He added a second finger, pushing upward, searching

for her G-spot, finding it when she started to move more frantically. Moments later, he felt her pulsing around his fingers. She pulled his head to her pussy, held his mouth against her as she arched and cried his name on a long, low moan. Then she collapsed back against the counter.

Looking up at her, he continued stroking himself as he got to his feet. Reaching out, she brushed his hands aside, pulling him forward until she twisted her body around and took him in her mouth.

From the minute her mouth closed around him, he was already on the edge. She sucked him deeper toward the back of her throat. His balls got tight; he thrust deeper into her mouth as he started to come.

He tried to pull out, but she put her hands on his ass, keeping him close until he was empty. He braced his hands on either side of her body. She smiled up at him, the expression surprisingly sweet after the wildness of what had raged between.

As he touched the side of her face, emotion welled deep inside him—a sweet pain that she stirred in him. He'd always been so careful when he dated, but there was no caution with Jena. There should have been, but his body had claimed her.

His mind and soul weren't far behind.

She was his.

Not sure how that was going to work, but he knew it as surely as he knew he wasn't going to rest until he'd taken care of Vex.

Jena didn't do regrets, even if part of her wished she'd just said fuck it and taken Rick into her body. Pregnancy and STDs weren't something she was ready to think about right now, so sticking to oral had been the smart choice.

But damn. That man was fine in ways that made her lose her head. Made her want *everything*.

He carried her to the shower after he'd gotten his shoes off, leaving them both naked. Setting her on her feet, he adjusted the water temperature and then quirked one brow at her.

"Ridiculously hot shower?"

"I think you mean the correct temperature," she said.

She stepped under the spray and made it a smidge hotter. A shower couldn't be hot enough to suit her.

"Sorry, I should have known to set it as if we were bathing on the sun."

She threw her head back and laughed. It was long and hard and came from the battered part of her soul that hadn't thought there was anything good or fun left in the world.

He drew his hand down her back, cupping her ass before biting her shoulder gently. "I'll shower next door, or I'm going to be in you in the next five minutes."

He left before she could argue that it would be fine with her. There were luxury hair products and that fine-milled soap that they had in nice hotels. Rick…he was used to this life but he felt so…like her. Like a kid from the streets who was eking out a living. Maybe that was why it felt so right to be with him.

That all-consuming sadness that had swamped her ebbed. Most of her life she'd eschewed accepting comfort from anyone, thinking it was a pointless gesture. And most of the time, it had felt like pity. But not from Rick. He'd given her space to cry and rage and then…

Yeah, then.

What was she going to do about Rick?

She still wanted him. Getting off together was nice, but there was an emptiness inside…to be honest, it had been there for a long time. Rick was the first person who'd made her feel…less hollow.

Shaking her head, because that wasn't something she wanted to deal with at the moment, she reached for the shampoo and started to wash her hair.

Eyes on the prize.

It was the one thing her father ever said to her that was quasi positive or useful. She used it a lot. Focus on what you can control. That came from Ms. Kiefer.

She dressed in the workout clothes she'd brought into the bathroom—and got a sweet tingle down her spine as she glanced at the bathroom counter. She put her hair in a ponytail and went out into the gym.

"Hey."

"Hi," she replied to Rick. He had obviously showered and was on an arm machine, doing reps.

No shirt. Just some tiny workout shorts that made it damn hard for her to tear her eyes away from him. She didn't even pretend she wasn't staring at him when he stopped working out and tipped his head to the side.

She was halfway to him when his phone dinged. He cursed as he bent and grabbed it.

He read something, cursed again and got to his feet. "Aaron's back and has an update for us. You want to get changed before we go meet them?"

"I'm good," she said. She *was* good. She didn't want to put on her old clothes from Texas. In the last few days, she'd moved on from that girl.

He nodded. "Just leave your dirty clothes in the basket. They'll be laundered and returned to my place."

She followed him out of the gym noticing he grabbed a T-shirt and pulled it over his head. Inhaling, she watched the play of muscles on his back as he tugged it on.

"Darn."

Looking back at her, he quirked one eyebrow.

"Just miss the view," she said, smacking him on the ass as she walked out of the gym.

He caught her by the waist, pulling her flush against his front. "You're not going to miss it for long." He spoke directly into her ear, and shivers coursed down her body.

"I'm not?"

"Nope. As soon as we're done working, I'm taking you back to my place, locking the door, turning off the phones."

"And then?" she asked, swallowing around the excitement in her throat.

"Then we're going to get naked and stay that way until we can't move," he said, biting her neck before he let her go.

"That might do," she said.

He groaned and she smiled.

He didn't say anything else until they were in the conference room. Lee was sitting on Aaron's lap but they pulled apart as soon as they realized they weren't alone. "That was quick. Sorry you couldn't leave the Tower. Hope the gym was enough for you," Lee said.

"It'll do," she said.

Rick gave her a look that told her he wanted to respond but he kept it professional. They took a seat. She was surprised they didn't get started, but then Van walked in with a woman she didn't recognize.

The tall redheaded woman was one of the most beautiful people Jena had ever seen. She moved with grace even though she was dressed in a prison jumpsuit. She also scanned the room like she was in charge when clearly she wasn't.

Sans the prison part, Jena found herself wishing she

could be her when she grew up. That kind of confidence was awe inspiring.

"She's on loan from the penitentiary," Van said. "Cate, you know Aaron, Lee and Rick. This is Jena."

She didn't acknowledge any of them.

"What's she doing here?" Lee didn't sound too pleased to see the other woman.

Rick seemed tense as well. Clearly Cate was not welcome, so Jena was curious why she'd been brought in.

Rick didn't want the daughter of La Fortunata crime syndicate in the same space as Jena. Van's face gave nothing away, but he knew his boss must have had a reason for bringing that viper in. Gym shorts and a T-shirt had seemed fine earlier, but now he wished he had a weapon on him.

She wasn't even trying to look meek as she took a seat next to Van. Her hands were in elastic binders, like that was going to be any kind of hindrance. Was that for Jena's sake?

The rest of them knew how lethal and deceptive she was.

"Why'd you borrow her?" Rick asked, not bothering to hide his distaste for the woman who'd infiltrated the FBI terror crime unit and betrayed her team—Van and Lee—leaving them for dead. So yeah, excuse the fuck out of him if he wasn't all on board with using any "help" she offered.

"She knows Vex."

"Knows him how?" Jena asked, sitting forward.

Van glanced at Cate, who slowly blinked and then rolled her shoulders before she said, "He's a sleeper. Someone that we kept quiet. If he's here, then Perses is very much active. Which I warned you would happen."

"Excuse us if we didn't take the word of the woman who almost killed us," Lee said. "Also, that's a very convenient conjecture without proof."

The look that Cate cut to Lee spoke volumes. The two of them still had unfinished business. Rick looked back to Van. The older man's face was stony, not giving a thing away. But Rick noticed that the angel wings on his neck pulsed every time Cate spoke.

He wasn't as unflappable as he was pretending to be—and he didn't like bringing her into the building either.

"So what do you know about him? My friend was present when he killed someone in New York. Do you know what that was?"

"If your friend was there, she's dead," Cate said.

"Yeah, you're right. Her battered and raped body was left by the side of the road," Jena said.

"Cut to the good stuff," he warned Cate.

"Fine. If it was in New York, then he would have killed Montoro or Alvarez. Two East Coast biggies to take their spot. Then he'd move west," she said.

Aaron sent a message on his phone with the names while Lee's fingers were already moving on her laptop. They leaned their heads together, conferring, and then nodded at Van.

"Montoro. His gang now reports to Vex. Is that enough for the girl to get killed?" Aaron asked.

"The dead one or her?" Cate angled her head toward Jena. Rick barely kept himself in his seat, but Jena put her hand on his thigh. Cate's disrespect toward the Price team, he could handle, but not toward Jena.

"Watch your mouth," he warned her.

She rolled her eyes. "You're all being so vague like you don't want me to know what you know. Who am I going to tell? I'm in solitary. Before this field trip, the only people I've seen have been the guard who delivers my meals and lets me outside for an hour each day."

"You just said your father was active."

"I said Perses. He's not my father. It's a name that passes on once the old Perses falls. Like royalty."

"I don't have time to argue semantics. Just tell us what you know," Rick said.

"Vex is probably being positioned to be the new head of La Fortunata until the trial. Your friend must have heard something or witnessed something that made her a liability. Not just the murder—since he brought her with him, I'm guessing he didn't mind her seeing that."

"Is the organization still functioning?" Aaron asked.

"Of course. There are always contingencies in place," she said.

Aaron cursed under his breath. Rick guessed that he'd hoped they were a bit more disorganized. They all had. But La Fortunata had been around so long and were so deeply entrenched in every part of the government that might have been a fool's hope.

"Do you know what he'd need a key for?" Jena asked. "He's accused me of stealing one from him."

"Did you?"

"No."

Cate eyed Jena, trying to make her squirm—but his girl just squared her shoulders and stared her down.

"The key would have been taken from Montoro. Each box is different, so I'm not sure what would be in his. Probably contacts, money, IDs—and information. It's handed down from one boss to the next."

Well, that was helpful. Now they knew why Vex needed it back.

"Anything else?" Van asked the table.

"Do you know where to find what the key unlocks?" Rick asked her, following Jena's lead and not mentioning the fact that they knew it was a safety deposit key.

"The keys are all to safety deposit boxes in the American National Bank Beverly Hills branch," she said. "But you know they aren't going to just point the box out to you and open it up for you."

"Thanks," Van said sardonically.

"I want the names of the new people," Aaron said.

"Ah, darling, I only agreed to share about Vex. That other stuff is going to require more negotiation," Cate said.

Aaron flipped her off, and Van got to his feet and escorted her out of the office. Jena started to speak, but Rick shook his head. "Not until Van's back and we know she's out of the building."

"What could she do? She was handcuffed," Jena said.

"Listening device, maybe," Rick suggested. Lee got up and went to examine the spot where Cate had been sitting.

"Nothing," Lee said.

"Do you have to know the box number to open it?"

"Yes," Aaron said. "What's the play here? The contents of that box could take down what's left of La Fortunata."

There was more than good luck following Jena around. Because if she'd confronted Vex with the key, she'd be dead.

Chapter 13

Jena had never really been part of a team. At the bank, she had coworkers, but they each sort of did their own thing unless someone was out sick and they had to cover for them. Usually it was everyone for themselves. Which she thought she liked—but now she wasn't sure.

"She didn't really give us much," Jena said, still not entirely sure what Van had expected to glean from Cate. He'd returned to the room even more quiet and tense.

"Except the bank where the box is," he said in that low, gravelly voice of his.

"Did she? Or did she send us on a wild goose chase?" Lee asked. "I don't trust her. I sure as hell don't like that she was in this building."

"I don't either," Rick said.

"What's the story with her?" Jena asked.

Van rubbed his finger and thumb on his eyes, and Lee crossed her arms over her chest. Rick took a deep breath.

"She's got history with Lee and Van. She used to be an FBI agent who double-crossed them. Everyone thought she was dead, but instead she was running a human-trafficking operation for the La Fortunata crime syndicate."

Oh.

"So Vex is into that too?"

Maybe the polite thing would have been to offer condolences to the others for what they'd been through...but honestly, Jena's focus was Vex—not Cate and what she might have done in the past. Rick gave her a side smile and then shook his head.

"Aaron?"

"Just drugs, from what I can tell," he said. "But given the previous setup, I wasn't really expecting one new head of the organization. From what Cate said, Perses is definitely still running things just who exactly is the new Perses?" Aaron asked.

"So do we think Brianne was killed because she took the key, or something else? Or the key *and* something else?" Rick asked.

"The key. Cate was too cagey about the contents. There is something crucial in there," Van said.

"That's what I was thinking," Jena added. "Why kill her for money when he could take it from one of the houses?"

"Exactly," Rick said. "Boss, did you go to her, or did she reach out to you?"

"I reached out to her. But it was your boss, Aaron, who suggested we do the meeting here."

"Is that significant?" Jena asked.

Rick turned toward here. "La Fortunata had connections in all levels of law enforcement. Aaron's boss seemed solid last year and was instrumental to bringing down the gang."

The statement wasn't exactly reassuring. There was

clearly a lot more going on than whatever Brianne had stumbled into.

"So next steps for now. Lee, keep trying to find the bank using Montoro's name. Rick and Jena—retrace Vex's steps. See if he tried to go to the bank."

"Did he, in the time you were following him?" Rick asked her.

"Not that I recall. But he spent a lot of time on Rodeo Drive. I don't blend in there, so I had to keep my distance and wait until he left," she said.

"We'll go and check it out," Rick said. "It'll get us out of the Tower and maybe spook Vex into doing something reckless."

"You sure you want that?" Van asked.

"Oh, hell yeah. I could use some exercise," Rick said dryly.

She could too. Plus, if that key cost Brianne her life, Jena was determined to use it first. The rest of the team were given assignments. Following Rick back to his apartment, she remembered everything that had happened in the gym.

"My thought is for us to triangulate the patterns in locations you noticed when you followed Vex. See if there are any bank branches in the area," Rick said. "Lee's sent the list of branches to my phone."

"Great," she said, very aware that they were alone again. "I have the screenshots of the locations where he stopped. Want to start cross-referencing them while I get changed?"

"Yeah," he said. "Let me grab my clothes first."

She followed him into his bedroom, trying to keep her eyes away from Rick as he moved to the dresser. That T-shirt hugged his torso, and she wanted nothing more than to pull him over to the bed and finish what they'd started earlier. Except the mood had changed.

That desire for him was still there, but her desire for justice was stronger. Hearing Cate talk about life and death like it meant nothing had angered her. "Do you think about Brianne the way Cate does?"

She hadn't meant to blurt that out.

"Definitely not. I doubt I have anything in common with her. To her, the only life that matters is her own. Everyone else is just a pawn in the game she's playing with her dad."

"Yeah, what was that about?"

"I'm not sure. I thought they were on the same side but perhaps he's cut her loose since she was arrested. He might blame her since Lee and Van helped bring him down. Don't really care since she's a world-class bitch.

"I guess we all have fucked-up families," Jena said.

"Yeah. Maybe. Don't feel sorry for her," Rick said, coming closer to her. "If she knew you had the key, she'd turn you over or kill you and take it. You can't trust her."

He didn't need to tell her that. "I don't trust anyone."

"Even me?"

"I'm not sure about you," she admitted. Which was a total lie because she trusted him. That was why she'd been in his arms in the gym and why she was about to share the intel she'd gathered on Vex. She trusted him to help her find the bank and get the information in it. But she wasn't sure yet if she trusted him to get a confession from Vex.

The day wasn't going at all to plan. Van bringing Cate in hadn't set well with him. Cate was dangerous and not trustworthy in the least. What was the boss playing at? He wanted to get Jena out of the Tower in case they'd been followed.

Van stopped by his apartment while Jena was changing. "What's up?"

"Cate...something's not right with her setup. I think that Malcom O'Dell, formerly Perses, is still running things from prison. She brought that key up when I walked back downstairs."

Rick wasn't surprised. They all knew it had to mean more. "So?"

"Just spitballing here, but what if Vex was meant to deliver it to Perses? He's been in LA too long for someone who intends to keep running that East Coast gang. Even Aaron doesn't like it."

"Good to know. Why you telling me all this?"

"Watch your back. I think Jena stumbled into an already tense situation that could get her killed. This isn't just Vex wanting revenge or his property back. Something's turning. I can feel it."

Rick could too. At the same time, there was tension with Jena that wasn't helping him keep a clear head. "Me too. The sooner we have the contents of the safety deposit box, the better."

"Agree. Get it and get back here," Van said.

"I will," he agreed as the door opened and Jena walked out.

She had on a pair of skinny jeans and a sleeveless blouse. Her hair was up in a ponytail, and he noticed that the bruises and cuts on her neck and shoulder were started to heal. Their eyes met; he couldn't help remembering what she'd said to him about starting to trust him.

How could he expect her to? The proof of what she'd been through was there for him to see. And if he was honest, he knew that trust might not help her with her goal of getting justice for her friend. Jena wanted Vex, personally, to pay—but Rick was very aware that the system might not work that way. If Vex turned on Perses then Rick knew that he could get a deal.

"Hi, Van," she said.

"Hiya. Just wanted to make sure you were both on guard when you left the Tower," he said.

"Rick always is. You didn't see him in the parking lot," Jena said.

"Didn't have to. My boy always comes through. What about you?"

"Apparently I don't need a gun," she said, shooting Rick a look. "But I think I'm getting better at hand to hand."

"Which you also shouldn't need," Rick said. "I've got you."

"What if I have to have you?" Standing up as she finished putting on her shoes.

Van laughed.

"You'll do, Jena Maxwell," Van said as he walked out of the apartment.

Rick shook his head as Jena grinned over at him. "I will do. What was he really here for?"

"Just warning me that Vex might be feeling pressure to get that key from you now that he knows you have it. He knows what you look like and that you aren't going to stop coming for him," Rick said. "That makes you dangerous and a risk to yourself. He's going to use that."

"You think so? I'm using him," she said, but her fingers knotted together. "I'm going to get justice for Brianne."

"It all comes down to us getting into that box before he does," Rick said.

"I'm not sure I follow," Jena said as Rick grabbed his work duffel bag that had weapons, clothes, money and other essentials and headed for the door.

"We need to have control of that information so we can use it to bring down the head of La Fortunata. If Vex gets there first, then even if we get him arrested for Brianne's murder, he can use that info to bargain for a lighter sentence."

She followed him out and down toward the elevator. "They'd let him off in exchange for it."

"I'm not going to let that happen."

"Yeah even you can't stop that," she said.

"Not going to be an issue, "Rick said. One way or another, Vex would pay for Brianne and for what he'd done to Jena. If the law was going to give him a deal, then Rick would take matters into his own hands.

He didn't say that easily. He respected the law and would always try to work within it. But he wasn't going to allow a man like Tomas Vectra to walk away from this. He either did time for Brianne's murder or Rick would deliver justice the way he had for his sister's killer. There were times when there were no other options.

Jena was quiet as they got down to the Dodge. She synched her phone to the car, pulling up the routes she'd used over the last two weeks while she'd trailed Vex.

He added in the locations that Lee had sent, and within fifteen minutes, they were able to narrow it down to two branches. He punched in the directions to the first one.

"Ready?"

"I guess. I really hope that this key works. Also, what name am I going to give them?" she asked.

"We'll figure that out. Do you know the procedures for accessing boxes?" he asked to give her something to think about.

"I do. I've never worked in that part of the bank but I like to read so I've read all of the procedures for every job."

"Every job?"

"Yeah. Some days, being a loan officer is pretty slow," she said.

"Do you like it?" he asked as he drove out of the underground parking lot.

"You know, I do."

"Why?" he asked her.

"I feel normal."

Just that one simple sentiment, but he got it. He understood why that job mattered to her.

Normal had always been the goal. She wasn't sure when it started or when she became aware her life wasn't like others—and that she would prefer theirs. But that boring job, with coworkers she had nothing in common with, had given her something she'd always craved.

Brianne had been her family and the bank her normalcy. Now Brianne was gone and all the fake normal in the world hadn't saved her. Jena had slipped out of the world she'd carefully built. That one that made her feel safe but not really alive.

Driving in the late afternoon sun in LA, she still couldn't quite believe she was here. Never imagined a time when she'd give up her day-to-day and that routine that she'd craved. But now it was almost hard to imagine going back to it. Avenging Brianne might have drawn her here but there were other reasons for her to want to stay.

"Want to walk through what we'll do when we get inside?" Rick asked as he pulled into the parking lot for the bank.

"Uh, I guess I'll just say I want to open my box, but I suck with numbers and can't remember it."

"Will that work?" he asked. She noticed he'd put on a

shoulder holster before they'd gotten into the car. He was being so nonchalant about it that she knew he didn't want her to comment on it.

That was in addition to the weapon she knew he had in an ankle holster and the one holstered at the small of his back. She wasn't entirely sure what he thought they were going to be up against, but he was armed for anything.

Which made her nervous.

"I don't know. I mean, we're not even sure of the name on the account, and I definitely don't have ID to match it. So there's a chance they'll deny me entry."

"Let me check with Lee before we go in," Rick said. He picked up his phone and she turned away. Looking around the parking lot, she noticed Vex's car.

"He's here."

"What?"

"Vex. He's here. We were right. This is the bank," she said. The rush of adrenaline she felt was similar to the one she'd had when she first located him. "He's too predictable."

"He is," Rick noted.

"What should we do? I wish I had put on one of the other wigs," she said.

"Why?"

"So I could go in. We could hear what name he gives the teller," she said. "But even dressed like this, I'm pretty sure he'll clock me."

"Yeah. I'm not sure he didn't spot the Dodge too," Rick said. "We're leaving."

"What? This is our chance."

"It's too risky."

"For who?" she asked. "Vex doesn't know you. Why don't you go in after him?"

"For one, he does know me. His goons would have reported back after I shot at them," he said.

"For two?"

"I'm in charge and I said no."

She took in a harsh breath. Like...she got it. She knew the dangers involved in going after Vex now. But at the same time, what were the risks? She had to make up her mind soon. Vex had gotten out of his car and Rick might be on to something about recognizing the Dodge, because even though he had on dark sunglasses, he seemed to glance at them as he straightened his tie.

"Risks," she said.

"He knows you have the key. He'll kill you for it and search your body," Rick said.

"He'd have to get close to me. I think I can do this, Rick. I've worked in a bank for a while now. They have guards and protections in place."

"What are you talking about?"

"Don't get mad. I'll be safe while I'm inside."

With that, she opened the door and walked with a helluva a lot more confidence than she felt toward the branch's entrance. Vex noticed her reflection in the glass, and a slight smile that played across his lips almost made her miss a step.

He was menacing.

She pushed her sunglasses up with her middle finger and kept walking toward the branch as Rick slipped up next to her.

"Wait for me, honey," he said, putting his arm around her waist and slowly her down.

"I'm not going back to the car," she said between clenched teeth.

"It's too late for that now. We have to play this out," he said.

Vex had already entered the bank when they got to the door. Rick opened it, moving her to his left side so he had his dominant hand free to get to a weapon if he needed it.

A rush of air-conditioned air wrapped around her. She barely noticed it. Glancing over, she saw that Vex had checked in and was seated.

Bravado had taken her this far, but she had no idea what to do next. Rick hadn't taken his sunglasses off and was scanning the lobby, looking for a threat.

She went to get in line for the cashiers. Rick followed her, leaning over her shoulder and acting like he was kissing her ear. "What are you doing?"

"Opening an account. That will give me a chance to listen to what Vex is doing," she said.

"Great. What about when we leave?"

"One problem at a time, right?"

Rick let out a low breath and shook his head as the cashier beckoned them up.

"We want to open a joint account," Jena said. "We're moving in together. If that works out, then we're getting married."

While she talked, she looked down at the bank screen. They used the same log-on system that Jena's bank did. She recognized the bank system as well. Information that she knew would help Lee when digging into this branch's files.

"Of course. Have a seat by the gentleman over there, and someone will be with you shortly."

Rick's hand on her waist tightened, and she knew he wasn't pleased that they were now going to be sitting near Vex. But they were close, and the information that they really had no hope of guessing was now at last in their grasp.

Chapter 14

"We're not sitting next to him," Rick said. "We're leaving now."

"I'm not," she said, putting her hand on his chest and coming close. "Stop telling me what to do."

It took all his will power not to lift her off her feet and carry her out of the bank by force. "This is too risky."

"Risky. That's all I've got now," she said.

There was something wild and untamed in her expression. Not what he wanted. There were certain security measures in the bank but not enough to be reassuring. He was armed but more than likely Vex was as well. It was odd that he'd come in by himself. Rick hadn't had time to make sure that Vex hadn't left anyone outside when he'd had to follow Jena.

She'd thrown him off-balance, and when they got through this, he was going to rip her a new one. But for now they had to play this through. "Let's go."

There were plenty of seats available. Rick took the one directly across from the other man. He left his sunglasses on because they filtered out the light and made his vision sharper.

Vex's name was called, Tomas Vectra so he hadn't given an alias. He walked past them without a glance or word. Rick noted the office that Vex was taken to. There was a window, but short of outright staring, as Jena was doing, there was no way to watch it.

"Stop. He can see you."

"Good. I want him to know," she said. "I'm going to the bathroom."

She was on her feet and heading down that hallway before he could stop her. Rick was on his feet a few paces behind her when a tallish woman called the name Jena had given the cashier.

"Sorry. I've got to run to the bathroom. You can take my boyfriend with you," Jena said. "Just use a fake name until I get back and we'll say we changed our minds when they ask for ID."

Rick shook his head. "I've got to go too. Give us a minute."

Jena's glare told him that she was up to something, but he still didn't know what. When they got to the unisex bathroom, he followed her in before she could lock him out.

"What are you doing?" he asked as soon as they were inside.

"I was going to tie my shoe and try to listen at the door."

His face must have registered his incredulity.

"What? I saw it in a movie. We need the name and box number," she reminded him, flushing the toilet before washing her hands and using the hand dryer. "Your turn."

"To what?"

"Fake pee. We can't stay in here too long," she urged him. "Vex might have already left."

He flushed the toilet and then nudged her toward the door. "Let's go, Junie B. Jones."

A smile toyed at the corners of her lips before she opened the door. Vex was coming out at the same time they were, and Jena rushed forward, pretending to stumble into the other man. She knocked him into the doorjamb and pushed the papers in his hands out of them. They fell to the floor.

Rick stepped forward to pull Jena back, but not before he noticed Vex whispering something in her ear. Rick bent to scoop up the papers, glancing at the name on the top. He only read part of the box number before the other man took the papers from him.

Jena's face was white as the bank employee asked if they were all okay. Vex's eyes never left Rick, clearly sizing him up. Rick stood taller, stretching to every inch of his six-foot-five frame, squared his shoulders.

Vex nodded to him and turned to leave.

Jena was shaking as the bank employee went to walk the other man out. The woman who'd been waiting to help them open their account hovered.

"I'm sorry. We are going to have to come back later. We had an emergency call," Jena said, taking Rick's hand. He wasn't sure he wanted to walk straight out of the bank after Vex, but they didn't have much of a choice. The other man was already in his car, driving slowly by the two of them. The passenger window came down and Rick had his hand on the butt of his Glock as Vex mimed firing a gun at Jena before he left.

Jena was shaking. Rick memorized the plate before force-marching Jena back to the Dodge. He started to get into the car, then realized he hadn't checked for wires or bombs. "Stay put. I'm not joking."

"Okay."

He dropped down and checked under the car but didn't see any signs of disturbances. He got back in and turned on the air.

"I got the name."

"We're too late," she said.

"What?"

"He told me that he didn't need the key and that I was dead."

Rick reached over to rub her shoulder. Part of him wanted to offer comfort—and another part of him wanted to shake some sense into her. She'd done this. Put herself in danger. "You're not dead."

"He's going to try to kill me."

"He's going to succeed if you don't start listening to me and learning some caution."

Her eyes flashed at him; he was glad to see that spark, because seeing fear on her face wasn't something that he liked.

"I got us in there," she said.

"Yes. And I got the name. Why did you say it was too late?"

"He said it was."

"He just wants you to feel like he's won. We have the key and the name now, and I'm going to have Lee make us an ID. I think we can beat him at his own game."

Rick had already decided the other man was going to lose. But now he was more determined than ever to make that happen. He just needed to find a way to keep Jena from being so reckless.

* * *

Her nerves were totally shot. Rick drove not back toward the Tower, but toward the beach—a place she'd driven to when she'd first got out here. She'd never seen the Pacific Ocean before. She'd never even seen the Atlantic, just the Gulf. on a trip to Galveston with Brianne. She'd always wanted to go to the ocean so the visit was the girls' trip she and Brianne had never been able to take.

Rick hadn't spoken since they'd left the bank. Vex's voice had been so full of menace when he'd whispered in her ear. Telling her that he was going to have more fun with her than he had with Brianne before he sent her to meet her bestie.

She kept running her hands up and down her arms.

"I'm trying to be chill, but we are going to have a come-to-Jesus talk," Rick said after he'd parked the car at the Santa Monica Pier. "Let's walk so that there are people around."

The Santa Monica Pier had an amusement park on it with a large Ferris wheel. She wasn't a fan of heights so hadn't ever been on one. They had food and merchandise shops along the boardwalk. It teemed with tourists and locals. There were shops lining the street behind them where she had read celebrities could be seen drinking coffee and smoking.

But she hadn't been interested in them. She hadn't come to LA to spot celebs.

"Is it safe?"

"I've got you," he said. "I don't think Vex is going to follow you now."

"Why not? I would," she said.

"You're impulsive, he's not. He's strategic. He's allowing the fear he planted when he talked to you to build. Fear makes people do dumb things."

She could hear the unspoken *like walking into the bank* tacked on to the end. "We needed to change the dynamic. Trying to find the bank, the name, the box number. It was too much. Even Lee wasn't making any progress."

"Granted. But taking a fucking second before getting out of the car would have been beneficial."

"In what way?" She was ticked off too. Mainly at herself because up close she'd realized how much she'd underestimated Vex. She'd thought it was the drug and skill that had gotten her away from him that night at Mistral's, but now she was leaning heavily toward Rick's theory of luck.

There was a part of that wasn't sure she'd ever feel truly safe again.

"Maybe we could have had an actual plan."

"It worked out."

"Barely."

He barked the word at her as he took her upper arm in a powerful grip. It didn't hurt her but left no doubt she couldn't escape him as he drew them toward one of the large pylons under the pier, turning to pin her against it.

As soon as they were out of sight, she wrapped her arm around his waist, burying her face against his chest. His ragged exhalation and the way he wrapped his arms around her and hugged her tight told her how upset he'd been.

"I was scared but determined to ensure we are the ones who get that box," she explained.

Yeah, her plans weren't always great. Junie B. Jones and most detectives she'd read growing up had just taken chances and always made it through them in one piece. But Vex wasn't some fictional bad guy. This was a gang member who'd murdered his way to the top, leaving not only Brianne and Montoro dead but probably countless more.

"You fucking scared me too," he said. "You have to trust me. I'm not letting the bastard walk for what he did to Brianne or you. But no more running into a situation like that. If I say stay—"

"I'll try to keep still."

"Jena—"

"I don't want to promise something I'm not sure I can deliver."

"You're reckless."

She couldn't respond to that. She'd never been reckless before…but that old normal was gone. There was just this weird quagmire of time where Brianne was gone and she had a chance to make Vex pay for it.

"I know."

He cursed under his breath, and then she felt his mouth on hers. The adrenaline she'd been trying to control found an outlet. God, she wanted this man. Wanted him naked underneath her. One brush of his lips, and fire coursed through her.

It didn't matter that they were on the beach under the pier, beachgoers and homeless people wandering around them. She tunneled her fingers into that thick blond hair of his, holding his head to her while she went up on tiptoe to deepen the kiss. Trying so hard to wash away that fear that Vex had wrapped around her.

"We need to work on our timing," he said, rubbing his erection against her. She rocked her hips against it, sighing when he pulled away.

"Let's walk."

"Why are we here?"

"You wanted to get out of the Tower," he said. "This

place is pretty chaotic, but you'll be safe here. There are too many people for Vex's gang to target you here."

He laced his fingers through hers and pulled her toward the boardwalk. They didn't look out of place even though they were dressed for the bank and not the beach.

"Was it Montoro's name?" she asked after he got her a burger basket with fries from Beach Burger.

"No. It wasn't Alvarez either. It was Pallus. So either Cate fed us bad information, or she doesn't know he's dead."

"Aaron didn't either," she pointed out.

"His people didn't, you're right. We need to be careful what happens next. Aaron's trustworthy, but I'm less sure about his superiors."

"Do you trust the DEA?" she asked.

"I did when I worked for them," he said as they walked toward the end of the pier and he stopped so they could look out over the water.

She thought about what Rick had said—and what he *hadn't* said. He'd trusted the DEA before. But not now?

"I love the ocean. When my sister was still alive, we'd always find a way down here. Usually it involved sneaking on the bus behind someone, but whatever it took, once a month she made sure we came here."

There was longing in his voice when he spoke of her. Jena wrapped her arm around his middle. Grief was like that, she realized. It never really left.

"What did you do when you got here?"

"Hustled people for food and ride tickets. Swam in the ocean sometimes. Stole surfers' wallets. They always leave them in their bags or vehicles," he said. "Those were my best days."

It did sound nice. Because they were together. The two of them taking control of their destiny for a day.

Going to Santa Monica had been an impulse. It was his and Andi's place. There was so much about Jena that reminded him of both himself and his sister. She took chances because life had taught her that was the only way. He got it. He'd been there. Hell, some days he still was.

There were ways to catch Vex but not if she kept going off like she did at the bank. He could only hope she'd heed his warning, because warning her was all he could do. He wasn't about to break her spirit. Not that he even could.

In her defense, they got the name on the box. But Rick wasn't sure they hadn't played too far into Vex's hands. Van would have something to say about that.

"You've got that serious look on your face," she said. "You've already lectured me."

"Yeah? Did it work?"

"As well as anything can. Thanks for sharing this place with me. I came out here when I first landed in LA."

"Did you think Vex would be here?" She seemed focused on Vex so it made sense. But if he had connections here then Rick had overestimated their safety.

"No. Brianne and I had planned to come one day. We'd only been to the Gulf so wanted to see a real ocean... In our head there was a difference." There was a softness to her when she talked about her friend. "So I just thought 'we're here, girl.' I cried, but I also felt like she was with me... I know that sounds odd."

"Not at all. I always feel Andi when I'm here," he admitted. "Sometimes I think I hear her laugh...probably just another kid."

God, why had he told her that?

"You do hear it. This is her happy place too," Jena said.

Maybe. Those summer days had been good but not exactly happy. They'd had to make sure the cops didn't notice them, which meant they had to be on their guard all the time. And hope their dad was stoned and wouldn't notice they'd been gone. If he was sober when they got home... it wasn't pretty.

"We need to get back to the Tower," he said. "I wanted you to have a break."

"Thanks. I think you also wanted to yell at me in private," she teased as she took his hand, leading him back toward where they parked the car.

"I didn't yell. Just...forcefully stated my position," he said.

He liked when she teased him. Too many people didn't. They just saw the worn-out man he was in his downtime or the on-duty bodyguard. Jena saw all the pieces behind the camouflage. He liked it.

Too much.

But not enough to stop it. He'd given up trying to control whatever was happening to him when he was around her. The awareness of her as a woman. The way she would drop a little comment and wait to see his reaction and then smile.

Her life had been hard lately, but she was still finding joy.

That was it.

Had he ever truly found joy? Even those beach days with Andi had been tainted with the reality of their lives.

"Forcefully. I'll remember that," she said.

"See that you do," he said. The cparking lot wasn't as busy as when they arrived, and he picked up two guys following them. They both had wetsuits on, and one had a board under his arm. Something about their body language wasn't right. He moved around so that Jena was slightly in front of him and reached under his jacket for his Glock that he had in the shoulder holster.

"What—"

"Be cool. Might be nothing. Two guys at eight o'clock."

"Huh?"

"To our back and left," he said.

"Why not just say that?"

He ignored that as the one with the board walked to a pickup truck and tossed the board while his friend lifted something out of a bag...a semiautomatic. "Down."

He shoved Jena toward the ground. She didn't hesitate. He felt her hand on his ankle holster pulling his spare gun as he turned into a shooter's position. Bullets whizzed toward them as the men came at them, giving up all pretense of being surfers.

He shoved his hand on Jena's thigh, giving her the keys. "Stay low. Get to the car and get in it."

"I'm not—"

"Go!" he barked out.

Her eyes went wide and she moved to the car, which was only two feet away. Staying low he watched her until she was in the Dodge. He took position behind the hood of a Chevy and waited until he had a clear shot. He hit the shoulder of the man with the semi, and the gun stuttered and dropped to the ground. He hit him again in the knee, watching him fall.

Then he turned to the other man, who was heading toward the car. Jena was safely behind the bulletproof body of the Dodge, and Rick stood for a better shot, thinking to disarm him with a shot in the shoulder.

The window of the Dodge opened and Jena's hand

popped out, firing in the general direction of the assailant. She hit him in the torso and then the hand. The other guy stumbled, then dropped to the ground.

Rick called Lee first to alert Price Security and then the cops and Detective Miller.

Chapter 15

"This is getting to be a habit," Van said after the cops had taken their statements and arrested the men who'd shot at them. Detective Miller wasn't too happy with them being in the middle of another shooting.

"I hope the detective doesn't believe we shot first," Jena said. She was drinking one of the Fantas he'd had in a cooler in the trunk of the Dodge.

"It's fine," Van said. "Lee is already pulling surveillance footage from the area. What was this side trip for?"

Rick knew that tone, and shrugged. Had he screwed up? Maybe. But Jena wasn't used to this kind of a life. She'd needed a break.

"We wanted to talk about the information we picked up at the bank."

Van's face told Rick they'd discuss that later when they were alone.

"It's my fault. I was impulsive at the bank, and Rick

sensed that it was from the tension of being cooped up in the Tower and everything that's happened since I showed up. He brought me here to help me calm down and gain some perspective."

He slanted a glance at her, and she just raised both eyebrows at him and smiled. Rick was pretty sure his boss wasn't buying it, but he nodded.

"You're both going back to the Tower now. Aaron's undercover guy heard that Vex wants you alive. I'm guessing those guys were going to try to kidnap you."

Jena's eyes went wide before she took a large swallow of the Fanta. This beach trip was starting to feel less and less like a good idea. He would keep Jena alive and safe, which meant being out in public was probably not a good idea.

"See you back there," Rick said.

An hour later they were back at the Tower in the conference room again. This time Daphne was there with her boyfriend, Kenji. Rick was glad to see his friend as Daphne spirited Jena away to do her lawyer thing.

"You've been having fun without me," Kenji said.

"*Fun* being a relative term," Rick responded, dropping down to sit by him.

"We all like a chance to do our thing," Xander added as he came in. Xander was as tall as Rick and built like an MMC fighter. He was British and highly intelligent, so all that brawn came with brains. Xander was also Aaron's brother though, the two men had been estranged for several decades until Aaron's undercover case had left him with no one to turn to but Xander.

"Yeah." Rick wasn't ready for an ooh-rah chat about the shootings.

"You good? Normally this is your kind of sitch."

"Yeah." He knew he was shutting down. Felt it happening but couldn't stop it. Talking about Andi was one thing. Seeing the hint of that desperation in Jena was something else.

"What's up? Don't try to play it off. Luna's on her way up, and you know she'll get it out of you," Xander said.

"Or don't. Not everyone likes to talk like you, X."

"Fair enough. Want to play some *Halo* later? That works for Kenji when he doesn't want to talk about his feelings."

Kenji flipped Xander the bird and Rick leaned farther back in his chair relaxing for the first time. His brothers were here with him. Things were going to be fine. There was something about having them at his side that made him feel like he was stronger.

"X, what are the chances someone at the DEA is rotten?"

"There's always a chance. Aaron doesn't know the new field manager. But we can trust his boss, Jayne Renner. You know that from working with her."

"Can we? We saw what she wanted us to see. Same with the FBI. I'm just asking if there is someone on the inside," Rick said.

"Why?" Lee asked, coming over. "Aaron doesn't trust anyone but his partner and us."

"The names that Aaron gave Cate...neither of them were on the form that Vex had filled out."

Lee went back and got her laptop. "What was the name?"

He gave it to her. Kenji and Xander were quietly listening to everything going on. "Cate could have been playing with you."

"I wouldn't put it past her. She threw out those names. Misdirection?" Lee suggested.

"Yeah, this dude has been dead...for six months. When did Jena say that Brianne started hooking up with Vex?" Lee asked.

"About that time," Rick said. "You've got her phone. Are there any pictures that aren't of her and Vex?"

Brianne's murder had always felt like something more. Something that wasn't just over a key. She had some serious intel on La Fortunata that she wasn't aware of. Rick didn't like the idea of the unknown. Chances were, Jena had that same information and that was why her life was on the line.

"I don't know what we are looking for...but now that we have the name...let me see if I can find any photos," Lee said.

Her fingers were busy moving over her keyboard. Soon, she got a hit on Sebastian Velasquez. She put it on the monitor wall. Then she gave them all access to Brianne's photos from the cloud.

"Start looking for anyone that looks like him," Lee said.

He and the boys were already going through them, taking their time to zoom in on every photo. They'd divided up the photos by months. Rick took the oldest ones. Seeing glimpses of Jena's life through Brianne's phone was interesting. There were some photos where Jena clearly wasn't aware there was a camera on her. Jena was so serious, and he liked her back in her normal life.

She had a comfy-looking apartment with low-cost furniture, but there were little details, like the pillows she'd put on the couch, that made it Jena.

He got to photos that were clearly in a club. Jena wasn't in them. Photos of drinks and a man's hand with a tattoo on his wrist that looked like barbed wire and two initials: S.V.

This could be something.

***

"Thanks so much for taking me as a client," Jena said. "I followed your advice during the questioning."

Daphne Amana was tall and glamourous. She had an easy smile but when she spoke, Jena realized she wasn't a pushover either.

"Not a problem. I'm not normally a defense attorney, so if this goes to trial you'll probably want a different lawyer. But I got you covered for questioning. Tell me everything," Daphne invited.

Jena did. Starting at the beginning of when Brianne met Vex and the relationship. She didn't add in the stuff they'd uncovered throughout their investigation because they were still figuring that all out. Once she'd caught Daphne up, the other woman stopped taking notes and leaned back.

"Wow. That was dangerous. Rick still has the Rohypnol you bought?"

"We gave it to Van," she said.

"Good. That can be tested and used as evidence if this goes to trial. The key... You didn't know you had it but you do?" Daphne asked.

"Yes. I think it's why Brianne was murdered."

"Probably, but the court doesn't care about that when it comes to this crime. We need to focus on you drugging Vex. At what point did he start attacking you?"

"He dragged me by my wrist across the club but didn't attack me until I ran and he caught up with me in the bathroom."

"So no witnesses?"

She shook her head.

"The knife came from him as well?"

"Yes. When I brought up Brianne's name, he pulled it

out and cut me here." Jena pointed to the spot where he'd cut her.

"Detective Miller got a photo of that?"

"Yes. She took all kinds of photos and took my clothes to see if she could get DNA off of them."

Daphne made more notes. "That first statement you gave her when you thought you killed Vectra is a gold mine for his attorneys. You confessed to stabbing him after he attacked you. If you are arrested, I'll try to have that quashed. I have to speak to some of my colleagues and see if we can do that without an arrest. Is there anything else you're worried about?"

"No. I don't want to go to jail. And I want Vex to go to jail for killing Brianne."

"Rick and the Price team are good at gathering evidence and finding answers. I think they'll help you there. In the meantime, I'll work on getting that statement sealed so that no one can read it. It will just give Vectra ammunition against you."

"Okay. I was just so scared. I thought I'd take my savings and run away to Europe, but Rick wouldn't help me get a fake ID."

Daphne smiled at her. "Probably for the best."

"It was. My first instinct was to run until I learned he was still alive. There is still a chance to get a confession."

"Be careful. He sounds like a very dangerous man."

"I will be," she said.

Daphne suggested they rejoin the rest of the team. When they did, they found a photo of a man up on the monitor wall while everyone scrolled through Brianne's photos looking for him.

She hated that these strangers were invading Brianne's privacy, but she knew that Brianne wouldn't have minded if it meant they were able to nail Vex. She took a seat across from Rick and next to Luna, who smiled a hello when she saw Jena.

Lee AirDropped the March photos to Jena. She thought she would be analytical, but the first photo was at the Dylan Wheeler concert at Gruene Hall in New Braunfels, Texas. They'd bought tickets in December. They'd both been so excited when they'd snapped the selfie right in front of the iconic Gruene Hall. They'd had dinner over the river, dressed in their short skirts, cowboy boots and cowboy hats.

Her hands shook and she balled them into fists until they steadied again. Brianne's life had been stolen from both of them. Jena wasn't going to let Vex and whatever secret he'd been trying to keep by killing her stay hidden. Flipping past the photo she saw one that was of the inside of her friend's purse. That helped settle her emotions down.

She kept glancing up at the man on the screen. Lee had asked that everyone zoom in and try to look in the background to find the man on the screen. Jena was pretty sure it was Pallus—the man whose name was on the safety deposit box.

Someone high enough in La Fortunata that everyone was trying to get their hands on his key...which Brianne had been smart enough to take. Jena wondered what else her friend knew and wished that Brianne had talked to her.

Why didn't you tell me? she asked the selfie of Brianne.

There could be no answer. Just that note that begged Jena to do something with the key.

It was slow going but finally Rick cleared his throat and shared a photo up on the screen. "I think this might be him."

The photos was of Brianne in front of Tiffany's on Fifth

Avenue in New York. She looked so gorgeous that tears stung Jena's eyes for a second. Then Rick zoomed in on the window. There, in the reflection, was a man. It was hard to say for sure that it was the same man who was on the screen.

But there was a resemblance.

"The date on this one is May fifteenth."

"That's three months before the note she wrote to me," Jena said. "Do you think that's the man that Vex killed?"

"No. That man was probably Montoro," Rick said. "This guy was killed earlier and his name wasn't floated around."

"So she met a man who was killed?" Jena asked.

"The photo with the tattoo S.V....do you think that could be Pallus?" she asked, finding the photo and showing it to the group.

"Might be," Rick said.

"She might have overheard something she wasn't meant to. What was she like when she came back? Was this a separate trip from the one where she was beaten up?"

"Yes. She went out there to see him twice that she told me, but maybe more because I didn't like him and she stopped mentioning him. When she came back she was excited. Vex had just gotten a promotion at work. He paid for her to move to a really nice apartment. She thought...they were going to get married. She told me that he couldn't leave her now."

Brianne must have believed that knowing Vex's secrets would keep her safe.

The tattoo on the wrist was a solid lead, as was the reflection in the window. Lee was working on street cameras, but most of that had been deleted if it wasn't part of an active investigation. Aaron looked stressed as he asked to use a private office to call his team.

It had been years since Rick had worked this closely with the DEA, but La Fortunata had somehow snagged all of Price Security back into that world. Jena seemed...not great. She was quiet, which wasn't at all what he expected from her. Possibly going through her friend's photos was harder on her than he'd expected.

"So that's Pallus. They are all in on the Perses mythology for La Fortunata, aren't they?" Rick asked. Perses was the elusive top boss of the crime syndicate and Cate's father. His real name was Malcom O'Dell.

"Indeed," Van said. "If that's Pallus then we have a possible motive for Vectra killing Brianne. Nothing that cops can act on. We have to keep looking."

"Were there any voice notes in the cloud?" Jena asked.

Rick glanced over at her, remembering the voice note she had on her own phone of her encounter with Vex. "Did you let Daphne listen to your recording?"

"Forgot about it. But yeah, I got Vex attacking me on a voice note."

Daphne smiled over at her. "That's good. Forward it to me, and we can try to isolate it. All of this will be good if you get arrested."

Jena nodded but waited to hear from Lee.

"Yes, there's... Whoa, there are a ton in here."

"Yeah, we used to send each other notes instead of texting," Jena said.

"I'll get to listening to them. I think it's going to take a few days for me to get through them all," Lee said.

Lee ran a search for a name with the initials S.V. "Looks as if Sebastian Velasquez had a box at America National Bank."

Rick realized that they were at a standstill for the day and most of them probably wanted to get out of the conference room. "One more thing. Now that we know the name of the box owner, and since he's not deceased officially, can we get the number and send someone to the bank with fake ID and the key?"

"I look the closest to him," Van said.

"I think you're going to have to mention that Vectra is trying to take your identity or something," Rick said. "You're better at this than I am."

"I like that idea," Van said. "The rest of you are good to go."

The team got up and left until it was just Rick, Jena and Van. With the name, Lee had been able to hack the bank and get the number. They had the key so Rick was convinced that getting to the box would be easy.

"You have to get there before Vectra comes back. They are probably going to have to 'find' the body and get a death certificate," Rick said.

"Yeah, Lee's watching for that. But it'll have to come out of Manhattan where the body must be."

"So we can't wait," Jena said. "Vex wants whatever is in that box badly. I'm pretty sure that if we let him have it, he'll find a way to kill me anyway."

"Not happening."

Rick had no doubts about his ability to keep her alive. But she wasn't wrong. Vex wasn't going to just let them take the box without starting a war with Price. And there were more people at stake than just Jena.

He glanced at Van. The boss got it too.

"Everyone moves back here. Even Nick," Van said as he pulled out his phone and sent an alert to the team's phones.

"Are you that sure he'll come after you?" Jena asked.

"Definitely. He already messed up once when he let Brianne get the key. He killed her but left a loose end—you. If he doesn't get the box, he's as good as dead. And men like Vectra don't go easy."

Rick glanced at his phone. The bank would be closing soon, so that meant they'd have to wait until the morning to go. "If we get everyone back here tonight, we can do a rotating tail and coverage for you tomorrow."

"Good plan. We'll work out the details later. You two have the night off. You can use the rooftop."

The rooftop was a secure patio with a lap pool. Actually the one place in the Tower that was just for leisure. They used it for Sunday dinners. Rick had never really thought about going up to it on his own. He was more of a "sit on his comfy couch and chill" guy. But the idea of bringing Jena there appealed to him.

Like a date.

Jena didn't say much until they were in his apartment. "I'm not sure that Van should go to the bank without me. I'm the one who has the key—"

"They saw you today. Everyone noticed you. You're not going back to the bank."

"Whatever. What's the deal with the rooftop?" she asked.

"I think the boss was offering it as a place to get away. You did say you needed some space. It's secure from snipers and pretty much anything other than an aerial assault."

"Really?"

"Yes. Want to get dolled up and go up there for dinner?" he asked.

"Dolled up? Really?"

"You're not the only one who watches old movies," he said, flushing a little.

"We can compare lists while we eat. Do you cook?"
"I don't. I'm okay with a grill. You?"
"I can heat things up," she said with a laugh. "I also make a passable salad."

Chapter 16

That elusive normal she'd been chasing for her entire life was starting to coalesce here in LA with Rick. She'd taken her time getting dressed, but not like she had when she'd gone to Mistral's. God, that felt like a lifetime ago. But tonight had nothing to do with putting on a false front or tricking anyone. She just wanted to look good for herself and for Rick.

She was exhausted from trying to make sense of what had happened to Brianne. Being beaten, raped and murdered…that was horrific. The grief and anger were still there just under the surface, but a part of her wanted to make it make sense. Point to something to say "this was why it happened."

Except there was every chance that Brianne had taken that key without knowing what it went to or its importance.

Rick rapped on the bedroom door to see if she was ready. She called back that she needed a few more minutes. He'd given her his room and had gone up to the gym to get ready himself. The gym. She wasn't sure she was ever going to be able to think of that place without remembering what happened there.

Taking out that instant photo of the two of them that she'd found in Brianne's bag, she smiled at her friend. "I met a guy. He's nice. Not rich. Sometimes a pain in the ass, but he's hot. His kisses make me gooey, like ice cream in summer. You'd like him."

Then she kissed her fingertip and pressed it to Brianne's face. "Wish you were here."

Would she ever be used to not having her best friend?

Probably not. But getting Vex's confession. Hearing him admit that he'd killed Brianne and then having him arrested and sent to jail. That would make that tight band around her heart loosen a little bit. Or at least she hoped it would.

Winking at herself in the mirror, she left the room and found Rick waiting for her. His big body was sprawled on the couch, his head resting on the back. As soon as he heard her, he got to his feet and smiled at her.

He wore a pair of casual shorts and a collared polo shirt. He'd obviously showered and shaved; the back of his hair was still damp. His gaze moved over her slim frame in the sundress she'd put on.

"You look great," he said.

"Thanks. You too."

They took the stairs up to the rooftop, which was lined with ten-foot-high bulletproof tinted glass. There was a lap pool near the far side. In the middle was a pergola structure with an outdoor kitchen and seating areas. There was a long table that could seat at least twenty.

A firepit was near one of the seating areas. A separate bar was behind it.

"This place looks like it's meant for parties."

"Yeah, that's what we usually use it for."

"Us…you guys are more like a family than coworkers," she said.

"Yeah. Not like that at the bank?"

"Definitely not," she said, trying to imagine if she lived in the same building as all her coworkers or even hung with them after work. They just didn't have that dynamic. Maybe other places did. She didn't know.

Rick opened the fridge. "We got everything here. Steak, chicken, ribs, sausages, fish…not my specialty."

"Steak works for me," she said. "I'll work on a salad while you do whatever is needed."

"Whatever is needed?"

"You know seasoning…making fire," she said.

He shook his head and made a grunting noise. "Give me meat."

She laughed as he took it over to the grill. She'd never actually cooked a meal with anyone. Maybe when she was little with Joey, but it hadn't been anything more elaborate than microwaving ramen or soup. But this…this was normal stuff.

She tried not to let that get into her head. Every single time she got within touching distance of normal, it disappeared. And she didn't want Rick to leave her life. It was easy to see that her feelings might stem from circumstance. Except that didn't feel like the truth.

That part of her that had been empty since Brianne's death was starting to feel again.

She washed vegetables, chopped them up and put them in a bowl, all the while chatting with him about everything and nothing. He was easygoing, self-deprecating when she pointed out something he was good at. But mostly he was just fun and made her feel like she was enough just as she was.

There weren't a lot of times she had felt that way.

"So those movies you watch. What's your favorite?" she asked as he went to the bar.

"I was joking—I don't watch a lot of movies. My boss used to say that when he had a date with his wife. That's where I got it from."

"Van's married?"

"Nah, Henry from the DEA. It was a long time ago. We got beer, wine, the makings for margaritas. What do you feel like?"

She was stuck on the word "date." "Are we on a date?"

He canted his head to the side. "Do you want to be?"

The temptation to ask him the same question was strong. But… "Yes."

"Then we are. Drink?"

"Rosé? And I like it with ice in it. Don't judge," she said.

"Why would I? You should have things the way you like them," he said.

Right now, the way she liked things was with Rick by her side. Watching her with those gray-blue eyes in a hungry way that made her feel very feminine and alive. The night was quiet up here, and the smell of the grill was enticing, but not as much as Rick.

Rick Stone was calling to her in a way that she hadn't ever experienced before. He made her hot and excited and comfortable. He made her think about a future. About a time after everything was settled with Brianne and Vex was in jail.

***

It had been years, maybe decades, since he'd been on a date. His job didn't lend itself to it. Technically he was acting as Jena's bodyguard, but she didn't feel like a client. He'd talked to Van privately and made it clear that he'd use his personal leave until she was safe, which Van hadn't had a problem with. The entire team working on the case wasn't what Rick had planned for, but he knew the boss. This was a family matter now that Jena was living with them.

Which might have explained why Van had suggested they use the rooftop tonight. No doubt everyone had picked up on the fact that he was different around Jena. It wasn't that he didn't go out occasionally and get laid, it was just… she was different.

The salad she made was…well, about like his steak. No one was going to be taking photos of the meal to post online.

"What?"

"Huh?"

"You just smiled."

"Was thinking that this dinner wouldn't make those online food photos," he said.

She snickered. "So true. But the steak smells delicious and—" She cut a delicate piece of the meat and put it in her mouth. Closed her eyes as she chewed it. "Delicious. Best steak anyone's every made for me."

"Is it also the only one?" he asked as he took a bite of his. It wasn't bad. He'd seasoned it with salt and pepper since that was what he liked.

"Yeah. You know how it is," she said.

It was nice not to have to pretend about his childhood. A lot of times he just faked up a nice family to talk about when he was out. "I thought all families were like mine. There is some truth to that. No one's family is perfect or normal like they are on TV."

"Even with Price?"

"Van...yeah he doesn't talk much about his family, but it's sort of the consensus that the man who drew a bunch of loners together and hobbled them into a team and eventually a family probably didn't start out with a great one."

Van didn't talk about his family. Actually none of them did. Luna had been raised in foster care, Xander had three brothers that he'd been close to until an accident had left one of them paraplegic. Kenji was an only child with a single mom who'd been dedicated to him until she died, Lee...her childhood was almost as messed up as his had been, but she'd had a grandfather to watch over her. Like Andi had tried to do for him until she'd met the wrong guy.

"Brianne's family was...well, she used to say they were the perfect family at church on Sunday but she couldn't live up to being perfect all the time. She left Oklahoma City and ended up in Houston. We were both at a homeless shelter together, and we hit it off. We both got jobs and it was hard, but there was this lady, Ms. Lenora, who showed us how to dress and let us live in her spare room."

There was always someone whose kindness made a difference. "Henry was like that for me. I had started working with a local drug gang to find the guy who'd killed Andi. Henry was undercover and saw something in me. He took a chance after his sting was done and brought me in. Offered me a job and I took it," he said.

"You did the same thing for Joey," she said.

"I did." It seemed a shame to keep losing generations of kids to the streets because they had no one to show them there was another way. "Turned out pretty good."

"Yeah, it did. Without him, I wouldn't have found you," she said.

"I would have regretted that," he admitted.

"Me too," she said, putting her hand on the table and the reaching for his. "I put a condom in my pocket."

"There's a pocket in that dress?" he asked. But despite his joking tone, he'd gone hard. His thumb rubbed over the back of her knuckles. Gooseflesh went up her arm, and he noticed that her nipples tightened against the bodice of her dress.

"There are two," she said. Her voice was huskier than it had been.

"I put one in my pocket too," he said, pushing his plate away and going around to her side of the table.

"Great minds," she said.

"Or horny bodies." He didn't want to admit this could be anything other than sex. His entire adult life, his relationships had been the people at Price Security and Henry or hooking up. That was it. He had never let anyone mean more to him than that.

He wasn't going to front or kid himself that Jena wasn't different. He knew she was. Knew that he was going to miss her when this was over and she went back to her life. Like he missed those long summer days with Andi.

He also knew better than to waste a minute of his time with her. He drew her to her feet, pulling her into his arms at the same time that she jumped into them. Her hands were on his ass as he pulled him flush against her.

"Kiss me like you did in the gym."

"If I do, I'm not stopping until I'm buried deep inside of your body."

"Perfect."

Her mouth met his. The kiss wasn't rushed because

this time he knew they had time. She tasted of the rosé and steak and something familiar that he realized was just Jena. Her hands on his butt drew his hips closer to hers. He felt her rub her center against his erection.

All that slow and easy he'd been hoping for to make love to her the first time went up in one white-hot flame. His arm around her waist, he pulled her off her feet and turned until he could set her on the table. She put her hands behind her spreading her legs and watching him.

Groaning, he took the condom out of his pocket and put it where he could reach it as she drew her skirt up to her waist and shimmied out of her panties.

The look in Rick's eyes sent a shiver through her to her very core. It made her so wet that she was glad she'd already taken her panties off. She spread her legs and he groaned again. The way he reacted to seeing her body made her feel like the sexiest woman on the planet. Something she knew wasn't remotely true. But she liked that in his eyes she was.

She was so ready for him. This night had been one in a million. A little oasis in the middle of the chaos that her life had become. She wanted him to see how much he turned her on. She'd had sex, a lot especially when she felt lonely. That had been especially true after Brianne's death.

But now she saw how fake that feeling had been. Being in Rick's arms was so much more than she'd experienced with those forgettable men in the past. The smell of his aftershave, the heat of him, the way his eyes moved over her body almost like a physical thing…that was what she'd been seeking.

Finally found.

She needed this because she was with Rick. He was what she'd been missing all along.

Her heart was beating so hard she wouldn't be surprised if he could hear as he leaned over her, his chest brushing against hers as he pushed her legs farther apart. The brush of his shorts against the inside of her thighs wasn't right. She wanted skin. Wanted to feel all of him against her.

She reached between them, undoing his pants and pushing them down his legs. He freed his dick as she leaned back to take his hot, hard length in her hand. She wanted to feel him inside her, filling her up.

She fumbled around for the condom, but Rick took it from her. "Not yet. I want to at least pretend that we can make this last."

"Why?"

"It's too good," he said, then leaned closer whispering in her ear. "Neither of us has had enough of the good stuff."

A shiver went through her straight to her heart. No use pretending that she wasn't falling for Rick. He got her, and he knew what she needed. Even things that she hadn't realized she wanted, he gave her.

She hugged him tight and he hugged her back. Moving around so he could touch her clit with the end of his dick as his pushed her back until she was prone on the table underneath him.

Pushing his hand aside, she took control of his erection, tapping it against her clit as he tore the condom open. With a smile she helped him roll it on. They didn't need to draw this out. The two of them knew how to hold on to the good moments. Knew how to cherish them. There was no denying that this was something she was never going to forget.

"Our first time."

She hadn't meant to say the words out loud, but he nodded. His mouth came down hard on hers, his tongue going deep into her mouth as she sucked on it. She felt the tip of him at her center, and then he was inside her. He stayed there for a long moment, letting her adjust to his size.

She loved that too-full feeling, and arched her hips as she tightened her pussy walls around him. He groaned and drew his hips back, beginning to thrust into her. He tore his mouth from hers. She wrapped her arms around his shoulders, her legs curled around his hips, using her feet to keep him thrusting harder, faster, deeper.

His mouth was on her neck, kissing, sucking. Shivers were spreading everywhere. She was so close to her orgasm and she wanted him to come with her. She caught the lobe of his ear between her teeth and bit it, then whispered to him what she wanted him to do.

Telling him how good he felt inside her and how she wanted him to keep fucking her forever.

He moaned her name. His finger was on her clit. "Come for me, baby," he pleaded. "Now because I'm—"

His words broke off as she clamped down hard on him and her orgasm shuddered through her. He thrust harder and faster, his hands tight and hard on her hips as he threw his head back and cried out as his own climax hit. He kept thrusting a few more times but then collapsed against her.

Her heart was racing so hard she could hear it in her ears and her body was one big tingle of delicious feelings that made her shiver. She wrapped her arms around him, and he rested his head on her shoulder, his breath brushing against her neck. She looked up at the stars in the sky.

So many nights had been spent alone and looking into the universe wondering what was out there waiting for her. This was it. He was it. Rick Stone was what she'd been waiting for.

That scared her more than being alone with Vex again. Tears stung her eyes as she tried to process how much he meant to her. How much she needed him. Because being with Rick wasn't going to be easy.

He had a dangerous job that he wouldn't give up. She had no future after this. She wasn't sure what her life would be when this was over, but she did know she wasn't going back to Houston or the bank.

Chapter 17

Rick woke the next morning and left Jena sleeping soundly in his bed. Last night had been incredible. But this morning reality beckoned. He wanted to give Jena what she needed, namely Vex behind bars and answers for why her friend had been killed. And that meant stepping away from the bliss of being with Jena and focusing back on the case.

Van was on his way to the bank with Luna as back up. Lee had worked all night until, at 4:00 a.m., she'd messaged the group she had the number. Rick went into the living room to wait for updates. Scrubbing his hand over his face, he walked to the tinted bulletproof glass windows and looked out at downtown. From his apartment on the seventh floor, he could see the street. That Mercedes Benz CLA 250 with black windows was still parked halfway up the block.

Lee had cameras set up all over the building, so he knew

she would run the plates once she was up again. The back of his neck itched.

If Van got the box and brought it back, everything was going to kick off. Vex was going to be super pissed...which Rick wished he could be there to see.

That asshole... Rick wanted to give him the beatdown he deserved. He'd seen the fear in Jena's eyes after their confrontation, but also he'd noted the satisfaction in Vex's. He got off on making her feel weak. Something that Rick was dying to repay.

His phone pinged, and he glanced down to see that Van and Luna were on their way back. He dialed his boss.

"I don't know what's in the box," Van said as soon as he answered.

"Did you get it?"

"Yes. It was another locked box that looks like it's going to take a safecracker to get into. You know anyone?"

"Not off the top of my head. But I bet I know someone who does. I'll put out some feelers."

"Good. How's Jena this morning?"

"Still sleeping. Thanks for suggesting the roof last night for our date," he said since he didn't plan on hiding the fact that he and Jena weren't just bodyguard and client. If Van had any issues with that, Rick wanted to deal with it now and not later.

"Nice. I hoped you'd enjoy it," Van said.

"That's it?"

"That's it. We should be back in forty minutes, depending on traffic," Van said.

"There's a black Mercedes half a block up north of the Tower. Watch it when you come in," Rick said. "I'll track you and go up to the roof in case you need cover."

"Thanks."

He disconnected the call and messaged in the group what Van had just shared with him as well as his plan to go to the roof. Kenji responded that he'd join him. Rick left a note for Jena and then walked out of his apartment.

Kenji was waiting by the roof elevator with his sniper rifle. Rick had stopped to get one in the armory on his way up.

"Morning. Where's this car?" Kenji asked.

Rick pointed it out, and his friend used the sight to check it out while Rick walked the perimeter of the roof to check for other vehicles. "I think there are two cars running a tradeoff pattern. I wish Lee was awake."

"She deserves her rest."

"Totally. But she's better at spotting these things than I am," Rick admitted.

"Where?"

He pointed to a blue Kia Sol and a Jeep Cherokee. Not exactly the vehicles he'd choose for an undercover op. Then he noticed a VW van that looked a lot like the one that Aaron had used during his undercover operation out of San Clemente.

"There are more than two," he said, texting Aaron. It looked like someone had mobilized the entire crime syndicate of all of the different gangs that operated in and around this southern California area.

"What's up?"

"Vex knows we are here," Rick said.

"Makes sense. He probably made you, and Cate would have given us up to get something for herself. La Fortunata is like a hydra that keeps regrowing it's heads," Kenji agreed.

Though she was in solitary, the La Fortunata crime syndicate had tentacles in every part of the government.

That pissed him off, but he had been expecting it.

Aaron strolled onto the roof a few minutes later, carrying another sniper rifle case. "I'm not as good as X, but figured you could use another gun."

None of them argued since they knew this type of situation wasn't going to end easily or well. The building was a goddamn fortress but no protection could last forever.

Jena woke to a very quiet and empty apartment. She saw Rick's note, took the time to make herself some coffee and curled up on the end of the couch. For a second it almost felt like a regular day. She messaged her boss because she needed to find out about her last paycheck and getting paid out for her sick/holiday and remaining vacations days.

Steven messaged back. I put you on unpaid leave. Your mom came in and told me that you got into some trouble in LA.

Her mom? The woman who'd been dead since Jena had been two probably hadn't appeared as an apparition to Steven.

Thanks for understanding. Not sure how much longer I'll be here.

Take your time. ☺

She thumbs-upped his message.

Not sure what that meant. That was weird. It had to be related to Vex and this quest to get that key from her. She hoped that her coworkers weren't in danger. They weren't friends or anything, but that didn't mean she wanted them to end up a victim to Vex and his gang.

A bunch of messages started to come into the Price Security group chat she'd been added to. Scanning them, she was relieved to learn that Van and Luna had gotten the box from the bank. Having it here would take away Vex's leverage—it meant that he couldn't trade whatever was in the box in a plea deal to avoid jail time for Brianne's murder. But then she started to worry as she read about the car on the street and Rick on the roof.

He was a bodyguard, right? Not a sniper.

Her heart was pounding as she realized that the safety she'd been taking for granted might have been false.

The entire team was on red alert because of the danger that she'd brought to their door.

If she'd either gotten a confession or killed Vex that very first night, then that would have been the end of everything. But instead, this had escalated into something much bigger. She had no skills to add on the rooftop but she was good at research.

She messaged the group about her boss's odd message, and Rick texted back to stay put and they'd figure out what that meant after Van got back.

Clearly they were all busy on the roof. She understood that, but that didn't mean she was happy about it. She totally hated when things weren't in her control. Now she was worried about Steven and the rest of the bank, Rick and all of Price Security. It was a lot.

She took a couple of deep breaths. What could she do?

That was what Joey had always said when they were growing up. What was in their control?

Jena got her laptop and opened the files she had on Vex, along with the notes that Lee had rescued from Brianne's cloud account.

She hadn't said anything yesterday, but the truth was

that Brianne left coded notes. They both had started to do it after Jena had dated a very possessive and emotionally abusive man who'd allowed her no privacy and used to check her phone every day.

The code wasn't that difficult. It was inspired by the movie *A Christmas Story* and the wheel Ralphie used to decode Drink More Ovaltine. They had made a wheel themselves. They just shifted the words around instead of the letters. So every third word in the note would be the important ones.

Jena dug in her bag for a notepad but didn't have one. Rick must have one someplace since he'd left her that note. She found it in the kitchen drawer, along with a small handgun that looked old-fashioned to her. She had no idea if it was loaded or not but took it and put it in her bag, just in case.

She wasn't taking a chance of being unarmed. Not now.

The first note wasn't a coded one. It was just a list of stuff she wanted Vex to buy for her.

Jena got it. Growing up poor…money was the answer to everything. Stuff was its cousin. Like if you had money and the right labels, then everything would be Gucci. Except that wasn't the case. Money didn't equal happy.

In Brianne's case, it had simply meant more problems.

Going to the next note, she found one that was definitely coded.

She jotted down the decoded message.

La fortune is working with Flynn Howard? Vex is going to be his second.

That name sounded familiar to Jena, but she wasn't sure where she knew it from.

Using her phone, she did a Google search and almost

dropped it when she realized that Flynn Howard was actually the head of the FBI. Holy crap.

Knowing that she needed to let Rick know, she started to get up but stopped herself. He was busy trying to protect Van. Sharing this news could wait.

There were two more coded notes.

The second one read: *Vex is crazy. Last night he killed a man. Not sure who.*

The last one: *Took something valuable to keep V in line. Must warn J.*

Well, that hadn't worked out. Jena drew a box around the last one. Brianne should never have kept this all to herself. They should have worked together. Yet even as the thought formed in her mind she knew how ridiculous it was. How was a loan officer and a part-time barista going to stop a major player in a criminal syndicate with connections to the government?

To be honest, it scared her to think of what that meant. Was there even anyone that could be trusted? Rick was the exception. Him, she trusted. But Van, who'd brought the daughter of the head of La Fortunata to the Tower…now she wasn't sure what his motive was now that she knew how highly connected the crime syndicate was…

Van and Luna made it into the underground garage without incident. The men on the roof all looked at each other, realizing that they were in a waiting game. The building was known to be well protected, to the point where even La Fortunata was probably going to think twice before attacking it.

But the criminals wanted everyone in Price Tower to know they were there.

Jena popped up at the top of the stairs and waved him over. "Van's back right?"

"Yeah. What's up?"

"Um...can I talk to you alone?"

He took her hand and led her down the stairwell until they were away from Kenji and Aaron. Kenji was staying on the roof, and Aaron was talking to his boss at the DEA.

"What's up?"

"I decoded a few of Brianne's notes from the cloud. She mentioned a name in association with La Fortunata that's...pretty disturbing."

Rick didn't like the way that Jena kept glancing over her shoulder and his. She spoke in hushed tones, wringing her hands together.

"Who?"

"I had to google him... He's the head of the FBI."

"What?"

"Yeah. I mean, I know you said you that you though there were connections in other organizations but this would give them access to all of the intelligence community, right?"

Rick shoved his hand through his hair, then took Jena's shoulder and urged her down the stairs until they were on his floor. He drew her into his apartment.

"Show me," he said.

She went to her laptop, and he saw she'd been using his yellow notepad.

The notes sounded like nonsense when he read them, but once he knew the code that she and Brianne used, he saw that she'd found the right message.

The sentences were crude, but what they contained wasn't.

"We need to take this to the team."

"Are you sure we can trust them?" she asked. "You said we couldn't trust Cate and yet Van brought her here. With this kind of connection to La Fortunata, could she be passing information out from solitary?"

"With my life and yours. I'm not saying this lightly, babe." When she still didn't look sure, he added, "You came to me. You know I'm not going to put you in danger," he said.

"I do. But what about your safety? I know what it's like to put my trust in the wrong person. I don't want that for you," she said.

"Who did you trust?"

"A boyfriend. It turned into a nightmare. But I didn't leave for a while. I thought I loved him and he loved me. I thought...that if I just tried harder I could make it work. I made excuses for stuff that didn't add up."

Like Van bringing Cate here. He understood her reasoning but Rick felt very certain Van would never betray them.

"Okay. I'm not saying you're right, but we take this to Van. We can ask him about Cate if that makes you feel better. Find out if she said anything to him when they were alone," Rick said.

"That's all I ask. If I don't feel safe here..."

There was tension between them. He got it. How could she trust the safety of the Tower when he was pretty sure Vex knew where they were?

"We leave."

She gave a short, tight nod. "Do you think they'll get the box open?"

"Yes. It might take a few days," Rick said. "I've reached out to a safecracker but he'll get back to me when he can. We need to go meet with the team. Catch them up on the notes you decoded. Stay to my left and behind me. If I tell you to go, run to the garage and my car. Don't take the elevator. Don't stop until you are locked inside."

He handed her his keys. "Wait for me there."

She took them and put them in her pocket. She reached for her bag and shoved her laptop and notes in it.

"I don't think that will happen," he said.

But he wasn't taking any chances. He trusted Van more than any other person on the planet. But he wanted answers.

They walked into the conference room, where Van and Luna were already seated around the table. Aaron was there, and Lee looked like she'd just gotten out of bed and smiled sleepily at them as they entered.

Van put his hands on the table to stand up. But Rick motioned for him to stay put.

"We would like to know why you brought Cate here," Rick said. "She's always been a dangerous woman. That didn't change just before she was arrested."

"You're right," Van said. "In fact, I've been asked by Hammond to use her as a contact to try to get to a mole in the FBI. Someone high up is believed to be part of La Fortunata," Van said, gesturing at Jena. "When you showed up, you brought us an advantage."

"How?"

"The entire syndicate is desperate for something, but we couldn't figure out what. This box is what has them in a tailspin. They are all scrambling to get it."

Rick glanced over at Jena, lifting one eyebrow. Was she satisfied with Van's answers about Cate?

"Brianne overheard that Vex was working with Flynn Howard...the head of the FBI," Jena said. "Vex is meant to be his number two."

A thick silence fell around the table. All of them had

connections to different government organizations so this was huge. After a minute, Rick shook his head.

"Do you trust Hammond?"

"Haven't had a reason not to, but that's as far as it goes," Van said. Then he looked over at Jena. "I wouldn't put you in danger."

He trusted the man, and what he'd just laid out made sense.

"Why'd you keep us in the dark?" Luna asked.

"It was need to know only," Van said.

"And you've always had a hard-on for getting your own back against La Fortunata and Cate," Lee said. "Next time don't keep me in the dark. We all take risks and lay it on the line for you, Van. We expect you to know we've got your back."

Van nodded. Rick knew there was more between the two of them than everyone else at Price Security. "Couldn't risk fucking up again and putting anyone else in danger."

"You were played by her in the past. We both were. It's hard to trust anything she says. Hammond shouldn't have asked you to use her for leverage," Lee said.

"It happens to everyone," Jena said quietly. "I think Brianne, to some extent, did that to Vex. She let him see her as nothing more than the part-time barista looking for a rich boyfriend. But once she realized he wasn't what she thought, she played him."

Rick took Jena's hand and squeezed it. Brianne had played Vex and the entire La Fortunata crime syndicate. Right now they were all panicking, wondering what all Jena knew.

Chapter 18

It wasn't as if surprises weren't part of her life now. But hearing Van's explanation...it wasn't what she'd expected. He was such a confident and forceful man that she thought he'd front and act like he hadn't made a mistake by bringing Cate O'Dell here. But it fit with what she knew of him. Risks were part of how he operated. His supreme confidence in Price Security and his team made it possible for him to do that. Hearing him own it tipped the scales toward believing in Rick and his team.

The tension in the conference room was so thick. Everyone seated around the table was on edge. Even Rick. There were so many variables now. The locked box. The cars surrounding the building. The bounty on Jena's head. In fact, Aaron's undercover contact had messaged to say that Vex had upped the reward on Jena.

"I think we need to have a plan that you share with your contacts. Maybe that you're taking me to a different safe house or something? That's the only way you're going to find out who is rotten in the government organizations that you are involved with," Jena said. "And anyway, I still want his confession to killing Brianne."

"No." Rick didn't even look over at her just dropped the word like it was final.

"Risking your life isn't a chance we'll take," Van said.

"I'm not asking you," Jena said. "I'm just as much a part of this team—"

"Screw that. You have no training," Rick said, turning to face her. She hadn't seen him angry before, and there was a look in his eyes that made her want to cower.

Except that wasn't her way. She'd had to fight for everything in her life. This was no different.

"You showed me how to disarm an attacker with a knife," she pointed out. "Stop treating me like I'm helpless."

"I'm not debating this."

"Good," she said. "Van, you pointed out how I changed your mission when I showed up. It would be ridiculous not to use me again." Rick grunted next to her. "I think with some backup this time, I could get the information and a confession."

She had no real idea how she'd do it, but she wasn't going to be left behind hiding some place while they went after Vex. Now that she realized the head of the FBI might be involved with the crime syndicate, she knew there would be other agendas at play. Rick had warned her, Vex might get a deal if he turned on someone big... she wasn't letting that happen. She had to be part of whatever plan was made.

"Backup is good. We could even have Luna or Lee disguised as you," Aaron added. "They have more training than you do."

"I'm taller than both of them by about five inches," Jena pointed out. "It has be me who is moved and then y'all can catch whoever tries to nab me."

This was the only way to throw the criminals off. Her impulsiveness had led to all of this. No one would know that La Fortunata was still operating or that someone high up in the FBI was involved. Her gut was sure of it. Was she scared? She'd have to be an idiot not to be, but at the same time, this was a chance she was willing to take. "I'll do whatever you tell me to. But we all know that I have to be involved."

What she really wanted…well, she wasn't going to share it with the group. If she got the chance, she was going to offer him that box in return for his confession to killing Brianne. Sure, she knew that there was a chance he wouldn't let her out alive, but that was where a whole hell of trust was going to come in. For the first time since Brianne's death, she had to believe that Rick would have her back. That he'd keep her alive and come in and rescue her.

"What if I I sneak out with the box—"

"What?"

"Definitely not."

Came from all around the room. "It's got to be used for leverage. By this point, he knows we got it from the bank."

"Yeah, and once you give it to him, he will kill you," Rick said.

"That's where you come in. You have to do your white knight thing and save me," she said.

"No. I told you I'm waiting for a call from a safe cracker. Your ideas…they make sense if we had no other options but right now we do."

At this point, she had no other ideas and she could tell that not all of them around the table felt the same way. But they weren't sure who they could trust, Jena guessed. The agencies and contacts that Price used to keep their clients secure might not be as reliable as they had thought.

All of them? Or just a handful. It was too much of a risk to tempt it. No one said anything and Rick took her by the wrist and led her out into the hallway.

He was doing some deep-breathing exercise, but when their eyes met he lost it. Pulling her into his arms, his mouth came down hard on hers. The kiss he gave her stripped bare all the pretense she'd been holding on to. All the bravado that had brought her from Houston to Los Angeles was gone.

She was running on nerves and this…this strength that she drew from Rick and their closeness. She'd found something in him that she'd never expected to. But she couldn't have a life with this man just yet.

She had to clear up the past before they could move forward. There was no other way.

She cared for this man. Hell, she might be in love with him. But having never really felt anything as intense and all-encompassing as this she wasn't sure if it was love or something more.

He lifted his head.

"I hate this."

"But you know I'm right. It has to be something risky. Every time I've done something unpredictable we've gotten results."

"Maybe."

Rick was conflicted in a way he'd never been before. He knew he was acting like one big macho hormone dragging her into the hallway just to kiss her. Her plan was logical, but that didn't mean that his gut—that primitive bastard she'd awakened the first night she'd shown up—was down for admitting it.

"I can't lose you."

Damn.

Had he said that out loud?

"I won't let you."

Yup.

He definitely had.

He pulled her to him, hugging her tightly. He wanted to be inside her, but this hallway wasn't the place and right now really wasn't the time. "I hate risky. If anyone comes up with anything else that's close to achievable, I'm voting for it instead. We are trying to figure out how to open the box."

"I hate risks too. I'm scared, but we can't sit here and wait for them to attack. And we both know that at some point they are going to."

She had a very good point. Why hadn't anyone attacked yet? Was it Aaron's contact or Van's who was waiting to see what they did next?

He opened the conference room door; Jena followed him back inside. "Why haven't any of the gang members cruising by this building made a move?"

Van shrugged, but Aaron was the one who answered. "Near as I can tell, they are waiting for an order from higher up."

"Higher than Vectra?" Rick asked.

Aaron nodded. "My contact, Denis, is deep undercover. I want to pull him out because if there is a mole in the DEA, he's as good as dead."

Rick knew that Denis was like a brother to Aaron. But

if they made a move to protect Denis, it could alert the gang that they were onto them.

Frigging hell.

There wasn't anything to do but discuss Jena's plan. She squeezed his shoulder as he came to the same conclusion she had already.

"We need to move. Luna and Jena, go train. If she's taking the box, then we need it rigged so it can't be opened. Is there any chance we can get a duplicate box?" Rick started spouting orders like he was in charge of the team. Normally he was a quiet team player, but not now. Lee got up and went over to her laptop, no doubt searching for a substitute for the box.

Van pulled the box closer and started to examine it.

"Kenji I need you as a sniper," Rick said.

"I know," he said. "Where's Denis?"

"He's been working a club downtown, but they pulled him off for a special job," Aaron said. "That was about six hours again and I haven't heard anything else since.

"Is that normal?" Rick asked. This not knowing who they could trust outside of Price Security was tough. Rick relied on his contacts in the DEA and other agencies that he'd come across over the years.

"Yes. I've got a tracker on him. He's at a house in Beverly Hills," Aaron said.

"If the intel I've been given can be trusted, Vectra is holed up in a house there," Van said.

Jena leaned forward. "I tracked Vex to a house in Beverly Hills."

Lee sent the block that Jena had identified to the monitor wall and Aaron shared Denis's location. They were very close. "Let's assume for now that is where everything will go down."

"Any chance we can get confirmation?"

"I'll go and check it out," Kenji said. "Daphne, you stay here."

"As if I was going to leave this place with a bunch of gang members on the street," she said dryly.

Kenji winked at his wife.

"I'd like to involve Detective Miller. She's proven herself to us. I don't like the idea of moving against La Fortunata with their web of government agents without some law enforcement on our side," Van said.

Jena didn't trust cops, but Rick always had. His gut told him that Detective Miller was could be relied on. "I agree."

"Sure," Jena said.

Not a ringing endorsement, but at least they were on the same page.

"She can't come here," Rick said.

"We could use Detective Miller with me," Jena said.

There was quiet around the table, but Rick knew that the team liked that idea.

"I'll go to her with the box. Whoever is watching can pick me up then. I'll have to call her."

Lee walked over to the table. "Not from here. This place is secure in and out. You'll have to go…up on the roof and make the call. Use your phone. We'll know if the government is listening based on what happens next."

The government. It didn't really help things that they had no idea who might be listening on the other end of a call. They needed to get into the box. He had a contact from a job he'd done while moonlighting for the DEA a few years ago. But that meant coming clean to Van about his side hustle.

Which, all things considered, wasn't that big of a deal. His phone pinged and he glanced down. "Just heard back from my contact... I might know a guy who can open the box."

"Great. Who?"

"Wexler. That's the only name I have."

"What's he do?" Jena asked.

"Jewel thief," Rick said.

He knew Jena was interested in knowing more, judging from the way her eyes sparked with interest. "Can he break into the box?"

"If anyone can tell us how to, it's him," Rick said.

Van steepled his fingers together. Rick knew his boss was putting all the facts together. "Call him. Luna and Jena, go to the gym. Everyone else has their assignments."

Everyone got up, leaving the conference room in couples until it was just him and Van.

"So where'd you met Wexler?" Van asked.

"Job a few months back." Rick had been on his forced yearly vacation.

"How long have you by working outside of Price?"

"Since the beginning. I told you, I don't do downtime," Rick said.

Van nodded. "Anything else I should know?"

Rick waited. His boss wasn't a man to hide his feelings, so if he wasn't saying anything more about Rick's moonlighting, then that meant he was cool with the explanation Rick had given.

"Nah. You?"

"Just want to find the bastard who's playing with us," Van said.

Rick couldn't agree more. What had started as helping out Jena had turned into protecting his family. No one was going to harm them.

* * *

Luna was quiet as she led the way to the gym. They both got changed. When she joined the other woman on the mat, she assessed Jena.

"What would you say is your strength?" Luna asked.

"I'm not sure. I mean, I'm scrappy and don't want to die," Jena said, then started laughing at her own words. "When Vex had me by the throat, I just kicked and hit out. I made contact a few times, and then when he got the knife out… I did get control of it but I feel like that was mostly luck."

"Don't discount luck," Luna said. "So what were you aiming for?"

Jena shrugged. Mainly she'd been following the advice from that Sandra Bullock movie *Miss Congeniality*. "Solar plexus, instep, nose or groin. I punched him in the nose and tried kicking him in the groin or kneeing him, but that really didn't have much impact."

"Those are good places to aim for. When you go for the nose, try to punch upward and with as much force as you can. Like you're trying to drive his nose up and into his brain. Don't be afraid to dig into your attackers eyes too. It's kind of gross but is effective," Luna said.

Luna went and got a punching dummy from the closet and waved her over. "So for the nose, you use the heel of your hand and drive it upward like this to maximize the impact."

Luna showed her a few times, then had her try it. It was awkward at first to think of hitting someone with the heel of her hand instead of her fist, but after Luna had her try it both ways, Jena realized she had more power with the heel.

"For the eyes, just dig your thumbs in," Luna said.

"Also, a punch to throat can be effective. Use your fist this time."

They practiced again on the dummy. "How'd you learn all this?"

"Ran away when I was seventeen. Had to learn how to protect myself. It was a good thing I did, because it turned out I had some skills. I started doing street fighting and then moved to MMA when a trainer took me under her wing. She let me live in her apartment until I had enough money to move out."

Jena could easily picture that life. "I ran away at seventeen, Brianne and I met on the street."

"I'm sorry. I felt like I didn't have any other choice. It was tough, but it made me into who I am."

Jena could see that. She thought about the gun she'd taken from Rick's apartment. "Will you show me how to use a handgun?"

"Yes. I doubt Vectra's people will let you bring one in with you though. The main thing with a gun is to use it as a last resort. There's always a chance that you will lose the gun and be shot with it," Luna said.

"That's what Rick's worried about. But I've only ever fired one, and Vex wears one, as do all of his men. I hit the target but I think it might have been luck."

"Yeah, better to be armed with the knowledge of what it's like to fire one than to shoot wild because you panicked," Luna agreed, leading the way to a room at the back of the gym that Jena hadn't noticed before.

It turned out to be a shooting range with two booths and targets on the back wall. She'd seen a larger version of one in the *Lethal Weapon* movies she'd seen. Luna went to a locked cabinet and used the retinal scanner to open it. Inside were all kinds of weapons.

A knot of fear bloomed in Jena's stomach. She thought of that guy she'd shot and killed and then about the little gun she'd taken from Rick's kitchen. Her heart raced. It wasn't as reassuring as she'd thought it would be. Luna took out a semiautomatic...which Jena could only identify because the other woman told her that was what it was.

"This is a Glock. Most of the guys like them. It comes with a standard clip that holds seventeen rounds of ammunition. It has a safety...right here. That means you have to click it off before you fire. "The semiautomatic bit means that it's self-loading. So as soon as you fire, another bullet goes into the chamber. But you only have what's in your clip," Luna said.

"This is the weapon I like because it feels right in my hand. Plus the Glock 19 has very little recoil," Luna said.

She checked the clip, which Jena noticed was empty, and then pushed it in. "You try it."

Jena did. Loading the clip and taking the safety off. Then putting it back on.

"Nice. I'll put some ammo in, and you can try firing a live round. I have to notify Van so he's aware of what we are doing," Luna said.

She went to a landline phone on the wall and made her call. When she came back, she gave Jena headphones and goggles, but Jena shook her head. "I'm going to be doing this as a last resort. I won't have all this stuff."

"I like the way you think," Luna said. "But use the headphones, we're in an enclosed room, a gunshot firing is really loud and can do permanent damage."

"Okay, I'll wear the headphones."

She helped Jena get into a shooting stance and then gave her the go-ahead to fire. Jena's first shot was wildly off target, but the second one hit dead center. She stopped closing her eyes on the third shot.

Luna gave her a few more tips before she tried again and put the weapon back in the gun safe before they both left. When they exited the range, Rick was lounging against the wall.

"Happy now?"

"She needed to know how to shoot one before she was in a situation where it was required," Luna said. "Knowledge is power, Rick."

"You're right."

Rick left them after that. Jena knew he wasn't happy about her being part of the team or taking risks, but too bad. Jena was starting to like the woman she was becoming.

Chapter 19

Rick was pleased that Jena had had Luna show her how to shoot. Luna was totally right that knowledge was power. He didn't like the idea of Jena in a situation where she'd need to shoot someone again.

He was protecting her. That was all there was to it.

Except, with the plan they were putting in place, there was a very big chance he wouldn't be able to have her back. Which he hated. But there was no helping it. Everyone at Price—except for Xander, who had Obie holed up in a safe house in South Dade county—was here. Daphne and Nick were working out of the third floor. It was the price they paid for being married to security experts who sometimes ended up in dangerous situations.

Wexler was available for video chat. The other man looked like he was living in a beach hut somewhere. Wearing an open Hawaiian shirt and a pair of board shorts, he reminded Rick of Aaron on the last mission.

"Dude, good to see you again," Wexler said.

"You too." He showed Wexler the box. "So have you seen one of these before?"

"The box itself is generic, but that's a Sargent & Greenleaf lock and those bitches are military grade. You won't be able to hack it or cut it open."

"Suggestions?" Rick asked.

"Well, it's got a digit keypad, and they usually generate a code that's good for ten minutes. I'd start with trying to get access to the phone of the person who owns the box."

Rick glanced over at Lee. "Can you do that?"

"Do we think that it's Vectra's phone or someone else's? Also, once we hit the button to get the code, they'll know we are trying to open the box.

"You could try smashing the box, but that's usually not viable. I used to have a backdoor code… See if you can get a serial number off it," Wexler said.

Jena leaned over Rick's shoulder as he tried to get to the number, but he didn't see anything. His eyesight wasn't what it used to be. Bending closer, she rubbed her finger over the bottom. "There's a number, but it's faded or been intentionally rubbed off."

"Might be a bit old-school, but if you have a jimmy you can probably pop the lock off. It might be wired to set off an alarm, but I'm guessing they already know you are breaking it," Wexler said. "Let me know how it goes."

"Later," Rick said, disconnecting the call.

Van had left the room and Luna went to her large bag. "I might have something."

"I have a file," Jena said. She pulled it out of her bag and handed it to Rick. It bent when he tried it, since it wasn't made of materials sturdy enough to get a good wedge under the lock.

"Try this one," Luna said, coming over.

He got a little farther with the low, flat tool she handed him, but not enough to get good leverage.

Kenji tried the butt of his Glock, hitting it hard and repeatedly against the side. The lock stayed in place.

"Where's X when we need that big brute? He could probably snap it off with his bare hands," Kenji said.

"I've got something," Van said, walking back in with several tools. There was a security key, which should have the strength not to bend or break. Plus, it was ridiculously thin.

When they tried that, they got up underneath the lock, which provided a small opening. Van shoved the tip of a wedge into it. They all took turns shoving it in, but it would only go so far. Finally, Kenji hit it again with the butt of his Glock, which worked. It took a good fifteen minutes, but they had the lock busted off the safe.

A red light started flashing on it, and they knew an alarm had been triggered. But, as Wexler had pointed out, there wasn't any hiding the fact they had the box and were breaking into it.

Rick drew Jena over to his side. She had the right to see what was in the box first. After all, this was the reason her friend had been killed.

He guessed she was thinking the same thing, as he noticed her hand trembling as she touched the box.

"Go ahead," Rick urged her.

She had to wedge the security key tool into the box to open it. There was an electric charge that went up her arm, and she dropped the tool, but it had shorted out the fuse and the box opened.

Rick rubbed Jena's hand and arm, knowing that kind of jolt would leave it numb for a few minutes. They both leaned over to see a black leather folder. She tugged her hand from his and pulled it out.

He didn't know what was in that folder but expected it to be damning. She opened it up. There were three jump drive type devices in slots on the left side. Just that.

"Bit of a letdown," Jena said.

"Yeah, I was expecting… I don't know, something old-school, like papers," Rick said.

"Me too."

"La Fortunata are ahead of the curve," Van said. "They have people placed high up in the tech industry. We saw that when they kidnapped those kids to try to get control of border security."

"That's right. So I guess Lee's up," Rick said.

She walked over to take the jump drives out of the portfolio. They lifted up to reveal photos buried in the bottom. They were photos of Malcom O'Dell, aka Perses, with different members of the intelligence committee, including Flynn Howard and two five-star generals.

Seems Sebastian Velasquez might have known he was marked.

Jena put her hand on Rick's shoulder. "Who are these people? That one guy looks like the head of the FBI. I googled him when his name showed up in Brianne's notes."

"He is. This is—"

"A dangerous clusterfuck. This confirms everything Brianne put her in note," Van said. "I trust Hammond, but this is his boss. Plus the deputy heads of the DEA and CIA. This is bigger than just the FBI."

The tension in the room ratcheted up as they all went to sit down, trying to process that even though they'd cut the head off of La Fortunata, it seemed to have more than one and it was far reaching.

* * *

Van left the room to call his contact. Kenji and Luna went to find their spouses, and Aaron was still out talking to Denis so he could try to find out where Vex was located. The house in Beverly Hills was a likely option, but they couldn't say for sure. Jena was confident the only way she was getting that confession was if she went to Vex. But at the same time, there was a knot in the pit of her stomach as she worried about not having any backup.

The sun was setting beyond the floor-to-ceiling windows. Another day had passed. She couldn't keep track of them anymore. Just felt like she'd been in this place for a lifetime. Everything before she'd run around that corner and spotted Rick was a blur.

That man.

He had on a button-down shirt; he'd loosened his tie and wore a pair of khaki pants that hugged his ass when he leaned over the table. She'd forced herself to focus on everything that had been going on, but Rick was hard to resist.

She'd used every excuse to get close to him. She knew the other people at Price Security would do everything to keep her safe, but her only real sense of safety came from him.

There was something about him. That hardcore steel that made up so much of him underneath that warm teddy bear vibe.

He called to her like nothing and no one else ever had. Not even trying to be normal. Being with him made her feel like she'd finally figured out who Jena was. The real Jena. Not the one trying so desperately to fit in with the suburbanites. That girl who had been formed in the quiet, lonely existence of her childhood.

"You're staring at me, babe," Rick said, his voice low and raspy.

"Can't help it," she said.

"Want to go back to my apartment and chill?" Rick asked.

Chill? More like jump his bones and then hope that would distract her from what was coming. No one had said it officially, but she got that as soon as Van talked to his contact she was going to be heading out.

She'd volunteered and wasn't backing down. But the knot in her gut...

"Sure."

She was so on edge it took all her concentration to follow him to the elevator. But she stopped walking when she was halfway there. Fear and anxiety were winning the battle in her body. Her legs were weak.

Those people in the photos were so high level. Honestly Brianne could have had no idea what she'd gotten into.

"You okay?" Rick asked, coming back to her. She hadn't realized she'd slid down the wall and was sitting on the floor until he crouched next to her.

"No. Not really. Is there any scenario where Brianne could have survived once she knew the name Pallus?"

"It's hard to say. Your friend sounds like she was smart and savvy about men. She was playing a good game. It just caught up with her when she took that key," Rick said.

"Exactly," Jena said. They were playing a good game right now and felt like they were winning, but that was because the cards had been falling their way. "No one wins all the time."

"It's not too late to back out of going out there," Rick said. "Now that someone is aware that we opened that box...it's a different world."

"So many variables. I wish things were straightforward, but they never are. I mean in *Lethal Weapon*, in the one where they put a bomb on the toilet...that's what this is. The box is the bomb on the toilet. I don't know if I should get off or stay where I am."

Rick put his hand on her thigh and squeezed, sending a little shiver up her body as their eyes met. "It's your choice."

Which made her feel slightly better. No one would judge her if she changed her mind. But she'd judge herself. Brianne had been gathering facts, and she might not have tied it all together, but her best friend had been onto something big...

"Why didn't I see this? That she had something else going on? Not Vex. What kind of friend am I just to assume it was a man?"

"Don't do that. There is no greater friend than you," Rick said, getting to his feet and offering her his hand so she could get up too. "You came out here, followed a known dangerous man and then attempted to get a confession that almost got you killed. You haven't stopped trying to get justice for her. There's no greater love than that."

Rick was a soothing balm for her battered feelings and injured soul. It made her more determined to be the one who heard Vex's confession. Part of her wanted him to stare into her eyes as he admitted it.

She needed to see what he felt when he knew that he'd been caught. She took a deep breath and a new calm surrounded her. Did she have any idea what was going to happen? Hell no.

But she did know that no matter what, she wasn't going to give up.

* * *

Knowing he had absolutely zero intention of watching a movie with her when they got back to his apartment didn't bother him because she seemed to be on the same page. Something so light, almost like joy, had lit up his heart when she'd talked about *Lethal Weapon*. A girl who'd grown up the way she had shouldn't still have that innocent belief in…well, Hollywood endings, where everything ties up neat and tidy and all the good guys live happily ever after. But more than that, she believed in justice. She might have an uncommon way of believing it should be achieved. But he got it.

As soon as they were in the apartment, she leaned back against the door. There was something so sexy about every bit of her. The way she watched him as he let his gaze drop down her body. The way she pulled the ponytail holder out of her hair and shook it until it fell around her shoulders.

"You just going to stand there and watch?" she asked.

He leaned against the table he'd set up in the dining area, crossing his legs at the ankles and nodded. They both needed this. Something that felt fun and removed from the very dangerous situation they were in.

"Fair enough, since I was ogling you earlier."

"You were."

"You're hard to resist," she said, slowly undoing the buttons of her blouse, letting it hang free around her. The creamy skin of her stomach and the swells of her breasts visible. She shrugged out of the blouse and tossed it to him.

He caught it one-handed and brought it to his face, breathing in the scent of her. God, he loved the way she smelled.

She unhooked her bra and tossed that to him as well. He swallowed hard, watching those creamy breasts as she cupped them and then ran her hands down her stomach to the waistband of her jeans. She didn't undo them, but ran her hands around to her hips and ass, turning as she plucked a condom from her back pocket. Holding it with two fingers, she glanced over her shoulder at him.

"Want this?"

He groaned. A moment later, he was on his feet striding toward her. He took the condom with his teeth, his hands going to her flesh. Caressing her back and waist and then pushing them around to the front of her. He cupped her breasts and plucked at her nipples until she arched against him, moaning a little.

He slipped one hand lower, undoing her jeans. She shimmied out of them, rubbing her hips against his very hard and trapped erection. He enjoyed that for as long as he could stand it, then undid his pants and put the condom on.

He put his hand on the wall next to her head and bent her forward until the tip of his cock was at the entrance of her body. Her hand came up on his, and she turned her head until she was kissing his wrist.

He flicked his finger against her nipple, bringing his mouth down on the nape of her neck and sucking against her skin as he entered her.

He drove himself deep into her; her hips moved against him and her teeth bit his wrist. But he held himself still, wanting this moment to last. But it wouldn't. She felt too good.

Her hand slipped between her legs as she bent at the waist. He drove himself deeper as he felt her hand on his balls—squeezing. A red haze came over him. He started driving into her; sensation rushed down his spine, then all over his body. He reached between her legs and rubbed her clit as he continued to drive into her, knowing that he wasn't going to be able to wait for her climax.

His orgasm was riding him hard as her walls tightened around him with each stroke. He bit the back of her shoulder, trying to make the feelings last, but he exploded, shivering and shaking as he continued to thrust into her until he was empty.

He felt her driving back against him until she cried out his name. She slumped forward. He held her with his arm around her waist, his head buried between her shoulder blades.

What was he going to do if he lost her too?

There wasn't going to be a way to carry on if she did something reckless. And everything about Jena was reckless and spontaneous. He loved that about her.

Fuck him.

He loved her.

There was no pretending he didn't.

He also respected her, so as much as his gut was telling him to lock her in his apartment to keep her safe, he knew he couldn't.

Part of what he loved was the recklessness and that loyalty to her friend that had her willing to pursue justice at any cost.

That was a bit to unpack, but he ignored the fact that no one had stuck with him—aside from Price—the way that Jena was sticking to Brianne.

He pulled out and then carried her into his bathroom, where they showered together and he made love to her again. As if that was going to keep her safe.

When they were done, she got dressed in another pair of jeans with her wireless microphone taped between her boobs and her hair up. He wanted to ask her not to go. To tell her that he loved her.

But that would be manipulation. Not his thing.

"You're being very quiet," she said at last.

What could he say to that? "I am."

She leaned against his dresser, watching him where he lay on the bed. "I'm scared. I'm not stupid. Are you worried I don't realize that I am putting myself at risk?"

He sat up, putting his elbows on his knees but keeping his eyes on her. "I never doubted your intelligence. You know the stakes and do what's needed despite that."

"Does that bother you?"

Hell no. It turned him on. It made him want tie her up and keep her safe. But mostly it made him love her.

"Not at all."

Chapter 20

Rick settled into his usual mode when he was working. The sex with Jena had taken the edge off of his worry, but it was still there. Everyone was worried about the implications for them all with La Fortunata's connection to FBI Director Flynn Howard. No one had expected that, and the implications were far reaching. Jena was quietly waiting for Aaron to return.

Denis had been able to get a message out that Vex and some other members of the Malus syndicate had infiltrated LAPD and were waiting for Jena to show up for her meeting with Detective Miller. She'd gone a little white when she'd heard that, then tightened her lips. Aaron was going to escort her instead of having Detective Miller come to them because he was better trained in dealing with drug gangs.

Jena had that big messenger bag she'd brought with her the first time she'd run to him at Price Tower. He wasn't sure what she had stashed in it, but he got the sense that it was like a security blanket around her.

Van had done digging and found a connection between Cate O'Dell and Flynn Howard. They'd been at boarding school together until both were thirteen. "He definitely had her reach out to us. Vectra is dangerous, and he's cornered now. They will kill him for losing the box and for allowing their connection to get out."

"Which is why we need to move," Jena said. "Whatever you are trying to do...do it. As much as I hate the thought of an international criminal syndicate being imbedded in the FBI and with other government organizations, my main goal is to get that bastard to confess to killing Brianne."

Van put his hand up. "You're right. Tonight we will get that confession and make an arrest."

Rick wasn't sure about the arrest. "Who's going to do that?"

"The FBI. Hammond was lit when he heard what we'd found. He's on his way to LA as we speak."

"Do we have to wait for him?" Jena asked.

"It would be better," Van said. "But once we are ready to move, we will. Kenji's confirmed the location Vectra is using. Kenji is in position and has been watching the house."

Rick knew that his friend had reported a frenzy of activity at dusk with dark-windowed cars arriving. From the passive security cameras, Rick knew that the local SoCal gangs were still driving patterns around Price Tower. When they left...it was going to be an all-out run to see if they could make it anywhere.

He wasn't going to lie—the back of his neck itched with both anticipation and nerves. He hated waited. Jena's leg was bouncing up and down with nerves as well. The plans had been made. They were just waiting for Aaron's all clear from his undercover agent.

Lee was still trying to crack into the jump drives they'd recovered. The encryption was next level. Everyone had an earpiece, so Jena had untapped her microphone since she was now connected to the team. Lee would be their eyes as they all went into action.

There was nothing left to plan. Timing though...that was the one thing that was out of their hands.

"Detective Miller's here," Lee said, startling everyone.

"What? She's supposed to stay at the station."

"Yeah, and two guys just got out of the car across the street. We letting her in?"

"Yes," Van said, getting to his feet. Rick and Luna did the same.

They needed to provide cover from the roof in case Detective Miller didn't get inside quickly enough.

Jena looked around. "Should I stay here?"

"Yes."

He was behind Luna but caught up to her with his longer stride. They both were armed but a sniper rifle would be better for where they were going. "You're better with the Glock. I'll go get the rifle."

Luna went to the gun safe in the armory as Rick changed his path and went downstairs after Van. He hit the lobby just as his boss greeted Detective Miller. As she moved inside, the two gang members made their move, rushing the door that was sliding closed.

Firing as they ran, they hit the glass doors and Detective Miller. She staggered and fell to the floor. Van covered her as he fired from the ground. Rick dropped into a shooter's stance and got two bullets off before the doors closed, hitting the assailant closest to them in the shoulder and chest.

He crumpled to the ground. The bulletproof doors took a spate of bullets. They were good up to ninety, but Rick didn't want to chance it and went to the control panel to bring down the steel fire doors.

He was aware of Van talking to Detective Miller. Trying to make sure she was okay. They had a clinic in the building, but depending on where she was hit, she might need real medical attention.

"911, or do we take her to the hospital ourselves?" Rick asked.

"Ourselves. I'll do it," Van said. His face was tight and only someone who knew the other man as well as Rick did would recognized how angry he was at the moment.

"I want more than a confession," Van said.

"I'll get it. I'm bringing the entire Malus syndicate and their connection to La Fortunata down," Rick promised.

Van nodded. "Lee, alert the hospital I'm on my way in with a chest gunshot wound. I've applied a compress... Could use someone to hold it on while I drive."

"I'm in," Luna said. "I would be extra for Rick and Jena. Aaron's out there waiting for you guys, along with his DEA team."

"Jena, come down with Luna. Lee, we're all going mobile."

"The street is getting kind of crowded... Oh fuck, one of them has an RPG rocket launcher."

"I've got him," Luna said.

Van was on his way to the garage, ready to take Detective Miller to the hospital. Luna took the shot and Lee confirmed the hit. "I can't leave. Nick will go with you."

Nick showed up in the lobby as Luna spoke, so Lee

must have kept Daphne and Nick informed of what was going on. He took over holding the bandage on Detective Miller's chest, lifting her in his arms.

Jena met him in the garage. "What are we doing?"

"We'll go to the mansion. Vex brought his fight to our house, and we're going to hit him in his."

Waiting had been killing her, but this…this wasn't what she'd expected. Going one-on-one with Vex was something she had prepared herself for. But gang members firing at the building was next level. Lee was busy calling commands to the team which Lee heard both in the room and in her ear. She realized how insane things were getting and opened her bag to touch the gun she'd put in there earlier. The one she'd taken from Rick's kitchen. She realized she wanted the knife too. The one that Vex had used on Brianne.

"I'm going to the bathroom," she said to Lee, who acknowledged her with a wave.

She knew that the evidence bags were still being stored in the armory in a safe which had surprised her but until charges were brought against her, Detective Miller had been happy with Price keeping hold of them. Van and Rick had both shown it to her and given her access with a key fob. The same one that opened Rick's apartment.

Without given herself time to think, she opened the safe pushed aside the sequined dress bag and her wig. The memories of that night still sent a shiver down her spine. She pulled the knife toward her and just put it in her leather bag. She closed the safe and hurried back down to the garage as she heard that was where the team was moving.

Rick waited for her at the bottom of the stairs. His expression was full-on "warrior in overprotective mode."

She'd seen it a few times, so she recognized it. His hands were steady and his face tight. "You okay?"

"I was upstairs. Are you okay?" she asked. As he got closer she inspected him for any wounds from stray bullets or shrapnel.

"I'm good." Pulling her close with one arm, he dropped a hard kiss on her mouth. "Go get in the Dodge. I want to make sure Miller and Nick are secured in the back of the Hummer."

Rick, Van and Luna's husband got Detective Miller into the back of the Hummer. Nick had brought down a medical kit, and they were doing something to Detective Miller before Van the back door was closed cutting off her view. Van ran to the driver's side and got in.

Rick was in the Dodge a few minutes later.

"Ready one," Van said.

"Ready two," Rick responded.

"Clear at the garage exit," Luna said. "Head east."

"Maps downloaded to the in-car GPS. Daphne is with me in the safe room. We are secure," Lee said. "Move out now."

The Hummer went first, with Rick following closely so that the garage door wouldn't have to be open for too long. Jena realized she was breathing like she'd run a marathon and her heart was beating so fast she had to take a few calming breaths. Except they didn't help. At all.

Nothing in her life had prepared her for this. The Hummer burst out of the underground garage with them hot on its bumper. A rain of bullets hit the Dodge as Rick turned, driving with more speed than he ever had before.

"Stay low," Rick warned. "We have an Audi 500 in pursuit. I can lose them, but he's firing pretty steadily at the back window. It should withstand the bullets, but I'm not taking any chances."

"Me either. You be safe."

"I always am," he said, flashing a grin that made her smile back despite the circumstances.

They turned left when the Hummer went right heading toward the hospital. "You've got one following you," Rick said. "I'll double back."

Rick looked over at her. "There's a sawed off shotgun in the glove box. Use your fob to open it."

She just did what he asked without question. "Load it with the box of shells...did Luna have a chance to show you you how?"

"Nope but I've seen Romancing The Stone and Jack loads one,," she said, just automatically doing what he asked.

Rick accelerated, getting close to the Audi in pursuit of the Hummer. The passenger was firing out his window. "I'm going to get close and bump them...see if that will jar them. Brace yourself."

Rick accelerated and rammed the Audi hard. She jerked forward, the seat belt cutting into her chest. It hurt, and she was scared.

The Audi didn't slow, but a gun appeared out the driver's side and he randomly fired back at them. Hitting the hood of the car.

"Hand me the shotgun," Rick said, holding his hand out to her.

"I'll steer," she said as she passed him the shotgun and took the wheel. This, she could do.

She took a deep breath as he opened the window and the tepid summer wind filled the car. Keeping her eyes just on the road and making sure the car stayed steady, she tried not to flinch when Rick fired the first shot. She was shocked at how loud the shotgun was.

Rick hit the back window of the Audi, and it fractured but didn't shatter. He spent a bullet so it would reload and then fired again. Jena realized he might need more ammo and took the box from the still open glove box, placing it between his legs as he prepared to fire again.

The next spray of bullets shattered the back window of the Audi, and then Rick hit the left rear tire sending it careening into oncoming traffic. He pulled his arm back in, took the wheel as he handed her back the weapon.

"Reload and then keep it on your lap," he said to her.

"Van, you're clear. We'll stay on you until you're in the hospital."

"Roger that," Van said.

They followed the Hummer into the ER parking and Rick got out holding his weapon in his hand but ordering her to stay put. He watched Van's back as he and Nick got Detective Miller on a gurney and followed the ER staff into the hospital.

"Thanks, Rick and Jena," Van said.

Jena wasn't sure what she'd done but knew that being calm had helped the situation. This was so different from when she'd been in Mistal's by herself. The team all covered each other, and she realized they drew strength from it.

Rick got back in the car. "You good?"

"Yeah," she said. "How did you turn your earpiece off?"

"You mute it by tapping it," he showed her.

She muted hers. "I'm freaking out a little bit. Van thanked me, but honestly—

He kissed her hard and quick.

"You were awesome."

* * *

Having Jena in the Dodge with him while they'd been on a high-speed pursuit wouldn't have been his first choice. But she'd handled herself like the champ she was. She took what life threw at her—whatever that was—and just survived. She just kept going, learning, evolving. He'd noticed it while she'd been at Price Tower, but it hadn't registered until this moment.

Somehow part of him still saw her as that girl who'd barreled around the side of the building in a tattered sequin dress with blood on her hands. It was hard to believe it had been less than ten days when it felt like a lifetime.

He had the car back, aware that they probably hadn't lost their tail. "Unmute your earpiece so you don't forget."

She did it as did he.

"This is two, en route to Beverly Hills."

"Roger that," Lee said. "Detective Miller's being taken into surgery. Van's not sure who we can trust on the force, so he's staying with Nick to wait for her. He's gone silent. All comms will go through me."

"Cool," Rick said. "Where's Luna?"

"Wrapping up here. Still debating how she's getting to the hospital," Lee said dryly. "Nick wants to send his chopper. But we don't have a landing pad."

"Something that needs to be remedied," Nick said. "Sorry, I took Van's earpiece. Is Luna okay?"

"I'm fine. We need to go silent so Rick can concentrate. I'm driving. The streets are clear now. I'll meet you at the hospital soon," Luna said.

"Be safe. You're my everything," Nick said.

"I know."

Lee laughed, as did Rick and Jena in the Dodge, and then their communication went quiet. Driving toward Beverly Hills was something he could do in his sleep. But it still took about forty minutes to get there. He drove as defensively as he could, made sure he kept his observation going the entire time.

"I thought Beverly Hills would be more impressive. But it is really just big houses... We have those in Texas," Jena said.

"What else were you expecting?"

"I don't know. Like sparkles or something to denote how glamorous it was."

"You get that on Rodeo Drive."

"Oh, believe me, I know. I've never felt more out of place than there. Brianne would have loved it. She would have put on her secondhand designer clothes and made herself up like Kim Kardashian and owned that street."

"Not you?"

"It's not my style."

"How did you two become friends?" he asked, wanting her to relax after the adrenaline rush that had been the car chase.

"At our core, we are very similar. We wanted someone to love and to love us in return. Neither of us had a sister until we met. I don't know how else to explain it."

She didn't have to say anything else; he got it. "That was me when Van hired me. I was sort of burned out from the DEA, but I still wanted protect people."

"You have a white knight thing," she said.

"I do. I like helping out and doing my part to keep the streets clean. Yeah, yeah, yeah, I know that's to be expected, but it's not just because of Andi. I mean, she's why I started, but I think I would have ended up here even if she'd lived."

Jena squeezed his thigh. "I can see that. What would she say if she saw you now?"

Rick thought about that for a minute. He always thought of Andi as the teenager she'd been when she died. What would his sister think of the man he'd become? She'd be surprised for sure. They'd hated the cops when they'd been kids, stealing food and money to survive. But now...

"I really don't know," he said.

"I bet she'd be proud. I know I'm impressed."

"Yeah?" he asked her, taking his eyes off the road for a second to look at her.

She nodded at him. "Joey was happy for me when I got the job at the bank, but I could tell he thought I could do better. Like I was settling."

"Were you?"

"I was. Brianne thought the same thing... The only time the two of them agreed on anything."

"What do think?" he asked as traffic slowed for them to turn off onto Mulholland Drive.

"They were right. I *was* settling but it was easier than being real with myself. If I learned anything from Brianne's death, it's that."

He wanted to say more but didn't know what else to add.

"She was the only one who loved me," Jena said. "Joey and I...we're not close like that. But Bri told me all the time that she did and I...felt the same about her. Could never say the words though. Didn't want to admit it and then have her leave...but she's gone anyway."

Rick thought about that long and hard. He wanted to stop the car and hold her, tell her how he felt but this wasn't the time. Not really.

"I bet she knew."

"Platitudes now? That's so not like you," Jena said.

"I want to make you feel better," he admitted. Slowing down as he got closer to the address.

"You do."

Chapter 21

Rick hadn't been a fan of the plan from the beginning, but now that he saw the high security walls and the armed guard at the gate as he drove passed it, he liked it even less. He continued past the house to the van parked on the side of the road where he knew that Aaron and his boss, Jayne, waited for them.

"Lee, we're here."

"Aaron's aware and I'm patching him in."

"Hey, you two. Park in front of the van. I'll be out to meet you in a minute. To save time, we are using numbers to identify. I'm one, Denis whose inside is two, Kenji's three, Rick you're four and Jena will be five. Mobile command is Lee. My boss Jayne is listening in from the DEA offices. We've been out here on surveillance all afternoon and have ID'ed two FBI agents, one of whom reports directly to Flynn."

"Parked," Rick said as he pulled the car to a stop in

front of the van. He muted his earpiece and Jena did the same to hers.

"Are you still good to do this?" he asked her. "No one will think less of you if you back out."

"That's not true. *I* would think less of me."

He started to get out of the car, but she stopped him with hand on his arms. "I... I care about you."

"I care about you too. And when this is over, we're going to have the chance to really talk about it."

She smiled. "Just in case. I want you to know that for the first time in my life, I feel normal. Like I'm okay in my skin. Thank you for that."

"You've done the same for me," he told her. "You're getting out of there alive."

He would die before he let anything happen to her.

"After Bri's death, I decided to not hold anything back the next time I found someone who I liked," she said.

The words really didn't reassure him. It felt like she was covering all her bases in case something happened to one of them. "I like you, too."

The words just sort of escaped him.

"What?"

Someone knocked on the window of the driver's side. Rick recognized Aaron as he cursed under his breath. "Later."

He opened the door to get out and heard Jena do the same on the other side of the car. "Hey, you two. What's going on?"

"We're good. Just making sure she was still good to go."

"Are you?" Aaron asked.

"Definitely."

"Great. So let's go. Rick, you coming with us?" Aaron asked.

"I am," he said, checking his weapons as Aaron verified they were both wearing bulletproof vests.

"We are," Rick confirmed. They both unmuted their earpieces.

"Two on the move. At the gate in two minutes," Denis said.

"We will be there," Aaron said.

They followed Aaron back up the street and waited in the shadow of the trees near the gate until they heard Denis give the all clear. The gate opened and they walked in.

Rick noticed the bodies of the guards slumped to one side. Aaron and Denis cuffed them and put duct tape over their mouths before signaling them to move forward. Rick took his weapon out. The feel of the Glock in his hand was a comforting weight as they moved toward the danger he knew was waiting for them.

The mansion was a large modern structure. There was a bridge that walked over and wading pools that resembled a moat surrounding the entire complex.

The house itself was all painted concrete and glass. There was a large blown-glass sculpture in the yard that looked like a cyclone.

"What's that?" Jena asked.

"Perses, the god of destruction. Cate's father fancies himself the god of war. He had this made."

"He's in jail now?" Jena asked.

"Yes, but still apparently in charge. Given his connections, that makes sense," Aaron said.

They moved down a lush tropical path that led to the side of the mansion. He noticed a patio off what appeared to be the kitchen. "We'll go in here."

Electronic dance music was pumping inside the house

and lights were strobing around like in a club. Rick wondered if that was to throw them off.

"Does he know we are coming?"

"It'd be foolish to think he doesn't," Aaron said. "Denis?"

"He's hopeful. When we heard the Dodge left Price Tower, he got his boys ready. The FBI guys are staying back. They don't want any part of the killing probably leaving that to Vex, but they want the box. I think there's a good chance they plan to capture and torture you to find out where it is and then attempt to ransom you for it."

"More than a chance."

Rick turned at the heavily accented voice. The man standing there was Tomas Vectra. He was tall and solid, his hair thick and black. His eyes were dark, and he had a scar that ran down the left side of his neck but it was covered in tattoos. He smiled at them.

"Dion... I never figured you for a snitch," Vex said, and before Denis could respond, Vex shot him twice in the chest.

Denis flew backward and fell to the ground. Jena cried out and started over to him, but Vex turned the weapon on her.

"Not so fast... Gia...wasn't that your name? Except that was a lie. You're Jena, Brianne's friend," he said.

"Wow, you've gotten a lot smarter than the last time we met," Jena said.

Vex didn't like that and motioned with his gun for two of his men to grab her. Before Rick could move, he was Tased along with Aaron. Rick fought off the men who were attacking him trying to keep his eye on Jena. He hoped she remembered everything he'd shown her in the gym, because she was going to need it to get out of this.

* * *

Jena struggled against the men who held her. In her rush of panic, she forgot everything she'd learned from both Luna and Rick. Then she saw Rick go down, and she got pissed. He'd said he like her...she wasn't ready to lose him.

Slowing her breathing, she remembered how Rick had shown her to break free of holds. With that, she was able to get loose from one of the men. Once she had her feet underneath her, she drew back her fist and punched him as hard as she could in the throat and followed it with a kick to the balls.

The other guy still had a grip on her, though. He punched her in the side, which hurt a lot and made her see stars.

"Fall," Rick yelled.

He was struggling and slurring a little since he'd been Tased. But she realized what he was telling her and let her body go limp falling toward the ground. Her arm wrenched hard and pain burned up her shoulder as she collapsed to the ground, but it worked—the other man lost his hold on her. She rolled as she hit the ground straight into Denis's prone body. He groaned. A feeling of relief went through her knowing that the other man wasn't dead.

Her hard hit on the ground jarred the earpiece she wore, and it fell to the ground. She picked it up, holding it in her fist as she struggled to her feet. But then Vex was there, his hand in her hair as he yanked her to her feet. Pain shot through her head, her eyes watered. He dragged her up into the house, moving so fast that she tripped and stumbled alongside him. Jena had to change the momentum. It was up to her. Get the confession.

"Enough. What do you think you're going to gain by yanking my hair out?" she demanded.

His grip on her head loosened, and she slumped onto the marble floor. She got to her feet. Knowing she still had the gun and the knife gave her a little comfort—but not much. After all the violence in the other room, and with her head aching, she wasn't sure of anything.

She was so scared her hands shook, but at the same time, she was determined. "Listen, those assholes have their own agenda. I don't care about that. I just want you to admit that you killed Brianne. Help me understand how you could do that. She loved you."

His eyes narrowed. He was so close to her that she inhaled his aftershave with every breath, making her nauseous. She had to get control of the situation. He was clearly a man with nothing left to lose. The suave charm he'd had at Mistral's had been stripped away to reveal the monster he was.

His jaw was covered in stubble; his suit looked as if he'd worn it since she'd seen him at the bank. There was desperation in his eyes that worried her.

She hadn't been able to get her earpiece back in, so she had no idea what was happening outside. Her one hope was that if she kept talking, it would give Rick enough time to get to her.

And she wanted this bastard to admit he'd killed Brianne. She needed to hear him say the words.

"She loved the money, not me. Even you can't be that naive."

"So you admit you knew her."

"I never denied it.

"Just made sure that no one could connect you two," Jena said.

"She wasn't the kind of woman I could have linked to me."

Jena shook her head. Anger pulsing through her. "I know what you want, and I know where it is. You're not getting it back unless you give me what I want."

"And what is it you think I want, chica?"

"Pallus's lockbox," she said succinctly. Stars danced around her vision. Checking out the large hallway, she spotted a bench against one of the walls and walked over to it, dropping down on it hard. Her arms hurt, her head hurt and Vex stood where she'd left him watching her.

"Did you open it?"

"Why would I care what's in that box? All I give a shit about is having you admit what you did to Brianne."

"So then what?"

"I walk away and you duke it out with them," she said.

Vex let out a low, humorless laugh, dropping down next to her on the bench. "Not happening."

"Which part?"

"You're not leaving here alive," he said. "One last bit of pleasure out of this fuckup. Your friend wasn't enough of a great fuck. Totally not worth the trouble she caused me."

Jena saw red, turning toward him to claw his face with her nails, feeling them break as he grabbed her hand, twisting hard. Pain shot up her arm, and the look on his face told her that was just the beginning.

"Come on, chica. We have so much to do," he said, yanking her to her feet and dragging her up the stairs.

The pain made her realize she wasn't getting out of this mansion alive. He was going to kill her. Struggling, she managed to shove the earpiece back in. Wasn't sure if it was live until she heard Lee ordering Aaron and Rick to stay down so Kenji could get a shot off.

"I'm in the house. He's going to kill me."

She got those words out as Vex dragged her into a large

bedroom at the top of the stairs. Shoved her down onto a chair that had straps on the arms and legs. He gestured to two of his men, who waited to bind her to it.

He went to the sideboard and poured a glass of whiskey and took his time in savoring it. His eyes never leaving her body.

He fucking hated being Tased. Every muscle in his body tensed. He was just grateful that he'd had it happen enough that he didn't piss himself. He ripped the Taser out of his neck and used his momentum to ram the guy who'd Tased him hard. Aaron was doing something similar but Rick concentrated on Jena who was in a fight with the guy who'd grabbed her.

"Four, drop to the ground," Kenji ordered in Rick's ear. He hit the ground, couldn't hear the sound of the bullet but saw the guy who'd been attacking him hit the ground. Blood splatter from the chest wound hit Rick in the face. He wiped it off with one hand, struggling to his feet.

It took a while for his body to fully shake off the effects of being Tased. But he started to move as Kenji hit the second man who'd been attacking Jena. Counting on Kenji to keep an eye on Jena he went after the other man on Aaron. They were blocked by that big statue and other pillars around the patio area.

The house had seemed open and easy to cover when Rick had first glimpsed it but now he knew that was deceptive.

Rolling his neck and flexing his fingers he pulled his Glock and got off two shots. The assailant attacking Aaron slumped onto the other man who shoved him off.

"Fucking hate being Tased," Aaron said as he ripped it out of his arm. "Bastards. Where's Jena?"

"In the house. She's gone silent. Might have lost her earpiece. Kenji's moving into a better position. Denis?" Lee asked.

"Not great, but not awful. The vest took the brunt," Denis said climbing slowly to his feet.

"That's a good thing because you've got six guys—paramilitary, from the looks of it—coming around the side of the building," Kenji said. "I can get—"

Kenji broke off, and the sound of a fight came from his end of the comms. There went their sniper. Everything with this operation was going to shit. He muted his earpiece and turned to Aaron, who did the same.

"Someone sold us out."

"Jayne or Hammond," Aaron replied.

"Or both," Rick said. "La Fortunata has deep connections."

"Yeah. Lee's going to be pissed if we stay off comms. But be aware the enemy is probably listening."

Denis made his way over to them. He heard what they'd said and had muted his earpiece as well. "My money is on Hammond, but hey, it could be Jayne. They both were really close to us taking down the human trafficking and drug running operation. There would be opportunity for either of them."

Aaron nodded. "So six—I guess that's two for each of us."

There was a note of almost excitement in the other man's voice. If Jena wasn't missing, Rick would have joined him. He liked a good fight but his woman was in danger. He knew it.

"Back to comms. I'll take care of mine and then head inside unless you can handle three each?"

"I was just shot," Denis said.

"Yeah, and? We were Tased. Suck it up, mate," Aaron said.

But the time for chitchat was over as the assailants, dressed all in black, came over the garden wall. Rick turned his comms back on in time to hear Lee going off on them.

"Where the hell are you?"

"Here. Just making a plan," Aaron said.

The line buzzed, and there was the sound of the channel being changed. "Price comms only. This line is secure."

"Denis and Jena?" Rick asked.

"Yes. I'm blocking Jayne and Hammond. It has to be one—or both—of them. Van's on his way. Detective Miller is still in surgery. Kenji?" Lee asked.

There was a grunt as an answer.

The time for talk was over as Rick ran full-out toward the assailant closest to him. He clocked the guy hard in the neck, driving the body backward with his shoulder until he was pinned between Rick and one of those pillars. He clocked the guy hard with his weapon until he passed out. He bound his hands with the zip ties he'd found in one of the guy's utility pockets.

A sound behind him alerted him, and he turned and fired as another operative lurched at him with a knife in one hand. The shot hit the assailant in the chest but he kept on coming the knife slicing down and cutting Rick's upper arm.

It hurt like a bitch, but he just added it to the list of aches and pains. He swung his leg around, kicking the other person's legs out from under them. As she came down, she hit him the nuts. Rick groaned and grabbed her hand pushing it back toward her body. He hit her with the butt of the Glock and then bound her hands as well.

"My two are down. They are Special Ops, Lee. No ID," he reported. "Who can get the Special Forces?"

"Either of the joint chiefs who were in that picture," Lee responded.

"I'm in the house. Vex is going to kill me," Jena said.

Rick scrambled to his feet and into the mansion. "Where are you?"

He waited for an answer as he thundered into the large marble-floored hallway. "Upstairs bedroom."

"Is your bodyguard coming?" Vex asked in a menacing voice.

Rick started up the stairs, keeping to the wall, guessing that Vex would send his men out to stop him. Rick wanted to storm up the stairs but went slowly and cautiously. As soon as the first person appeared at the top of the stairs, Rick recognized him as a gang member from Aaron's last op.

He fired to take the other man out. One shot to the kneecap, shattering the bone as the man fell. His automatic rifle fired a burst of shots until Rick ripped it from his hands. He slung the strap over his shoulder as he heard Jena's scream coming from the first room on the left.

He fired two quick bullets to bring down the second guard and ran full-out toward her.

Chapter 22

Jena's wrist ached, but she managed to pull the knife out of her bag before the first man got to her, throwing herself out of the chair and onto the ground.

"Enough," Vex said firmly. "Go. Make sure no one disturbs us."

He gestured with his gun toward two men she hadn't realized were still in the room. They left each carrying a semiautomatic weapon. She was scared for Rick, knowing he must be on his way to get her.

He would have heard her the same as Lee had. Jena knew she had to provide a distraction but honestly she was so sore at this point. She wasn't sure what else she could do. Vex came toward her and looked at the knife she'd taken from him.

His knee on came down hard on her chest, forcing a scream out of her lips. She couldn't breathe and entire chest cavity and back felt like it was on fire.

He was over her, his hand on her neck as he wrenched the knife free from her grip.

"I don't like to use a knife to kill more than once," he said, turning it over in his palm, studying the knife.

"That's why you left it behind?" she said. "After you killed Brianne." Saying it out loud so Lee could get it recorded.

"It is. How'd you get it?"

"The cops thought it was Brianne's. They gave it to me," Jena said. Rage at the Houston cop she'd talked to boiled over, giving her the strength to shove at Vex but he wasn't budging. He took the knife and held it to her throat, leaning over her until his mouth was right next to her ear.

"Brianne talked about you. Told me how the two of you met and bonded. How you shared everything. She wanted you to live with us when we got married," he said with a laugh.

"That wasn't ever going to happen, was it?" she asked, realizing that Vex had picked Brianne to play with. She had been selected because…maybe he got off on having a woman fall in love with him before he started to break her. She hated that.

"No. Marriage isn't for me and especially not to a street rat like Brianne," he said in a tone that made it seem as if Brianne and even Jena were dumb to assume that it might result in that.

Jena had already guessed that. "How'd you fuck up enough to let her find that key?"

Vex pushed the blade harder against Jena's throat. It stung as the air reacted with the cut. She knew she was crying. She wished she could stop so he wouldn't know how hurt and mad and angry she was. But the tears just wouldn't stop. They flowed down the sides of her face and into her hair, which was also matted with blood from where he'd grabbed her and pulled her earlier.

"Underestimated her. Fucking bitch. Shouldn't have let her go the first time. When she went back to you, she changed."

"After you fucking beat her. What did you expect?" Jena demanded even though it was hard to get the words out with his knee on her.

She'd never struggled to breathe like this before. She really didn't like it. She was scared, but a part of her was glad she was getting this confession.

"That she liked it rough like you, chica. Don't deny it. You were gagging for it."

"Asshole. The only thing I was gagging for was you behind bars."

That humorless laugh of his rang out again. "Yeah, that's not happening."

"I'm not leaving here—"

"You're definitely not," he said.

Leaning over her, he put the knife to her neck again. "I know the two of you liked to share everything, so it's fitting that you'll both die at my hands by this knife."

He spoke right into her ear. His fetid breath brushed over her cheek and made her gag. He lifted his knee off her chest as he shifted around for a better position, and Jena let out a loud scream as he brought the knife down toward her. She wanted to roll away but she couldn't move as it cut through the top she wore, all the way through her shoulder blade. The wound burned as the air got to it.

She tried to block his neck cut but he put his knee on her shoulder blade, slicing up her arm. She screamed again, trying to get away from him. She tried to remember all the stuff she'd been taught. But her mind was a haze of pain and fear.

There was no time for a calming breath. No one was coming to save her. She was going to die here. At least he'd admitted he'd killed Brianne. Lee probably got the recording.

Jena brought her knee up hard, twisting her body, trying to knock Vex off-balance. It worked to a certain extent but he still brought that knife down hard straight toward her sternum, the same way he'd killed Brianne.

The look on his face was a blend of desire and excitement that made her gag again as he brought that knife down a second time, only to frown in disappointment when he realized that she wore Kevlar. He drew the knife tip around the edge of the vest. She felt the blood running down under the vest as he did it.

"That's not going to stop me, chica," he said.

Rick roared as he came through the door, Vex noted his presence and then brought the knife down hard on her neck and shoulder. It went deep and hurt so much. Stars danced again until she passed out.

The yell was ripped from the most primal part of his soul. Jena was on the ground under Vex as he drove the knife straight toward her neck. Without a thought, Rick fired two shots to take out the men who'd moved toward him.

Aware that they had hit the ground, he focused on Vex, hitting him hard in the chest.

"Jena's down. Get EMTs now," Rick said, running full force at Vectra until he had the other man under him. He wasn't even aware of what he was doing. A red haze had engulfed him, much like the one that had been on him the day he'd found the bastard who had killed Andi and beaten the other man to death.

He kept hitting Vex until the man's face was bloodied.

Aaron entered the room, pulling Rick off Vex. "He's good."

Rick wiped his bloodied hands on his pants as he moved over to Jena. Denis had a compression bandage on her neck. "Feels like it missed the carotid artery," was all the man said as he moved away.

Rick lifted her into his arms and thought about what she said about love. God, why hadn't he said that to her, so that she'd know? But he hadn't, and now it might be too late. Leaning low over her now, he brushed his lips against her forehead. He wasn't sure she'd pull through this. She was losing blood in a number of places; she looked blue and small in his arms.

"Lee, where is the ambulance? We might need a medivac," Rick said.

"En route. Hammond's on the ground."

"Is he our guy?"

"He was supposed to be in DC," Lee said.

"Fuck him."

Aaron was on his feet, as was Rick. He couldn't leave Jena, but Hammond, that fucker, was responsible for this, and he needed to pay. He'd been the one to send Cate O'Dell to them, which had set a lot of this in motion.

"Denis, you watch her," Rick said as he ejected the clip in his Glock, seeing Aaron do the same. They both reloaded as they went to the door of the room as Hammond got to the top of the stairs.

"Nice work," Hammond said. "I take it Tomas Vectra is out of the picture."

"No. Just bound and waiting for arrest. He's ready to

talk and tell us everything," Rick said. "In fact, he was glad to see us. He knew that the La Fortunata syndicate was going to send someone to kill him."

"Did he tell you who?" Hammond asked, reaching for his pocket.

"He didn't have to," Van said, coming up behind Hammond putting his gun in the other man's back. "We already knew it was you. Hands where we can see them."

Hammond put his hands up...and then pivoted toward Van, attempting to shove the other man. But Van was solid as a brick wall, and Rick and Aaron opened fire on Hammond. Rick wanted him down but not out. There was still a lot they didn't know about La Fortunata, and he wouldn't rest until they had answers. But at the same time, he wanted Hammond to remember this night for the rest of his life. So he hit him in the top of his thigh, then in the shoulder of his gun arm and finally one more shot very close to the other man's groin.

Hammond crumpled to the ground as Lee told them that LAPD and the medical chopper were on the ground.

Kenji checked in saying they had all of the Special Forces operatives bound together. Rick ran back to Jena's side, lifting her into his arms and carrying her down the stairs and out onto the grounds, where the lights had been turned on and the chopper landed.

The EMTs rushed to take her from him. There wasn't room in the chopper for him. He didn't want to let her go alone, but he had no choice.

Van told him to head to the hospital as Price Security and DEA boss Jayne took over cleaning up the mansion. He also shared that Hammond's connection to La Fortunata came way back when he'd set Van and Lee up with Cate O'Dell. She'd turned him then, offering him the money he needed to support his gambling habit.

Rick was glad he wasn't sticking around to hear more of that story. Jayne nodded at him as he left. It was like he'd told Jena there were always good cops and bad cops. The good ones were worth their weight in gold.

The EMTS checked him out and bandaged him up, but he was anxious to get to the hospital and check on Jena. Kenji waited with his own black Dodge at the end of the drive. "Hop in."

They didn't talk as Kenji drove. All that Rick could think about was Jena. He hoped... He wasn't going to allow himself to think that another drug dealer could take a woman he loved.

He'd only loved two women, and it didn't seem right that they'd both been involved in the drug world.

"That's life," Kenji said, making Rick aware he'd spoken out loud. "We can't control what happens to our woman even when we try."

Rick hated the way that sounded. "Daphne's safe enough now."

"Until she takes her next big case."

"How do you do it?" Rick asked.

Kenji glanced over at him. "Truth is, time with her makes it worth it. I know I'll give my life to keep her safe and she'd give her life to protect the rights of others."

Which worked for them. "Jena's a loan officer."

"Typically not dangerous work, but I don't think that's what she's going to want to do after this. She was hard to keep down. She played it cool and smart," Kenji said. "I like her."

"I love her. And I didn't get a chance to tell her," Rick said.

Kenji pulled up in front of the ER doors, taking his hand off the wheel he put it on Rick's shoulder. "You will."

Getting out of the car, he walked into the ER. Was met by Nick and Luna.

"She's still in surgery up on the sixth floor," Luna said after she gave him a hug.

"How's Detective Miller?"

"Detective Miller's in recovery. Doing well," Nick said.

"I'm glad," he said. And he was. But he'd asked because he needed to keep his mind off his own worst fears that he'd never get to tell Jena how much he loved her.

Jena's throat hurt as she blinked her eyes. She glanced around the darkened room, heard the heartbeat monitor, and the IV pump. Obviously she was in a hospital room. She had no memory of how she got here. Still, she was grateful she was alive. The last thing she remembered was…not good.

Putting her hand to the bandage on her throat she tried to sit up.

"Steady there. You're in a rough way," Rick's deep voice came out of the darkness.

He stood over her, put his hand on hers. "What do you need?"

"Vex?"

"Dead."

"Did… Lee…get—"

"Rest your voice. I'm not sure if you can have water. Let me call the nurse," he said, hitting the button.

"Vex told me he killed Brianne," Jena said, determined to get the words out through her dry throat. She was probably drugged, because she didn't hurt half as bad as she had the last time she'd been conscious.

"She got his confession. She got it all. Hammond was the traitor, working directly with Flynn Howard. He's been on the La Fortunata payroll for a long time. Brianne is a national heroine. Jayne from the DEA was clean. She was fed different information than Hammond."

The nurse came in, and Rick stepped back so she could check Jena's vitals and give her water. The nurse explained all of Jena's injuries and how they'd been treated. Her left wrist was in a cast having been broken by Vex—she wasn't surprised to hear that. They'd bandaged and cleaned most of the scrapes. The cut on her neck was deep and required stitches but had only nicked her artery which would heal in time. The contusions on her head, and her cracked ribs would also heal.

She had been required to stay in the hospital overnight for observation. They explained that nurse would be only a click away and that the IV was keeping her hydrated. There was also a morphine pump that Jena was able to use if her pain was too intense.

Jena thought she probably wouldn't. She already felt so dazed, and drugs weren't going to help. She had more questions for Rick, which she assumed he'd answer once the nurse was gone. Most of all, she wanted to know how bad his own injuries were.

He looked good to her, but he had a bandage on his neck and arm. His face was black and blue, and unless she was wrong he'd broken his nose. He watched her with that quiet intensity that she expected from him now, but when he noticed her looking at him, he gave her that comforting teddy bear smile of his.

She was so happy he was mostly okay. So glad that Lee had gotten a recording of Vex's confession. This moment was one she'd dreamed of but hadn't thought they'd actually get to.

As soon as the nurse left, Rick was back. His hand gently on the side of her face, touching her.

"Babe, I thought I'd lost you," he said, his voice thick with emotion as he kissed her so softly.

"Me too. Both of us. That was so scary," she admitted. "I want to know everything."

"Okay, well, Jayne was given the information about Detective Miller being the hospital. She was also told that that was where the box was being taken as we wanted it in police custody. Hammond was told that the box would be with us when we went to Vex's mansion."

"So that's how you smoked out the mole. Nice. Why wasn't I in on that?" she asked.

"None of us were. That was Van's plan. He's the one who fed the information to them as Detective Miller was rushed to the hospital. He knew that information was being leaked and lives were at stake," Rick said, his tone suggesting he and his boss might have had words about that. "Also it was Hammond's idea to call your boss to put pressure on you—make you fear for your coworkers."

"Are you okay? I've heard getting Tased is intense."

"Yeah, I'm fine. What about you?" he asked. "When I heard your scream, I saw red."

"I'm fine now. I mean, everything aches," she said, tears leaking out. "Damn. I'm crying again just thinking about it. I've never been in that much pain. I hate that Vex saw me cry."

"I'm sorry too," he said, stroking her hair. She'd never seen him like this.

"Are you okay?" she asked again. "Not physically... emotionally."

"Fuck no."

Oh. She wasn't sure what that meant.

"Is your job always like that?" she asked.

"Rarely. Normally my clients are corporate types who need a bodyguard. Like big oil or pharma executives. I've done a few jobs at the UN, but those people mostly have their own guards… Why are we talking about this?"

She remembered how easy it was for Brianne to just tell Jena she loved her. Her friend had no problem saying the words, but for Jena they were stuck in her throat. Even though she hadn't wanted to die with them unsaid. But now that he was next to her bed, in this darkened hospital room the feels swamped her.

What if he didn't love her back?

Returning the words to someone she knew loved her had been a challenge. She'd never felt worthy of love. Yeah, that was something to probably unpack with a therapist, but honestly they were expensive and she just sucked things up and moved on.

Not this time.

This time…

"I love you," she said quietly.

Rick straightened up. She couldn't read his expression. She knew he cared about her at least a little. Maybe for him it had been the intensity of the job, remembering his sister and perhaps seeing a bit of Andi in her. But for Jena she these feelings were too deep, too strong and too all-consuming to be anything else.

"You don't have to say it back. But these emotions I have for you… I kept thinking 'I don't want to die without Rick knowing. I love him.'"

Chapter 23

Rick wanted to answer her and tell her he loved her too, but there wasn't a chance, as the doctor came in.

"How's my patient this morning?" he asked Jena as Rick moved out of the way. He watched her laying on the bed as she talked with the doctor. She looked young and fragile.

But he knew how tough she was, which just made that love he felt in his heart ache a bit more. He'd been struggling with the fact that he might not get to tell her how he felt and now that the moment was here…the words were stuck in the back of his throat.

He wanted to admit it. No one had said those words to him since Andi had died, and he wanted her to know that she wasn't the only one in love.

There was no doubting what she felt; it was there on her face and in her eyes. But he found himself thinking about the man he'd been tonight, worried about the monster that had taken over as he'd attacked Vex. After the life Jena had lived maybe she deserved a better man.

Also, she had a life back in Texas. Rick wasn't sure he wanted to go back there. He could return to the DEA for one thing. Though he'd been doing odd jobs for them for the last few years, he wasn't entirely sure he wanted to continue. He wasn't prepared to leave LA or Price.

Van would work with him. Rick knew that but…that was why he struggling with the idea of letting go of this place. Los Angeles was his home. The one place he'd found where he felt safe. He wasn't shy about admitting that even though he was tough and could take on whatever life threw at him, he had always felt like that scared little boy inside. Not sure where his next meal would come from. Not sure if his dad was going to beat him or his sister. Not sure if Andi was going to come home when she went out. It had taken Van Price to get him to the point where he mostly stopped that worry.

He'd made himself into a better man because of it. But there was still a lot he wasn't sure he was ready for. And it broke his heart to think of letting Jena down.

Letting her go would hurt, and he'd ache for the rest of his life, but if that was the way she had a better life, he'd do it.

Was that selfish?

His fear was driving him now. He thought of the cigarette he'd left in his trench coat back at Price Tower. He hadn't been wearing the coat or playing with that cigarette since Jena arrived. In a way she'd become his new touchstone. His new addiction.

Oh God, why hadn't he realized it sooner? This wasn't just love this was something more. She was the woman he'd been waiting for. Out of all the clients and people he'd saved in his years of working for the DEA and Price Security...they were all just a warmup to save her.

That moment when he'd seen Vectra drive that knife toward her throat, Rick's hands had shook and rage and fear mixed together in a dangerous cocktail that nearly drove him to his knees.

"Rick?"

Jena and the doctor were both looking at him.

"Huh?"

"The doctor needs to discharge me into someone's care," she said.

"Of course. I'm taking her home. I'll be with her 24/7 until she's recovered."

The doctor started to give Rick instructions, so there was no time to keep debating his own feelings and worth. She needed someone and he was the only one she had. No, the only one she needed.

The doctor left with the promise to send in a nurse to remove the stent from the IV. Then they'd have to sign some paperwork and they'd be good to go.

"You sure you're okay with this?" Jena asked.

"More than okay," he said.

She loved him.

Even though she didn't need to hear the words back. He needed to say them to her. Even if he was letting her go. His feelings for her were going to be with him until he died.

Time to figure out if he could say the words out loud or if he they were going to be stuck in his throat for the rest of his life.

"I want to tell you how I feel," he said, because he guessed she had to be wondering if he cared about her too.

"Not yet," she said. "You have to have doubts about this, right?"

Of course he did. There were other things to consider. He'd never been in a serious relationship with a woman. Everything felt new to him. What if he fucked it up?

Jena put her hand out to him. "I keep wondering what if this is a fluke. You know, since the two of us have been thrown together for the last…how long has it been, a week or ten days?"

He stood up so that he could see her expression better, looking down on her face. "Do you doubt how you feel or how I do?"

She shrugged and then flinched. "Both. Neither. I don't know. Love is new to me."

"Me too," he admitted. "But I'll tell you this. I haven't thought about smoking since you came into my life. I haven't been trying to project that calm agent that everyone expects me to be. Instead I've just been myself. The cranky, craggy parts and all. And somehow you still fell in love with me."

She smiled, reaching up to touch his face. "I did. I like those parts."

"We'll figure this out," he promised her.

One week later, she wasn't sure they were any closer to figuring anything out. Rick had moved her into his apartment and had been sleeping on the couch so he didn't jostle her while they were sleeping. Van had been in to visit her as had everyone else on the Price team. They all wanted to make sure she was okay.

It was nice, she wasn't going to lie. She was starting to get to know them as people and maybe friends. Not just acquaintances she needed to get justice for Brianne.

And she'd done more than that.

Her murder had been solved now and Brianne was being hailed as a heroine who'd helped take down a crime syndicate that had moles in most government agencies. Jayne Renner of the DEA had been promoted for her work in helping untangle it.

Jayne had been the only one they could work with after Hamond had been revealed to be part of La Fortunata. Malcom O'Dell might still be connected to the gangs as Perses but his power was being stunted. He was in solitary confinement with no visitors allowed including his daughter Cate.

Everyone had assumed Cate was working with Hamond but she'd been just as shocked as they were that he was part of La Fortunata. Something Jena didn't believe.

Jena had also been given accolades for her part in taking down the syndicate, but she wasn't comfortable with that.

The path to getting Vex had been bumpy and uncomfortable. Not the way she thought it should have gone. But she was happy he was dead.

So yeah, things were great as far as the reason she'd come to California. But that left Rick. Who still hadn't told her how he felt.

She had no doubts that he cared deeply about her. While he was "giving her time to recover" she'd formally terminated her employment at bank back in Houston and arranged for movers to pack up her apartment. Her boxes would arrive in two days' time. Right now she had them going to a storage unit until she figured out what was next for her and Rick.

Leaving the bedroom, she went out to find him sitting on the couch. "We need to talk."

"Yes, we do. But not here. Do you feel up to a drive?" he asked her.

She nodded. She was ready to get out of the Tower for a little while. "Am I dressed okay?"

She wore a pair of gym shorts and one of his T-shirts.

"Perfect. Grab your sunnies. I was thinking we would drive to the beach," he said.

She went and got them, bringing just her phone with her.

The drive took a while, as traffic in LA was always the worst. Rick didn't say much as they drove just put the windows down so the warm summer air blew around them. She liked it.

The breeze wiped away the last of the cobwebs in her head, and she knew with perfect clarity that she loved this man. And she was going to tell him exactly that. It might take him a while to realize that she was sincere, but she'd accepted that. Growing up the way both of them had love wasn't something they were familiar with. But she'd persist until he believed her.

He parked where they had the last time when they'd been attacked by Vex's gang. "God, remember the last time we were here?"

"I do. You don't have to worry about your safety today."

"I know," she said quietly. He got out, coming around to take her hand when she exited the car.

He still stayed silent until they were walking down the pier. At the end, he stopped, having found a semi-quiet place for the two of them.

He leaned against the railing, the Pacific Ocean and an endless horizon behind him.

"Why'd you bring me here?" she asked.

He pushed his sunglasses up onto the top of his head.

"It's my happy place, and I wanted to be here when I told you I love you."

The words spread through her like sunshine as she wrapped her good arm around him and rested her head on his chest. "I love you too."

"It took me some time to process that. No one has since Andi died. I just needed some time to figure out how to tell you and not get choked up," he said, his voice husky with choked feelings.

"I don't mind," she admitted.

"Why didn't you say it again?" he asked.

"I was waiting for you to be ready to hear it. But I thought it all the time—especially when I was lying in your bed. I missed you in there by the way. Why didn't you sleep with me?"

"I want you. You needed time to recover and I needed space to realize you had recovered," he admitted. He took her hand as they started walking toward the very end of the pier.

"Well, I'm better now."

"Thank God," he said.

"I love you so much," she said. "I didn't think I'd find anything like this. I was okay with being alone and having just Bri but with you... I don't want to be alone anymore. I want a life with you."

"I want that too," he admitted. "I've talked to Van. I can work remotely from Houston."

She laughed and shook her head. "You won't have to. I'm moving here."

"You are?"

"Hired a moving company yesterday and booked a storage unit since I didn't know how you felt."

"Are you sure?" he asked her. "Are you going to work at a bank out here?"

She had decided that was done settling. Rick had given that to her. "I'd like to go back to school and maybe study criminology. There are a lot of other women like Bri whose cases go unsolved. I want to try to solve them."

"I like that. I can support you while you go to school," he said.

"Lee offered me a job as her assistant. Doing research and the like," Jena said.

"She did? Why didn't anyone tell me?" he asked.

"I asked them not to. I needed to know that I could do it on my own, without you pulling any strings for me. I asked her and told her I'd understand if she said no, but she liked the research I'd done to find Vex," Jena said with a shrug.

"Sounds like you've got it all figured out."

"It was easy once I realized that I wanted to be close to the man I loved so he could figure out that he loved me too."

"Glad I did," he said.

"Me too," she admitted.

He pulled her into his arms kissing her as the sunset. It was such a perfect moment for two people whose lives had always been imperfect.

Jena felt like Brianne was smiling down on her and happy that she'd solved her murder and found Rick.

* * * * *